Readers Love GAYLEEN FROESE

The Girl Whose Luck Ran Out

"Definitely recommended for those who like to follow mysteries, enjoy engaging characters, and second chance romances."

—Nat Kennedy Reviews

"…the story boasts a soothing, balm-like quality that seeks to heal what has been slivered."

—Delphic Reviews

"I can't wait to read the next book in the series. I believe once more people hear about this book, Gayleen Froese will have a hit on her hands."

—Gina Rae Mitchell Reviews

The Man Who Lost His Pen

"I could read a thousand Ben Ames mysteries and can't wait for another installment!"

—Emily's Hurricane Reviews

By GAYLEEN FROESE

BEN AMES CASE FILES
The Girl Whose Luck Ran Out
The Man Who Lost His Pen
The Man Who Hated Clouds

DISCHORD
Lightning Strike Blues

SEVEN LEAGUES
The Dominion

Published by DSP PUBLICATIONS
www.dsppublications.com

GAYLEEN FROESE

THE MAN WHO HATED CLOUDS

DSP PUBLICATIONS

Published by
DSP Publications

8219 Woodville Hwy #1245
Woodville, FL 32362 USA
www.dsppublications.com

This is a work of fiction. Names, characters, places, and incidents either are the product of author imagination or are used fictitiously, and any resemblance to actual persons, living or dead, business establishments, events, or locales is entirely coincidental.

The Man Who Hated Clouds
© 2024 Gayleen Froese

Cover Art
© 2024 Cover Art by L.C. Chase
http://www.lcchase.com
Cover content is for illustrative purposes only and any person depicted on the cover is a model.

Mass Market Paperback ISBN: 978-1-64108-759-9
Trade Paperback ISBN: 978-1-64108-758-2
Digital ISBN: 978-1-64108-757-5
Mass Marker Paperback published December 2024
v. 1.0

Printed in the United States of America

To Edmonton. Sorry about my detective.
You know how Calgarians are.

Acknowledgments

Thanks as always to the team at DSP, especially Gin and Andi, as well as to fellow author and housemate Laird Ryan States. I'm especially grateful to Robert and Cori for their behind-the-scenes notes on the Edmonton Folk Festival after-party (all resemblance to persons, festivals, ragers, and hotels, living and dead, are coincidental.)

FOREWARD

I've written introductions for two of Ben's case files and I was looking forward to writing a third. However, as much as I enjoyed Ben's retelling of his latest case, I thought there might be something more important I could do with this space. After a full and frank discussion with Ben, he agreed. I now turn this foreword over to Ben for an important statement.

-Gayleen Froese

DEAR READER,

In the interest of fairness, I want to make it clear that Edmonton bears little to no resemblance to the setting of *Escape from New York* and is instead a pleasant mid-size city with an enviable amount of forested parkland.

Though my life was in danger more than once during my latest visit to Edmonton, this was related to my work as a private investigator and not to be expected by a typical tourist.

The people of Edmonton are no drunker than anyone else.

The average Edmonton driver, when cut off in traffic, will not track you like a vengeful bull elephant. If this should happen to you, it is an aberration. If you are unable to navigate Edmonton's road system, you may be overly reliant upon such things as accurate road signs and lanes that do not end mid-block without warning. That is, obviously, on you.

West Edmonton Mall is not considered a foretaste of Hell in any mainstream religious doctrine.

I hope that clears things up for everyone and that all of you, including Edmontonians, enjoy this book.

-Ben Ames

GAYLEEN FROESE

THE
MAN
WHO
HATED
CLOUDS

CHAPTER ONE

SILLY ME, I'd thought I was on vacation. I was lying on a hill with my eyes closed, listening to a Chicago blues band from Helsinki play a song about New Orleans. I was soaking up the sun from the cloudless sky and the warmed ground under my blanket. There wasn't a crime anywhere in the vicinity, or at least not one I was paid to care about. Heaven.

I was so relaxed that I didn't even open my eyes when a slight darkening and coolness told me someone was standing next to me, or when a familiar voice came from the same direction.

"You all right down there, Grampa? Did you have a fall?"

Izzy.

Isobel Wagner was a musician I'd met a few months earlier, backstage at one of my boyfriend's gigs. She was pretty sharp for someone who still wore pull-up diapers to preschool.

"Old people need naps," I told her. "What are you doing here? I didn't see Ash Rose in the lineup."

Another change in the light and a soft rustling. She'd sat down. It was probably rude to keep lying there with my eyes closed. I sat up, squinting against the sun. Izzy was cross-legged on the grass in frayed white denim cut-offs and a pink Powerpuff Girls T-shirt that matched her hair. She had sunglasses on, but it was still easy to read her irritation as she said, "We're not. We broke up."

Reliable sources, like my boyfriend, had told me the three-piece she'd been in was good enough to go places. But she and her bandmates had also been full of opinions and the youthful energy to fight about them, so I wasn't too surprised it had fallen apart.

"That's too bad," I offered.

She shrugged. "Yeah, sucks. I couldn't even afford to come this year."

In the abstract, that was also not surprising. The Edmonton Folk Festival was a big three-day show, and tickets did not come cheap. Not in the abstract, though, as she was sitting next to me, very much inside the fences.

"I guess that's why you're not here," I said.

"You're still so funny. I'm a volunteer. Party Crew." She slipped the edge of a badge from the pocket of her shorts. "Clashes with my shirt."

That, or she didn't want anyone to know who she was. Her band hadn't been the biggest on the local scene, but they'd been big enough, and this was a music-loving crowd.

I'd picked a spot behind the audience at one of the less popular stages, so it wasn't likely either of us would be bothered. The hill sloped down before us, covered in middle-to-upper-class Edmontonians pretending to be hippies for a weekend. Most had arrived with the full package of low-rise festival chairs, overpriced vacuum bottles, and non-GMO, cruelty-free vegan sunscreen from whatever stood in for Whole Foods in their town.

Past the pseudo-granolas and the stage with the Finnish blues band, across the North Saskatchewan River, the Edmonton skyline glinted in the sun. One of the glass buildings was an improbable pink, nearly the same as Izzy's hair. The heat gave everything a haze of unreality. I grabbed my own sunglasses and put them on.

"Good," Izzy said. "Now no one will know you're a rock star."

"You're also still funny," I told her. "Did you come over here because I looked too peaceful?"

That got a smile out of her, though only half her mouth was involved.

"I want to say yes. But no. I'm supposed to find out if you're going to the party tonight."

I didn't have to ask which one. The folk festival held after-parties in a local hotel. These were performer-, crew-, and VIP-only events where people with Junos got legendarily shellacked and spilled their beers on even drunker Grammy winners. The parties were considered fabulous or notorious, depending on your point of view—or how many beers you'd had spilled on you.

"Jess is going," I said. "I thought I'd tag along."

"No one will give a shit that you're with Jess. You need your own badge."

I pulled the Performer badge from the back pocket of my shorts. I wasn't a performer, which was to the benefit of everyone, but it marked me as part of Jesse's entourage. In this case, a small entourage consisting of me. Izzy took a quick look and nodded

"'Kay. I didn't know if you knew the rules."

"Can you tell me why someone wanted you to find out if I'd be there? Are they planning an assassination?"

"You're not—" she started, then paused. "Actually, how famous do you have to be before it's an assassination and not a murder? You and Jess are pretty famous these days."

"Eh," I said. "We've had our fifteen minutes. Or I have. It's not like I was famous for myself."

What I'd done, the night I met Izzy, was solve the murder of an A-list actor. His fame had rubbed off on me, and some of it was still hanging on, like a club stamp that was slow to wash away. But the paparazzi had fucked off, thank God, and I was something like a nobody again. Jess, who was better known as rock star Jack Lowe, would never be a nobody. He'd one day become a has-been. But he was back to his baseline of quasi-famous for now.

"Probably just a murder," Izzy concluded. "But they don't want to murder you, I don't think. I think they want to hire you."

"I'm in the book," I said. Off Izzy's puzzled frown, I added, "It's a figure of speech. From when there were phone books. I'm saying if someone wants to hire me, they can find me. I run a detective agency. I'm not hiding."

Izzy smiled again and gestured at my low-key location.

"I mean…."

"I have a business number and an email and a contact form on my website. If someone insists on contacting me through social media, they can do that. There's no need to send their best friend to find out if I like them too."

Izzy laughed.

"Oh my God. It's not like that, but can you imagine? I'm not their friend. They just knew I knew you because of the whole murder thing. I don't know why they never called you. They said they wanted to talk to you about a job, and could I find out if you'd be at the party. That's all I got."

"And this person is?"

"I can't tell you. They said if you go to the party, they'll find you."

"You can tell me," I said. "You know who it is and you know how to talk."

"Yeah, but I said I wouldn't, so I won't. You're gonna have to go and see. Or don't go and don't see."

"It's someone very famous, isn't it? That's why they don't think they have to behave like a reasonable adult."

Izzy was pulling up blades of grass, slow and careful. I'd done that as a kid. The idea was to get the root, the soft white part that was good to chew on. In this place, you could get nachos from one of a dozen food trucks, but maybe food tasted better if you pulled it out of a hill yourself.

"You should go," she said. "They'll bug Jess if you're not there, and he'll agree to whatever this person wants, and it'll be like you went anyway."

For someone who hadn't known Jess long or well, Izzy had a decent grasp of his nature. Not that he was a pushover, but he liked a good case as much as I did. More than I did, in fact.

"I'll go," I conceded. "So I can turn down the case."

"You do you," Izzy said. "I'm gonna catch the end of Jesse's workshop. I totally thought I'd find you in that crowd, but you weren't there."

"Because I was here."

She frowned, drawing lines in her thick foundation.

"Didn't you want to see him? And the Twist? They're your friends too."

"I thought I'd be more anonymous over here," I told her. It was true, if not the whole truth. I figured I'd leave the rest out, but she was ahead of me.

"I asked Jess backstage, and he said he was fucked if he knew where you were. He's crabby. You guys aren't fighting, are you? Are my not-real-dads tearing this family apart?"

"I don't think we're fighting," I said. Not a great answer but the truth, which was all I had. "He's in a mood. I don't know why."

"Well." She stood without needing her hands to push up from the ground. She'd recall that with nostalgia one day. "Maybe you should ask him, Gramps. I think that's what boyfriends are for."

I didn't follow her to Jesse's workshop because it would have seemed like I was following orders, which I rarely do, and especially not when they're coming from children. Instead I stayed for the rest of the blues band's set before I jostled my way to the far stage.

I heard them before I saw them. As I understood it, a workshop was meant to be a chance for musicians to develop songs together. Let the audience in on the process. If any work had occurred at this particular workshop, it was over now, because I recognized a rowdy version of "We're Here For a Good Time (Not A Long Time)," and the audience was singing along.

Rounding the edge of a merch tent, I could finally see the stage. Jess was at the right, next to two of our friends from the Twist. Next to them was a Montreal singer-songwriter who'd been the flavour of the day about a decade earlier. He was dressed for casual day at the office, in khakis and a white dress shirt. Finishing off the row was someone I didn't recognize, an artfully scruffy woman about Izzy's age. It was hard to say which had taken her more time: making herself look like she'd just fallen out of bed, or finding the perfect Janis Joplin glasses on Amazon.

This was not a typical setting for Jess, or really his alter ego, Jack Lowe. Jack did a mix of glam, power-pop and goth-tinged alternative rock, usually with spectacle and never without eyeliner. But Brennan, the

Twist's singer, had been clear when he'd invited Jess on the festival's behalf. *It's not fancy, mate. Dress down, bring an acoustic guitar, and we'll kick songs around.*

I suspected Jess had agreed because he was toying with a new image, one where he was a songwriter and artist first and a hero to furious goth kids second, if at all. Whether dusting off classic Trooper with a pack of roots rockers was the image he was going for, I could not have said.

They wrapped it up, thanked everyone in sight, and disappeared backstage. The audience seemed to understand that there would be no encore, and though a few stuck around to yell "I love you" to Jess, most dispersed quickly. I saw Janis Glasses slip away with them. Probably heard there was a sale on love beads at a souvenir booth.

A small group of fans was being led away by guards as I approached the backstage area, and the remaining guard gave my pass more than a cursory eyeball before allowing me to enter. I didn't need a second guess as to what had brought that on. I wouldn't go so far as to call Jesse's fans reprobates, at least not around him, but sometimes a quadrupled security team speaks for itself.

I found the musicians in a tight circle, packing up instruments and dodging crew members who were setting up for the next act. As I approached, they were laughing about something. Brennan's Geordie accent rang out loudest.

"And I'm looking at everyone like, are we gonna go for it? Does Liv even know there's a key change? Where is Liv, anyway?"

"She was meeting someone after," Jess said. Liv must have been Janis Glasses. So Jess had at least felt sociable enough to chat with the kid.

"Ay, it's Poirot!"

That was Brennan, and he was not only calling me Poirot because I'd solved a murder in front of him, but also because I'd hauled all the suspects into one room to do it. I'd made a speech and everything. I hadn't started it with "You may be wondering why I gathered you here," but I should have, and I regretted my failing.

At Brennan's words, his co-writer, Reiss, turned to look at me. Jess kept packing his guitar into its case, which did not take as long as he was making it take. The Montreal folkie vanished like he'd been waiting for the chance.

"You hold one murderer reveal dog-and-pony show…," I said.

"…and you can't wait to hold another," Reiss finished for me. He and Brennan came over for an awkward, is-this-a-handshake-or-a-hug greeting. Hugs, it turned out. Jess hung back.

"You coming to the thing tonight?" Reiss asked.

"I'd better," I said, "since I have an appointment."

Reiss and Brennan exchanged a glance. Standing so close to them, I could see sunburns starting on the sharp points of their faces.

"Do you mean the same thing when you say 'the thing tonight'?" Brennan asked. "I think Reiss was talking about the after-party."

"Yeah, I know. I have an appointment. Izzy tracked me down and said some mysterious big deal wanted to hire me for something. They're going to find me at the party."

Reiss cocked his head. "Does this mystery person know what parties are for?"

"Networking," Brennan said. "'Twas always thus."

He slapped my arm, the all-purpose aloha of guys, and trailed a threat to get me "well off my tits" later as he and Reiss left.

And there I was, alone with Jess. Jess was not getting a sunburn, since he always wore enough sunblock to withstand a nuclear meltdown. He was still, his expression flat and his eyes gazing through me. To infinity and beyond.

"How'd it go?" I asked.

He shrugged. His face didn't change. "Fine."

"I'm glad you got the good-time versus long-time debate settled," I said, and he smiled. It wasn't enthusiastic, but he at least meant it.

"They said it wouldn't be solved in our lifetimes."

"Izzy said she talked to you," I said.

"Briefly," Jess acknowledged. I reached past him to grab the handle of his guitar case. If I was going to be the entourage, I might as well pull my weight.

"She didn't drop any hints about this mystery celebrity?" I asked.

He shook his head. "She asked for you. That was pretty much it. I can carry my guitar."

"I know you can," I told him and kept hold of it. "Where are we headed?"

"The car? Unless you need to talk to Izzy or something."

I gave him a moment to reconsider. We were surrounded by good music and passable food. Aside from his fans, people weren't likely to get too far up in his business if he tried to enjoy those things. Many people wouldn't even have recognized him, looking as non-Jack Lowe as he did today. And we could have stuck to the musician and crew areas if he really didn't want to talk to strangers.

He stood there, giving me nothing. Like a video-game character waiting for its next cue.

"Is everything okay?" I asked.

He blinked. "It's fine. I'm just tired. I want to sleep for a few hours before the party. I can get a runner to take me if you want to stay here."

"No, we can go," I said. "I should get out of here before someone finds out I don't know the words to 'Four Strong Winds.'"

That got a laugh out of him. He moved closer and leaned against me a little, companionably, as we made our way to the secure parking lot. No one stopped us or even spoke to us along the way. The skyline was still hazy, and calypso was bouncing on the currents of the air.

It took almost no time to locate my plain brown car, which looked like it had been dropped into that lot by a scrap-yard magnet. It wasn't that old, and I kept it in decent shape, but it didn't belong there in the shadows of tour buses and menaced by aggressively swooping sports cars. Even the runners had a fleet of shiny Navigators. I would have made a joke about it, but Jess would then have offered to buy me a fancy new car, as he did once a week or so, and I would have had to turn him down again. The steps to that dance were getting so familiar, we could do them with barely a thought.

I wondered whether he'd make a play for the driver's seat while I was putting his guitar into the trunk. He'd insisted on driving on the way up from Calgary, but that was the QE2. They called it the Alberta Autobahn, and it was a tempting drive for someone with a lead foot and no sense of their own mortality. I'd once had someone on that highway honk at me for going a mere fifty over the speed limit in the passing lane.

But now we were in Edmonton, and no one would mistake driving in Edmonton for fun.

Jess seemed to have figured that out because he got in on the passenger side. He was already staring out the side window as I got in. No grabbing of a pop from the cooler or a bag of Cheezies from the glove box. No change to the radio station I'd set on the way into town. Only stillness and that same distance I'd sensed in him earlier.

"You sure you're okay?" I asked as I started the car and put on the AC. He hadn't even rolled down his window, the usual prelude to my telling him to roll it back up so the AC could work and him saying he'd roll it up once the AC started working.

"M'okay."

Our hotel was almost directly across the river, which should have made it easy to get to, but Edmonton didn't believe in easy. The winding roads down the valley slopes to the many and varied bridges made no sense at the best of times. Mid-festival was far from the best of times since half of those roads were blocked. The bridges themselves were two-way, one-way, or no ways today, because they're doing construction on two lanes and there's an accident in the third. Good luck guessing which was which before you'd gone too far down the wrong road. I'd long felt they should give out Xanax and apologies at the city limits.

I gave my phone the hotel's address and hoped for the best. Normally Jess would have been putting the address into his iPhone so we could bet on whether Apple or Google would bitch up the directions worse, but his phone was on his lap, and he clearly had other things on his mind.

"Do you want food?" I asked as we waited behind a row of cars to cross what was probably the wrong bridge. "Before the hotel? Or I could bring something back for when you wake up."

He glanced at his phone and tapped it to light the screen, like he wasn't sure what time it was, though he'd finished a set not half an hour earlier and usually had an inner stopwatch on performance days.

"It's around six," I told him and pointed helpfully at the car's clock. I was a helpful guy.

"Don't worry about me," he said. "I'll get food later if I feel like it."

Like most of the performers, Jess was booked into one of the fancier downtown hotels. It was easier to have people in one place if you were going to be carting them back and forth, and the hotel probably knew by now to set aside a certain number of rooms each summer. Like a well-oiled machine, except when that machine got COVID and had to shut down for a few years. But they seemed to be back in the swing of things now.

The other reason to have everyone in one hotel, of course, was that it was the site of the after-party. Letting that many people party in one place, then disperse to a dozen hotels, would put enough drunks on the 3:00 a.m. streets that even Edmonton might notice. This way they were bused from the festival site to the hotel, got as drunk as their hearts desired, and had only to stumble to their rooms when they were done.

"I'll park anyway," I told him. I could have gone anywhere and done anything for the next few hours, but there was nowhere I could think of going that was worth driving to get there. He nodded as if he'd heard me.

We parted ways in the elevator, me leaving at the main floor and Jess continuing up to the room. As the doors closed, he was leaning against the elevator wall with his eyes shut.

For lack of anything better to do, I went for a walk. Down to the river valley, past the CPR hotel Jess had been hoping the festival would use. Those old hotels had been dropped across the country like charms on a giant bracelet, obviously from the same set but unique in the details. They were so much like castles, at least on the outside, that confused graphic designers sometimes put photos of Canadian cities in European tourism brochures. I hadn't known Jess to have any particular affinity for them, but he'd probably stayed at most of them over the years, and maybe he needed the Macdonald to collect the set.

Though Edmonton was farther from the mountains than Calgary, it had the more dramatic river valley— steep and craggy and thick with trees. It was full of people on this warm evening, walking dogs or jogging. Zipping past the pedestrians on their bikes and scooters and taking the glass-walled funicular between trails. Even this late in the summer, the height of the sun gave the impression that time wasn't going anywhere, or at least wasn't in a hurry. I wasn't either, so I bypassed the rows of rental bikes and strolled instead.

Kayaks, canoes, and a riverboat full of tourists were sharing the North Saskatchewan with a pack of optimists who'd made some kind of floating island out of rafts and air mattresses. It was hard to tell how much danger they were in, but no one around them seemed alarmed, and the police boat upstream was ignoring them, so probably they were fine as long as they managed not to float into the riverboat.

I had the automatic thought that it was a good thing Jesse wasn't with me, since his usual impulse on seeing a group of reckless idiots was to join them. But he wouldn't have been in the mood today… for whatever reason. Maybe I should have known what that reason was, but in my defence, it was hard to figure out what was going on when the witness wouldn't admit that anything was wrong.

The other mystery of the day, that one was easier. Who wanted to talk to me at the party? As I'd said to Izzy, it had to be someone famous enough that it wouldn't even occur to them to call my office like a peasant. There were a few of those hanging around the festival, between performers and their significant others. But they would also have to be willing to speak to the likes of Isobel Wagner, and that narrowed the field. Hell, they would have had to reach out to Izzy because, unlike many of the other volunteers, the Party Crew weren't hanging around backstage where the performers could run into them.

Somebody, in other words, knew Izzy personally.

I got closer to the water, where the air was cooler, and parked myself on a bench. I had to shield my phone with a hand to see the screen. That slowed me down a little, but I still managed, in under an hour, to trace the histories and connections of one of my suspects back far enough to find the crossed paths.

Putting pieces together was always satisfying work, much better than sitting around outside a motel room waiting to photograph adulterers. Then again, most things were.

I took my time heading back to the hotel and grabbed food from a donair place on the way. It was quieter on the downtown streets than in the river valley, mostly people on their way between one place and another. Someone was busking far up the road. A pit bull was tied up outside the restaurant, looking forlorn, so I gave him a pat and a kind word. He would likely have preferred a donair.

My own dog was spending the day with my friend Luna, who insisted on being referred to as his auntie Luna and who would likely have bought him a carload of toys, a side of beef, and a tuxedo by the time I got back. That last thing wasn't a guess—a few weeks earlier, she'd texted Jess a photo of the tuxedo to ask what he thought of it, then texted me for Frank's measurements. She didn't seem to think we would put that together. What formal event she was planning to attend with an eighty-pound mongrel remained unknown.

Back in the hotel, I ate and showered and changed and flipped through TV channels while Jess slept. He'd had a shower before crawling into the bed nearest the window, and he'd pulled the blackout drapes until only a thin line of orange light broke through. There was no sign he'd done anything else, like ordering food or checking his email. His phone and guitar were both lying on a table, just inside the door. His clothes were in a pile on the bathroom floor.

That hint of light between the curtains grew slowly darker until the sunset was replaced by city lights. I was thinking I might have to wake Jesse, or go to the party without him. I wasn't certain I'd be allowed in without my personal celebrity, but as Izzy had noted, I did have my own pass. I was about to turn off the TV when Jess rolled over and half opened his eyes. Twin green lines between dark lashes that did not quite match his hair.

"What time is it?" he asked.

"Eleven," I told him. "I was thinking of going down."

"God, I slept that long?"

He sounded surprised but not accusatory, which was good because it was not my job to wake him or to set alarms. When we traveled together, he was pretty good at remembering that he wasn't on tour and that I wasn't a roadie, but I stayed vigilant in case he forgot.

"There's a donair in the fridge," I said.

"'Kay."

He clambered off the bed and went into the bathroom to do whatever he imagined he needed to do in order to show his face at a party. I was fine with my face as it was, so I stayed put. Checked the weather—still fifteen above—and considered getting out the donair in case he wanted it. Except I wasn't his roadie.

"Are you hungry?" I asked through the door.

"It's yours if you want it," he replied, which would instead have been an answer to "Do you want the donair?" It was possible he did want something to eat, but a donair wasn't it. I considered pointing that out, but I didn't think he was in the mood for semantics, and it didn't matter anyhow. They'd have food at the party, and he was a grown-up who could feed himself.

I turned off the TV and turned on the room lights so we could find our phones and ID cards and anything else we might need before going downstairs. As I moved Jess's guitar case to the floor, I saw a copy of the *Journal* on the table. I knew there was a story inside about Jess's last-minute addition to the roster, because Jess had brought this up on the drive from Calgary. He'd said a number of choice things about it, in fact, mainly regarding how the festival had chosen to characterize him. Jack Lowe, ex-boyfriend of an A-list murder victim, recent murder suspect. Brusher of shoulders, and so much else, with the ultra-famous.

Being painted as an edgy star-fucker was a ridiculous thing for him to complain about, considering that he'd known perfectly well what the festival was up to when he'd accepted their invitation. Also considering that he'd sold enough of his own tickets off that reputation.

Still, seeing the offending paper in his hotel room couldn't have improved his mood. I rolled it up and slid it into the wastepaper basket.

He emerged from the bathroom a little fancier than he'd been at the showcase. Still in a T-shirt and jeans, but with more makeup and product and overall effort given to looking like a star. I'd watched him do the magic more than once and still couldn't have said what all went into it.

He'd left the bathroom light on, and as he crossed from that bright space to the larger, darker room, the contrast between the backlight and the shadows made it hard to see his expression. I didn't need to see his face, though. I could tell by his shoulders, tense but low, and the overall slouch of him that he wasn't excited about our plans.

"You know we don't have to go," I said.

"I'm not obligated," he agreed. "But I thought you were meeting someone."

"I'm also not obligated," I said. "We can drive home. Or we can drive to Jasper. Or order in room service and hide under the blankets."

"Fuck it. I'm going," he told me and went past me to the door. I held out his phone, and he paused before taking it, as if I'd surprised him. Because he'd nearly forgotten it. I opened my mouth to ask again if he was sure he was okay, but where would that have gotten me? Instead I checked that he had his pass and put my own phone into my pocket.

A swipe from Jess's key gave us access to locked party floors from the elevator. No stops on the way down since most of the party guests would have come directly from the headliner's show. But Jess startled a little each time the elevator's chime announced we were passing another floor.

When we did stop, Jess raised his head and pushed off the back wall of the elevator. I watched him do a fast change as he moved through the opening doors. Jesse to Jack, prey to party animal. Eyes bright, big smile. He showed his pass to security in the corridor, as if they needed to see it, and launched into the main hall like a missile. I showed my own pass and followed, or tried to. I lost sight of him in the dark and crowded room where jeans, T-shirts and black boots were not a rare sartorial choice.

People were everywhere and closer than I preferred, laughing and bumping into each other and me. Yelling over the music, which was coming from a band I didn't recognize. They were young and punkish for folkies, cranking out "Home for a Rest" with more energy than finesse. The bouncing chaos at the front of the stage said no one was worried about the finer points of the tin whistle, or likely anything else.

I didn't know where I'd find my prospective client, or whether he was even here yet. I did my best to search the hall in an organized way, wall to wall, a few steps forward, then across again. People insisted on moving around and would likely not have stopped even if I'd asked politely, so I wasn't sure how much progress I was making. A few people stepped on my feet, and more bumped into me, but at least I was managing to stay clear of the swaying Solo cups. Small victories.

I relocated Jess before I found my quarry. He was talking to the musician-turned-actor who'd hosted the Juno Awards earlier in the year. Though Jess had nothing against Carson DeJong, as far as I knew, I could tell he'd been cornered. I wandered over to see whether I could help him escape.

"...trying to thank you," DeJong was saying as I approached. He was waving his cup and leaning forward into the space Jess was trying to hold. Even in this well-oiled crowd, I could smell alcohol in the sweat that soaked the back of DeJong's white silk shirt. "I never said you were precious. I'm just telling you what I was hearing backstage. Far's I'm concerned, you can be as precious as you want if it gets me that kind of gig. You can be a rare fucking diamond. Why the hell not?"

"Sorry to interrupt," I said from over DeJong's shoulder. I had enough height on him that it had to feel like I was looming, and besides I'd come out of nowhere, so he jumped a little. Good thing his drink was nearly empty. "Jess? Timmy's trapped in the well."

It was a bit we hadn't used since college, a transparent little back and forth that we'd do before fleeing a party.

Woof, woof!

What's that, Lassie old girl? Timmy's trapped in the well?

Jess blinked in surprise but came back fast enough. "Shit. We gotta get him out of there." He gave DeJong a tight smile. "Good talking to you, man."

He moved sideways, forward, and under my outstretched arm like he was following dance steps painted on the floor. Neat and smooth.

"Scotty should slow down," I said. DeJong had been in a short-lived streaming reboot of the original *Star Trek*, a few years before. Not the best work of his career. Jess laughed.

"Scotty should have slowed down hours ago."

"What was that about?"

Jess steered us to a place in the shadows at the front of the room and past the stage, where the music was about half as loud. I could still hear the band yelling something about Isambard Brunel, which was British even for this party.

"Thanking me for turning down the Junos," Jess said, close to my ear.

It was accurate but incomplete to say Jess had turned down an offer to host the Junos.

They'd called Jesse with surprising speed after the Calgary murder. Many times before that, I'd teased Jess that he'd never get that gig on account of his shameful trash mouth. In truth, it had puzzled me that no one had offered it to him. He had charisma to burn, he was professional despite his persona, and—most important of all—he'd gotten famous in the States. Nothing impresses Canadians more.

But it had never happened until he'd been in a blood-drenched scandal, which suggested the offer had nothing to do with Jess and everything to do with... well, scandal. Same as the reason he was at the festival now. And so he'd turned them down and then some. Though he'd never admitted it to me, I suspected Jess and his famous trash mouth had told them exactly what he thought of them for asking.

"I didn't know people knew I got the offer," Jess said, "and turned it down."

I raised my brows at him. "You didn't think people knew that. Interesting. Did you get into entertainment ten minutes ago?"

"I thought the organizers would keep it a secret out of shame. So ten minutes ago sounds right. Oh, also, I'm precious. Did you know?"

"You're a gem," I told him. "Why are you letting this get to you?"

We'd been connecting, his eyes on mine, a quickness in his face. Now he seemed to fade, like a painting turning into a sketch. Only the outlines of him were left. Then he slipped past me, back into the crowd.

I knew there was no point going after him, even if I could see where he'd gone.

I took advantage of my position at the front of the room to look for my target—or if not *for* him, exactly, for what I expected to see around him.

The etiquette in places like this was to be chill. Even if your lifelong idol was standing on your foot, you were not to react. At most, nicely ask them to get off your foot. But some people seemed to get clusters around them. Indifferent clusters of crew and the younger, less famous musicians, all standing around a central point for no particular reason.

In the back left corner, I saw an eddy in the irregular ripples of the crowd. I moved to the edge of the room and hugged the wall as I went. Aside from the occasional wallflower, that path was clear.

By the time I reached the edge of the circle, I could hear stray words under the music. People talking about the headliner's show, or how they'd gotten into him after it was cool and before it became cool again. No one was discussing anything else. Bullseye.

I went straight for the centre of the group, a tactic that wouldn't have worked under normal circumstances but was fine here since people couldn't block my way without being obvious about crowding the star. I got where I was going without getting my hair mussed and offered a hand to the man in the middle.

"I'm Ben Ames," I said. "I hear you want to talk to me."

CHAPTER TWO

DENNY HILL cocked his head and offered a hand in return. Manicured, strong and calloused, the hand of a guy who played a lot of guitar and was paid well to do it.

"I do," he said. He had the annoyed but forbearing expression of a man who thought a child had done him wrong. I'd have to salvage Izzy's reputation later. "Let's find a quieter place."

People stepped quickly out of our way as we went into the corridor, almost as if they'd been paying more attention to Hill than they'd wanted him to think. Once we were in the corridor, I took out my room key and lifted my chin at the elevators.

"My room's quiet," I said, "if that works for you."

"No need to go that far," Hill said. Before he was done speaking, he was already looking past me. Over my head, in fact. That kind of thing surprises me on the rare occasions when it happens, since I'm taller than the average guy.

Hill waved a hand at someone behind me, and I turned to see a Party Crew volunteer approaching. She was a honey blond with chalk-white skin, impressive for a prairie dweller in August. Alberta could be what my friend Kent called "colder than a witch's tit" or a few degrees cooler than the inside of an active volcano, but it was usually sunny either way.

The crew ranged in age from teens to retirees, and this one was somewhere in the middle. I couldn't tell whether she was starstruck by Hill because she seemed slightly dazed by everything around her, the noise and lights and bodies going hither and yon. She got close to me and Hill and leaned in from her shoulders, like a pigeon.

"Yes?" she said. Her voice was low and soft, and despite her proximity, I strained to hear it.

"Is there a quiet room where my friend and I could talk?"

Hill's voice was effortless and conversational, as if we'd been chatting in a quiet café. Singers and stage actors were like that. They trained for years to be able to whisper to the back of a theatre and then told their boyfriends things like "I did tell you we were out of milk. You must not have heard me."

The blond kept eye contact with Hill, but she went inside herself somewhere. To a map of the building, maybe, or snapshots of the rooms they had available. One thing I'd learned when I'd started interviewing witnesses was that everyone's mental pictures worked differently. Some people didn't have them at all.

"Yes," she said finally. "We do. If no one's in it."

She took a few steps down the corridor before looking back over her shoulder and waving a few fingers to tell us to follow. We did, all the way down and around a corner to a door that she knocked on, listened at, and finally opened a crack to peer inside. Satisfied, she pushed it open and did that same slight wave of her fingers to direct us inside.

"It's a sensory room," she said. "If someone needs it, you'll have to go."

"Of course," Hill said, as if he understood both the room's purpose and her request. I'd have bet he understood neither.

I hadn't seen a lot of sensory rooms, but to my eyes, this was a pretty good knock-up for a room that wasn't purpose-built. Someone had taped a dark blue gel over the ceiling light, and LED strings were tacked to the walls. Furniture had been replaced with beanbags and foam mats. A plush basket between the bean bags was filled with Koosh balls, and someone had left an open adult colouring book and set of markers on the floor. The overall effect was of a playroom for kids with hangovers.

Fortunately, a few stacking banquet chairs had been left in one corner. Hill and I wouldn't have to find out whether we'd be able to get into beanbag chairs or, if we did, whether we'd ever get out again.

As we moved the chairs, I noticed a small white-noise generator that had been hidden behind them. It was doing its plucky best to combat the Celtic punks, whose music was leaking in through the gaps around the door.

Once Hill and I were seated, he gave the room a once-over.

"Not exactly what I had in mind," he said, "but it'll do. Did she call this a sense room?"

"Sensory room," I said. "For people who get overstimulated."

He raised his brows, which had been shaped by a professional.

"Do those people enjoy parties?"

"To a point, I guess," I told him. I didn't tell him that I also enjoyed parties to a point, or that the point was usually within half an hour of my arrival.

"I feel like I should be dropping acid," he said. "Does that date me? I don't think anyone does that anymore."

"You'd have to ask Izzy," I suggested.

He smiled. "Missy L'Izzy. I assume she told you to find me?"

"Nope," I said firmly. "She told me that someone wanted to hire me, that they'd find me at the party, and that she couldn't tell me who they were. Just like you asked."

He cocked his head. "Then how…?"

"It was easy to figure out you were one of the more famous people here," I said. "No offense, but it's not usual to summon people the way you did. I don't think even Jess would try it. Then I thought, why Izzy? Party Crew volunteers aren't hanging around backstage. You didn't pick her at random. You had to have her number. Once I realized that, I had to ask myself who the biggest stars were and find out which of them had that connection."

He smiled. It was a charming smile, because it had better be for a man in his line of work.

"I'm not as clandestine as I thought. Ben, I summoned you, if you want to put it that way, because I didn't want to talk about this on the phone. I wanted a chance to convince you to take this job. Face-to-face."

He had the amiable but distant manner I was used to seeing online and on TV. His jeans and long-sleeved cotton shirt might have looked casual if they hadn't been ironed, and I didn't think I'd ever seen him with a loose button or a crease where it shouldn't be. He was the visual equivalent of his sound.

Denny Hill had broken in the late 90s and early 2000s with burnished acoustic rock, the kind of thing anyone could tolerate and no one loved. Jess had once told me not to underestimate how many people bought an album or went to a show, not because they loved the artist, but because they didn't mind them. The fact that Hill had topped the US charts a few times bore that out.

He'd had actual fans too. What might feel generic to some was, to a lot of people, relatable. Some fans had turned their backs on him in the 2010s, as he'd moved on to string and piano ballads for popcorn flicks, but they were reapproaching his legacy now. Saying things like "deceptive simplicity" and "effortless." There'd been a *Rolling Stone* piece calling him an everyman.

Hence his appearance at the festival. Even the musicians who didn't buy his new valuation were excited to stand next to him, in case a secret to success fell out of his ironed pocket.

I waited as he crossed his legs at the knee and leaned forward with an elbow on one toned thigh and a thumb beneath his chin, like he was about to hold forth on the legacy of Peter Gzowski or the songbook of Neil Young. He paused like that, eyes on mine, making sure he had my full and complete attention. I gave him a nod so he could stop worrying about it.

"I'm here on behalf of my friend Charlie," he said. "He needs your help because someone has stolen his book."

What I pictured was someone setting a paperback down on a bench, walking away to use a water fountain, and coming back to find it gone. Out one John Grisham and at a loss for how to replace it. A private investigator wouldn't be most people's first thought.

"Stolen his book?" I repeated.

"Yes. He finished writing it last week, and a day later, it was gone."

Oh. That did make more sense.

"An author," I said. "So they stole a manuscript. How's his cat?"

Hill looked confused, as well he might. "He doesn't have a cat."

"It was a joke," I said. "There's a play from the seventies where the lead character gets his manuscript stolen and his cat dies."

"Oh, is that right? The 1970s? That would be before your time."

It wasn't before his time, but neither of us said so.

"I've heard of Shakespeare too. Anyway, the thing in the play is that the author only has one copy because he used a typewriter, which no one does anymore."

"Some people," Hill said, "do still use typewriters. Not Charlie, but it's similar. His laptop has no internet connection."

"No backup?" I said. "At all? What if his laptop died?"

"He uses a flash drive," Hill said. "That's been taken as well."

I nearly asked whether the drive had been plugged into the laptop at the time of the theft. An important question if you were a detective who had taken that case. Which was far from determined. I shut my mouth so hard I could hear my teeth click.

"The main goal is to get the manuscript back," Hill went on. "Finding out who took it, why they took it, making sure there are no other copies out there… those would also be good, of course. But the return of the manuscript is primary."

"The return of the manuscript," I told him, "is a tall order. I'm not sure I could do it. I'm not sure anyone could."

Hill blinked in surprise. At least I thought he did. The blue ceiling light and the LEDs were interacting in a way that made lines, even the lines of his face, jittery.

"It would be like finding anything else, wouldn't it?" Hill said. "A stolen car? Stolen diamonds?"

I couldn't keep from laughing. I did manage to stop within ten seconds or so.

"I'm sorry," I said. "You have a funny idea of what I do for a living. I'm generally not on the trail of international jewel thieves."

"Oh no," Hill said. He was drumming lightly on his knees with the pads of his fingers. Jess was a nervous drummer too. "I don't think that. I used it for… dramatic effect, I guess. What I meant is, you find stolen things. Don't you?"

"Sometimes," I said. "If they seem findable. If someone took a bunch of recording equipment out of your studio? It's probably already two provinces over, but I can put up some flags and check the local fences. If you inherited the antique butter churn your sister wanted and now it's missing, I'd have an idea where to start. Does your friend even know why his book was taken?"

"Well, I…." Hill trailed off and ended with a shrug. "The usual reasons."

"For stealing manuscripts?" I said. "What are those?"

"You're the expert," Hill said, more prissily than was called for.

"Experts need data. I don't generate it. I get it from clients and witnesses, and then I use my expertise to make sense of it. You know this guy. Why do you think someone would steal his book? Are you even sure someone stole it? What if he left it on a bus or in a Starbucks?"

"He didn't," Hill said. "That laptop never leaves Charlie's house. I wonder if the theft might have something to do with the kind of book this is. Have you heard of Charlie Gudzyak? He has a pen name. He writes as Wolfgang Waltz."

"Jesus, why?"

It was out before I could stop it. Fortunately, Hill laughed. There was a hitching sound to it, different from his usual rolling chuckle, so I thought it was for real.

"Wolfgang because when he started out, he was convinced that German science fiction writers were taken more seriously. Waltz, I have no idea. What's that word for letters being the same? Alliteration."

"It has a, uh, ring to it," I said. "I know I haven't heard that name because there's no way I could forget it. But I don't read a lot of sci-fi."

Hill actually flinched, like I'd thrown a Koosh ball at him.

"Never say sci-fi in front of Charlie. It's science fiction. He will not tolerate that."

"Okay," I said. "Wolfgang writes science fiction. How's that connected to the theft? Does he think aliens did it?"

"I don't think so," Hill said, half to himself. It wasn't the worst possible answer he could have given, but it was up there. What kind of character was this Charlie? Hill gave his head a little shake and went on. "This isn't science fiction, this book. It's an autobiography. Or a memoir. I'm not clear about the difference."

"Me either," I said. "Has Charlie had an unusual life?"

"In some ways," Hill said. "He's actually very successful. Just not here. You know the term 'big in Japan'?"

"Yes. Is he?"

"No." Hill had gone from drumming his legs to picking at pieces of lint I couldn't see. "He's big in China. Huge market there. It's been lucrative. And I think Charlie likes the excuse not to interact directly with his readers. There are times I envy him."

He raised his head to look at me. Did I understand the plight of the poor little famous boy? God, did anyone?

"Fans can be intense," I said.

"They're… many of them are lonely. Always throwing out these lines for connection, like fishing lines, with hooks, and you have to step aside, but not too quickly because they can't know you're avoiding them."

It might have been my imagination, but I thought I saw his fingers curl around an imaginary pen, itching to capture that deathless imagery for a song.

"So," I said, "your friend is a big deal in China, and he wrote an autobiography for his fans. Were you in this autobiography?"

"Probably," Hill said. "Charlie and I grew up on the same street. We've been friends that long. I asked to read it, but he said no."

"Did he think you'd never see it?"

Hill smiled. "I think he knew everyone would see it eventually. But he's never liked for people to see things before publication. Not even his publisher, until he's ready to turn the finished manuscript in."

"And did he?" I asked. "You said it was done the day before it was stolen. Had he sent off a copy?"

Hill shook his head. "Charlie liked to let things marinate. He usually held on to a manuscript for a few days, maybe a week, in case he had any last-minute thoughts."

Was that commonly known? Would the thief have known they had some time before the book was sent away? Did it matter, since I was not taking the case? I shifted in my chair. It was like every stackable chair I'd ever sat in, designed more for stackability than comfort.

"Here's my expert opinion: It's not accurate to say I find things and so I can find this thing, because the manuscript isn't really a thing. It's digital. You could destroy it forever in a few seconds. A few minutes if you really wanted to make sure. Or you could hide a copy somewhere on the internet and destroy the original. You think I'm pessimistic about finding a laptop in the real world, you should hear the odds of me finding a digital thing on the internet."

To my surprise, Hill reached into the bucket between us and picked up a Koosh ball in his long, narrow fingers. He massaged it and stared at the opposite wall, next to the door.

"All right. I'll concede that it seems bleak. And I know people in your profession don't offer guarantees. I'm not asking for one. This was a terrible thing to happen to a good… to a good friend. He deserves to have someone at least try to help him. All you would have to do is try."

Why the stammer before "a good friend"? Had he tried to say Charlie was a good guy, a good person, and choked on the words?

"It's admirable," I said, "that you're going to this much trouble for your friend."

"He's always been there for me."

We looked at each other and nodded like we were both content with that answer. If Hill was personally worried about what his old friend Charlie had written, or who might have gotten their hands on that information, I wasn't going to hear him say so.

"Thank you for thinking of me," I said. "Sincerely. But I'm not taking the case. If your friend doesn't mind wasting his money, I'm sure he can hire someone else."

"Is there anything I can do to change your mind? You could name your price. I suppose you probably can most of the time these days."

"I can?" I said. "No one told me that."

Hill laughed again. "You're a private investigator to the stars," he said. "It's why I sought you out. That and Izzy's recommendation."

"If Izzy told you I specialize in celebrities, she was joking, and her sense of humour needs work. I live with a celebrity, and I happened to be around when another one died."

Hill patted my leg. It was a chummy thing to do. We were not chums.

"You understand things that most private investigators don't. Artists. Fame. The business side of it all. These insights matter."

I eyed his hand. He took it back and put it on his own leg. I wanted to say that everyone thought their thing was special, intricate, and impossible for an outsider to understand. People who stood around in bathrooms giving out towels for tips probably thought their job needed a decade of experience and a PhD. Instead I said, "I question the extent of my insight, but it doesn't matter. I don't want the case because I don't want the case. At the moment, I'm only taking work that interests me."

"Then you really should take this on. Charlie's interesting. He's a big idea guy. Big bold ideas."

I couldn't shake the feeling that there were things about Charlie that Hill was hiding. I'd have asked questions, except it didn't matter. "I'm still turning it down."

Hill pressed the heels of his hands into his legs and pushed to get himself standing. Once upright, he stretched and winced.

"You'll creak like this one day," he told me. "Thank you for hearing me out. I would like to give you my number in case you do change your mind."

I stood with less effort and creaking but a twinge in my legs. It was the chair's fault, not anyone's age.

"No harm in that," I said. We took out our phones and exchanged numbers. I saw a few texts from Izzy asking whether the client had found me yet, and one from Brennan asking where I was, what I was drinking, and where was the nearest bar to me.

Hill and I shook hands, and he left without putting his chair away because that was the kind of thing his butler or batman would take care of. I stayed behind for a minute to text Izzy that, yes, I had met the client. I didn't mention that I wasn't taking the case. Then I texted Brennan to say that, yes, he could buy me a drink, and I could meet him wherever he was. He sent back directions to a breakout room one floor down.

Brennan was a newer friend for both Jess and myself. We'd gone to school with a guy named Thom who'd become the keyboardist in the Twist, and Thom had recently introduced us to his bandmates.

The Twist had played the festival Friday night, a show Jess and I had missed, and the next day everyone but Brennan and Reiss had taken off for Jasper. Those two had stayed to do the workshop. They seemed to be trying to bond with me and Jess, and I appreciated the effort, kind of. I wasn't that social, but Jess was, and he'd been isolated from a lot of his musician pals since moving in with me. If I had to have a beer with an agreeable Englishman to encourage this friendship, so be it.

Brennan wasn't too hard to find, since the breakout rooms weren't large and he'd already said he'd be at the bar—which in this case was a table near the door where drinks were available from an ice tub. Live music was playing in this room, too, but it was a jazz combo, and they weren't trying to drown anyone out. They also weren't yelling about pirates or railway engineers, so already they had me on side.

"Hey, hey!" Red-faced and radiating sunburned heat, Brennan came to me for a hug and a slap on the back. He smelled good despite the clinging moisture of his T-shirt. Something like pepper and raw wood. When we pulled back, I looked around for Reiss and Jess and saw neither.

"You been abandoned?" I asked.

He grinned. "Little bit. You?"

"So it seems. I'm not sure where Jess is."

"He's with Reiss. They went somewhere to talk. I was not invited."

He grabbed beers for us both, and we found club chairs with a small table between.

"When did you get here?" I asked

"Twenty minutes? Dunno. We skipped out on Denny Hill's show to get dinner. Nice little Lebanese place up the street. Go in the back, it's a hookah. We stayed longer than we'd planned."

It sounded nice for some reason. Because a lot of things did in Brennan's Newcastle accent or because it was better than what I'd been doing with my time.

"I caught Denny's show a couple of minutes ago," I said. "One on one. He was trying to convince me to take a case for a friend of his."

Brennan grinned and took a pull on his beer. "Did he sing?"

I laughed. "Maybe he should have. I turned it down."

"Good plan. We opened for him out east. Wouldn't do it again."

We drank and listened to the band and watched the people milling around.

"Jesse did great today," Brennan said. "Not stagey. Fit right in."

I shrugged. "He's good at his job."

"He is. His usual job is quite different, though. If you think about it. Anyway, he acquitted himself well, and I hope he feels good about it tomorrow. Once he's past his hangover."

"I doubt he'll get that drunk," I said. "I know he used to, but that was part of the Jack Lowe show. He's trying to be himself."

Brennan gave me an odd look. "I'd say it's the Jack Lowe show tonight. You may want to check on him."

I didn't exactly want to, if he really was drunk off his ass. I'd gotten more than my fill of that back in Toronto. But it was starting to sound like I should.

"Any idea where he and Reiss went?"

Brennan shook his head. "Could be anywhere. But not upstairs. I have the room key. Unless they went to your room."

"I'll check the other breakout rooms," I said. "If I can't find them, I'll try the room."

"You could text him and ask where he is," Brennan pointed out.

"You could text Reiss," I said. "Or you could text Jess."

"Or you could text Reiss."

We stared at each other. Neither of us reached for our phones. I set my beer down and left.

I roamed for a while, sticking my nose into rooms, seeking Jesse's dark wings of hair or Reiss's curls. I wasn't listening for their voices because I didn't think I'd hear them over the music, but it turned out they'd found the only room around where the music was quiet enough that voices could beat it. Just a guy and his guitar in a chair, not even on a stage.

The door was open, and the first clear word that came through was my name, spoken by Jesse. They hadn't seen me yet, and I'll admit it, I stopped to hear what he had to say about me.

"...Ben told me to shut up. He said I didn't have real problems."

I couldn't recall having said either of those things to Jess. At least not recently. I edged closer.

"I know he doesn't like publicity! I've apologized a lot. A lot! And I didn't even murder anyone. And he's getting better cases now, so what's his fucking problem?"

"Also you do have real problems." That was Reiss.

"Fuck," Jess said. "I do, don't I? No one is going to take me seriously. Ever. Why would they? I'm a fucking goth clown. That guy in Kananaskis? He called me a cut-rate Marilyn Manson."

"That was uncalled for."

"That's what I fucking said. I should've shot him."

I went into the room and raised a hand as a wave, giving them the opportunity to tell me to fuck off. Instead, Reiss gave me a nod and Jess gave me a smile that was anemic but not forced. Apparently he was willing to overlook whatever he thought I'd done.

They were sitting on a pair of low and wide chairs that were better suited to height-challenged people, such as the two of them, than to me. I pulled a third chair in and sat beside them anyway.

"You find Bren?" Reiss asked me.

"Yeah. He's watching my beer."

Reiss's mouth twisted into a half smile. "You know you can carry open liquor around here, right, Officer?"

"I thought I could find more if I needed it." I glanced at Jesse's chair, which was surrounded by empty glasses. Tough to count in the dim light, but it was somewhere between enough glassware to host a small party and enough to open his own bar. "How're you doing, Jess?"

"I'm a fucking joke."

"Huh." I turned to Reiss. "How's your night going?"

"Been better," he said. "Been worse."

He didn't seem too bad, at least compared to the night we'd met. He wasn't drinking, though that didn't mean anything one way or another. I wasn't sure he was supposed to with the meds he was on. Reiss had the kind of complicated mental health condition that made Jess follow up complaints about his own depression with "but I'm not Reiss or anything." By which he meant some people have it worse. I was 100 per cent sure Reiss would not appreciate it and equally sure Jess would never say it to his face.

"Are you just doing one-off gigs this year, or are you touring?" I asked.

"We're working on the new album," Reiss said. "Can you see me working on it?"

I smiled. Jess scowled and stared at the floor. Possibly hunting for a not-quite-dead soldier.

"So it's happening at a leisurely pace?" I suggested.

Reiss laughed. "The thing about being mentally original," he said, "it is sometimes good for the writing. Sometimes, though, it is good for nothing."

Before I could say anything, Jess stood. Mostly. He got to his feet, knocking over a few bottles, put his hands on his knees, and hung his head. Getting ready to leave or to boot. I wasn't sure even Jesse knew which. I was torn between taking his arm to steady him and keeping out of the splash zone. He made the choice moot by shaking his head, standing more or less upright, and charging past me into the hall. He was moving at a good clip for someone who could have used a map to find his feet.

I exchanged "what're you gonna do?" looks with Reiss and went after Jess.

He was a pinball out in the hall, bouncing off people and walls and excusing himself roughly as often as a pinball does. I caught up and grabbed his arm for the safety of everyone.

"Where are we going?" I asked.

I could see he was about to say "to hell" or something equally witty, but he correctly guessed from my face that it wouldn't go over.

"Not here," he said.

In theory, "not here" could have included France or the tip of Ellesmere Island or the moon. In practice, there were likely to be fans hanging around outside the hotel, and Jesse was in no condition to face them. Not that he'd never met fans while drunk, high, or otherwise off his nut, but he was also in a mood, and I didn't know what he might do or say. The safest choice was our room. I steered him toward the elevators, and he went along with it, even using his card to swipe us in.

He leaned against the elevator's back wall in silence and let me choose our destination. Eyeballed his shoes for the whole ride. He was acting like I didn't exist, but I didn't take it personally. It wasn't my fault the human race had somehow disappointed him or that I was one eight-billionth of it.

No one seemed to be up and around on our floor, which made sense as musicians would still be downstairs and regular guests would be asleep. I got Jess into our room quickly, before that luck ran out, and opened the curtains while he went into the bathroom to, by the sound of it, splash water on his face. He was dripping from the hairline down when he emerged.

"Too drunk to talk?" I asked.

He sat on the bed he'd napped in. The blankets were a twisted mess, like he'd tried to tie knots in them while he slept. "About what?"

"I dunno. Maybe why you started two-fisting it the second you got out of my sight? Were you trying to get into a party mood?"

He regarded me through half-lidded eyes. "I feel like Izzy," he said.

"What?"

"You're not my real dad either."

That was a callback to Izzy's favourite bit, where one of us would give her some rational advice and she'd tell us we weren't her real dads. We were doing callbacks, because this was the comedy hour.

"I'm sincerely asking," I said. "You told me you'd stopped getting drunk or high to tolerate social events. This seems regressive. Why did you do it?"

"I'm not that drunk."

"You're not not drunk."

"I'm an adult."

I sat on the bed next to the window. My bed, as I was starting to think of it.

"I know that. You're the adult who told me he was going to stop doing this."

He was pulling at something on the blanket. A loose thread or a fleck of lint. "I didn't have anyone to be."

I lay back on the bed and looked at the ceiling, which was not feeling irrationally sorry for itself. As far as I knew.

"You couldn't be yourself?"

He was silent for what felt like a long time. A flash at the window drew my eye. Paparazzi, outside the nineteenth floor? It happened again, and I realized it was heat lightning. The first I'd seen that summer.

"Nothing's working," he said. His voice was thick. I felt a little shock in my chest, like a live wire had skipped across my heart.

"What do you mean?"

"I don't know."

I gave him time to think about it. If he came to any conclusions, he didn't share.

"I'm sorry about whatever I said in the car," I told him. "I don't know why it upsets you that people think you're the guy you've been pretending to be for the past eight years, but if it does… I'm sorry."

"I did it to myself. I did."

Not quite the words from the old song, but he sang them anyway.

"You piled up a mountain of money being that guy," I told him. "You can do whatever you want now."

More silence. On the other bed, Jess was lying on his side, looking at the wall. Missing the lightning. He hadn't even asked about my mystery client, I realized. And he loved a mystery. I opened my mouth and what came out was this: "Do you want to help me find a missing book?"

He rolled over to face me. I could barely see his features. "That's your job? Your new job?"

"Yes," I said. It was a lie, and this was a bad idea, but I could call Hill in the morning and tell him I'd take the case. God fucking help me. "I have to find a stolen manuscript. Digital. Should be nearly impossible."

Lightning flashed, and I thought I saw him smile. "Sounds fun."

"It's here in Edmonton. We'd have to stay for a while. I'm not sure how long."

I couldn't see him anymore, but I could hear that his smile had widened when he spoke again. "Trapped on the Orange Island. The horrible Oranges. The horror."

The Orange Island was the nickname Edmonton had earned by doggedly voting for socialists while the rest of the province went right. Most of the province, anyway. About half of Calgary had thrown in with the radical left the last time we'd gone to the polls.

"I'm not the one percenter in this room," I reminded him. "I won't be against the wall when the revolution comes."

He sighed so deep, I could hear his mattress move. "Goodnight, Ben."

He didn't come over to my bed or invite me to his. He didn't tell me to stay put, either, but I felt like it was implied. I turned toward the window and watched for lightning until I fell asleep.

Chapter THREE

JESS TRACKED me down just before 10:00 a.m. at the table behind city hall where I'd set myself up with a book and a respectable iced coffee. It would have been impressive that he'd managed to find me, a few blocks from the hotel in a busy downtown, but in fact I'd texted him my location and a photo to make it easier. He'd have seen that after the wake-up call I'd set up, likely while eating the pain au chocolate I'd left beside his bed.

He didn't seem too rough for a guy who'd overindulged the night before. That was no surprise. First, he hadn't been all that drunk—certainly not by the standards he'd been setting for years. And second, he'd spent those years developing skills in making himself presentable no matter what had gone on hours or even minutes earlier.

In fact he had done better than presentable. He was wearing casual basics, shorts and a T-shirt, but both fit better than anything I'd ever worn. A pair of pitch-black shades hid his eyes, and his hair was stirred by a breeze that was taking the edge off the heat. He'd also acquired a coffee, hot, which I hadn't left for him. It would only have gotten cold.

"Thank you for breakfast," he said. "Fuck you for the wake-up call."

"You're welcome for both." I waved a hand at the table's second chair, and he sat, taking off the oiled-leather satchel he'd been wearing crossbody. I hadn't seen it before, so either he'd bought it on impulse somewhere nearby or he'd only recently had it sent from Toronto. Most of his things were still in a Quay West condo I'd never seen.

"How's your head?" I asked.

He mulled for a moment before saying, "Fine."

"Good. We're meeting the client in an hour."

"The mystery client." He still didn't ask who it was. "Why is this city so obsessed with pyramids?"

That didn't come out of nowhere. The city hall building was made up of glass pyramids, oddly like the four-pyramid conservatory up the road from the folk festival site.

"Probably run by the Illuminati," I said.

We sipped coffee and thought about that. A seagull flew overhead. Between us and city hall, kids were playing in the fountain spray park as their parents watched from the grass.

"Sinister," Jess said. "Is the client meeting us here? Is it someone famous, like you thought?"

"It's Denny Hill."

"I was wondering." The smile that spread across his face was sly, like we were sharing gossip. "I didn't think anyone else would be that much of an ass."

"Bren doesn't like him either," I said. "He's been making friends all over the industry."

"It's not very Canadian," Jess said, "to think you're a big-ass deal. Did he write a book?"

I was lost for a moment. Then I remembered that I'd told Jess about the stolen manuscript the night before. He seemed to have pretty good recall. Maybe he really hadn't been that drunk. It was possible, in a party where people bobbed and flowed from space to space, that not all the empty glasses around his chair had been his.

"No," I told him. "The author's a friend of his. He'll pay, but it's his friend's book."

I didn't mention that the friend sounded like one of God's own originals. There'd be time for that later.

"So are we meeting Hill or the author?"

"The author. Hill texted me his address. I asked him to come along and make an introduction, but he declined, so we're going in cold."

"Did you say it was digital? I think you said that last night."

"Yeah. The guy doesn't trust the cloud. He writes on a laptop with no internet connection, and he saves his manuscript to a flash drive. That's what got stolen—the computer and the drive. He doesn't have any other copies."

"Why would someone steal a manuscript? Are they going to black market publish it or something? Is he that popular?"

"Maybe if it was one of his novels. But this one's a memoir. I'm thinking maybe someone didn't want to be written about."

Jesse's eyes went to the book I'd set on the table. I'd picked it up that morning at a bookstore a few blocks west along the main drag. I could have downloaded it cheaper, but I thought I might have to annotate the thing, and I preferred to do that on paper.

"That's one of his books? The novels?"

I picked it up and offered it to him. "*Side-Chain*. Wikipedia said it was the latest one."

Jess took the book and studied the cover, which was green and yellow with a leaves-and-chain-links design that reminded me of Magic Eye pictures. It might have been one—I hadn't tried to make it pop out.

"Wolfgang Waltz?" Jess raised his brows so high they appeared over his sunglasses.

"It's a pseudonym," I said. "He chose it."

"He's the one who has to live with it," Jess said absently as he studied the inside flaps. "No bio or author photo, hey?"

He turned the book over to read the back cover.

It's 2075, fifty years after the release of the Sak-2 bacteria, and most of Earth's non-organic plastic has been destroyed. In the aftermath of the Plastic Wars, multi-national Monor-Ascall is rebuilding the world's major cities while geneticist Harry Duvall and his team discover new mutations in Sak-2 that could have deadly implications for all life on Earth.

"It's a series," I said, as if Jess couldn't have figured that out.

"You said he was popular?"

"Yeah. Not here. He sells a lot of books in China. The guy's a rockstar in Beijing."

"I'm glad somebody is," Jess said. I detected no bitterness in his voice, just wry resignation. He was about a million times too out and proud for the Chinese government. I wasn't sure he'd ever been allowed to perform there. Even if he hadn't been gay, there was a good chance he'd have been banned for loucheness.

"If you feel like reading that, go ahead," I told him. "I thought I should get a sense of the guy's writing. I'm two chapters in, and I'm not sure how much further I can go."

I stood, and Jess did the same, tucking the book into his satchel. I'd take that as an offer to read the thing unless he said otherwise.

"Did you move the car?" I asked.

"No, I re-upped the room for tonight and left it in the parkade," Jess told me. "We can keep staying there, or we can get another hotel or an Airbnb or something. Depends how long you think we'll be here."

"And what Hill will pay for," I reminded him. "This is on him, not you."

Jess laughed. "Rent a mansion. He won't even notice. Did you tell him your fee yet? You should double it. And go two weeks on the retainer instead of one. You said this case was going to be impossible. That's got to mean two weeks at least."

I was keeping my eyes ahead since the sidewalk was packed with magazine dispensers and shop sandwich boards—and a stop sign lying on the ground for some reason—but I spared him a glance.

"Are you my manager now? Should I be giving you ten per cent?"

Jess looked to the sky and shook his head. No fear of tripping over stop signs or walking into light poles. He probably thought I'd swoop in to save him if he started to fall. I probably would.

"Where to even begin. First, if I'm negotiating rates for you, I'm not your manager, I'm your agent. In which case ten per cent is roughly fair. If I'm advising you that you don't charge enough but I'm not actually negotiating anything, then I'm your manager, and I get more than ten per cent."

"Why do managers get more money for doing less work?" I asked.

"Capitalism, Ben." He let that hang for a moment, then added, "I'm kidding. Sort of. Managers don't exactly do less work. They're supposed to be shaping your whole career. The shape of it, your longevity, how you adjust to change. They'll advise you to pass up a gig if they think it doesn't fit the plan. An agent will never tell you to pass up a gig."

"So you're my agent."

"Hah," he said. But neither did he deny it.

He offered to drive so I could text the financial details to Hill and get my retainer locked down. This may have been because Jesse was oddly efficient for a sybarite, or because Jess was worried I would drop the case at the first hiccup if I wasn't financially obligated to keep going. I had never dropped anything over a mere hiccup, but I had walked out on things that weren't how the client had described them, so he wasn't entirely wrong.

For a guy who'd played Edmonton any number of times but likely never driven in it, Jess did reasonably well with the city's wonky roads, spiteful drivers, and general lack of get-there-from-hereness. He and Google managed to get us deep into the neighbourhood we'd asked for, but the app sent us in circles after that and finally directed us to a place in one of Edmonton's bedroom communities, a half hour west of town. That was my cue to turn off my phone and go it alone.

In theory we should have been fine, since most of the city's streets were numbered, not named, and the numbers were supposedly consecutive, except when they weren't. If you wanted to go to 10010 130th Street, you could be forgiven for thinking you were home and dry once you'd found the corner of 100th Avenue and 128th Street. That was what Edmonton wanted you to think. In reality, the place could be anywhere, and so could you.

Jess and I drove around the same four blocks a dozen times and finally got out and roamed the streets, darting up front walks to check house numbers that were hidden behind tree branches or too small to read without a magnifying glass. When Jess stopped dead in front of me and demanded to know whether the client lived in "motherfucking Narnia," I could not blame him.

However sick of the neighbourhood we were getting, there was no denying it was a nice one. Mature trees, well-kept yards, handsome wood-and-brick houses. It was the kind of place that tenured university professors liked to live in and that assistant professors wished they could afford. Wealth wasn't displayed in gold chandeliers and marble gates but in the cost of the bikes racked on the roof of one's Subaru.

Jess finally figured it out. One corner of the street featured a nearly unbroken hedge that seemed like it was shared by the visible houses on either side. A narrow path of concrete blocks led through the hedge, and it seemed as if it must be a walkway to one of those houses. If you looked closely, though, you could see that it didn't go to either yard. It was an easement. Jess didn't use that word because, not having grown up on a farm, he'd probably never heard it. What he said was, "I think this goes somewhere."

He started down it without further comment. I followed and took a few hits to the shoulders from branches. The hedges along the path weren't untrimmed, but the path was barely wide enough for a grown human, and a branch only had to be a little ambitious to be long enough to block my way.

The path led to a plain metal-mesh gate, about three feet high, that swung into a pie-shaped lot with a house parked at the wide back. It was one of those faux-German houses with chocolate-brown wood stripes and a jagged alp of pointed gables. Raised flower beds framed the door.

If I had my geography right, and I might not have, we were near the top of the river bank. A risky place to stick an expensive house if you asked me, but this one seemed like it had been standing for a lot of years.

Jess and I stopped to regard our discovery. The black iron numbers nailed alongside the door matched the ones in my phone.

"Did you bring breadcrumbs?" Jess asked.

It did, in fact, seem like the kind of place where a witch would try to cook us.

"Denny knows we're here," I reassured him.

"Denny could have done a better job of telling us where here was."

He had a point about that, too.

It was impossible to tell from the shuttered windows whether anyone was home. I could see no way I could see to drive a car onto that lot, so that cue was also unavailable. I shrugged and went up the walk to the front door, which was solid dark wood with thin strips of lighter wood framing rows of rectangles along it. Around shoulder height, there was a brass lion's head door knocker that had either been well-used over the years, or had been antiqued to look that way. From the eave, a red light blinked at me.

I found a camera doorbell and pressed it. I could hear a long series of chimes inside the house. A bird sang back from the trees. We waited.

"No one home?" Jess said.

"Maybe not. Denny said his friend was usually home. But everyone goes out sometimes."

"Not everyone." Jess was eyeballing the camera. He'd been so well trained in noticing cameras and managing himself around them that it was practically physical by now, like an extra sense that overrode his motor skills until he'd considered his brand.

I'd almost talked myself into giving up and coming back later when the door opened.

Wolfgang Waltz's book did not have an author photo, as Jess had noted, and there was no photo on Charlie Gudzyak's brief Wikipedia page. I supposed the short red-haired woman who answered the door could be Charlie, but it didn't seem likely.

"Hello?"

She looked from one to the other of us. She didn't seem to recognize Jess, or if she did, she didn't care. Her face wasn't hostile, but her eyes were wide and moving fast. She didn't seem like a woman who believed in good surprises.

"I'm Ben Ames," I told her, handing over one of my cards. "Denny Hill sent me. I'm here to see Charlie Gudzyak."

She took my card between French-tipped nails. She was dressed for summer in a sleeveless white cotton top and a sturdy tan skirt that ended just above her knees. The heat had melted her foundation into the lines on her face, and the excess was washed up around the edges like silt. Between that and the specks of grey at the roots of her feathered bob, I put her somewhere north of fifty.

"A detective," she said. She was holding the card up high enough to watch me as she read, in case I tried to detect something when she wasn't looking.

"Yes."

"Well, I do not know. Is he expecting you?"

From the words alone, you'd think I'd buttonholed her outside a yacht club. Her way of speaking was like that, enunciated and lazy at once, but her tone was different. She really didn't know. Was Charlie expecting a detective? He could have been. Was Charlie expecting Cirque du Soleil riding a herd of unicorns? Also possible.

"I'm not sure," I said. "Denny may have called ahead."

Denny's name was the one thing that didn't seem mysterious to her. I wondered whether Denny had stopped by while he was in town. Given that he'd been in town for days and was up on the latest in Charlie's life, the odds were good.

"Well," she said again. She glanced over her shoulder, into the house. I couldn't see past the foyer, which was small and tidy with a wooden bench and brown tiled floor. "I suppose… come inside."

The unspoken part, expressed by a sudden droop in her posture and weariness in her eyes, was "fuck it." Jess and I exchanged a glance behind her back. I shrugged, and we followed. I hadn't introduced Jess, and she hadn't asked, but the invitation hadn't excluded him.

On entering the foyer, I could see a few pairs of shoes under the bench—men's leather slip-ons and hiking sandals, next to a pair of open-toe heels that were a fit for the redhead. A dirt-streaked blue windbreaker and a black quilted jacket were hanging on a black metal coat rack.

As neither Jess nor I had been raised in a barn, we paused and considered the shoe removal issue. Our host was charging ahead, wearing thick-strapped sandals, and the floors were washable, so we kept the shoes on.

It was immediately cooler once we were inside, more so than I'd have expected from shade alone. I couldn't hear fans going, and the coolness was steady, not moving on a breeze. Had to be an AC somewhere.

Past the foyer was a hall with a closed door at the back, stairs on the right, and a pair of open doorways on the left. The stairs had thick carved posts and a patterned rug running up the middle. With the stairs taking up half the space, the hall was narrow. Another set of stairs, below the ones going upstairs, led down to the basement.

To our left what I had expected to see was a normal living room. Some furniture, art, and photos on the walls, enough floor space to get from one end to the other without having to move anything. That was not what was on the other side of the archway.

It was a smallish living room, from what I could tell, though it was tough to be sure because it looked as if someone had taken the contents of a bookstore, a few comic shops, and a flea-market collectibles booth and shoved them into the space. Bookshelves lined the walls, and each was packed, with as few gaps as possible between items, but there were also bookshelves coming out from the walls at a perpendicular. The tops of the shelves held more of what I could only call "stuff," rising up to graze the stippled ceiling.

In the midst of this, on the one chair and next to the one end table afforded room amid the books, was a skinny guy with greying blond hair and rimless glasses. His round head was a little too big for his body, and the way he sat, twisted to one side with his legs crossed at the knees, made him resemble a bag of nuts and bolts that someone had dressed in a cowboy shirt and faded jeans. His watery blue eyes flicked back and forth over the intruders at the threshold. I'd have put him older than the fifty years Wikipedia claimed, but he was a contemporary of Denny's, so it did check out.

Jess and I stayed well back, because there was limited standing space once you got more than two or three feet into the room. What space existed, the redhead had already stepped into.

"Charlie, these people are here to see you," she told him. "Denny sent them."

"What for?"

The redhead looked at me. I stepped forward, and she moved back slightly to give me room. I extended a hand, which Charlie ignored.

"I'm Ben Ames. I'm a private investigator. Denny hired me to help you find something."

I didn't get specific since I had no idea who the redhead was or how much she was supposed to know, but she jumped right in.

"Oh! Charlie, your manuscript!"

He glanced at her, then back to me. I considered leaving my hand out for the shake that would never come, to see how uncomfortable that would get, but I had a feeling my arm would get tired of it before anyone else would. I took my hand back.

"He sent you to find my manuscript? Why would he do that?"

The volume of his reedy voice would have been appropriate for a conversion held across a ballroom or a mid-sized parking lot. That was often the sign of a person who didn't hear as well as they used to, so I made sure he had a good view of my face when I spoke again.

"Going out on a limb," I said, "could it be because you've lost it?"

"I know I've lost it. Well, not lost it. Someone took it."

"Denny thought I might be able to get it back for you."

"He did? Well, you can't."

He presented this not as opinion but fact. Could I jump from here to the moon? You can't.

"Maybe not," I allowed. "It's not going to be easy to find a missing laptop, and it'll be even harder to find a missing flash drive. Even if I do find them, your manuscript may have been deleted, and there's no guarantee it'll be possible to recover it. I told Denny all of that. He still wanted me to try."

"I'm not stupid. I get what he's after, but it's gone. I'll start the manuscript over."

From the corner of my eye, I saw the redhead's brows raise slightly. A tick up and back down. This was news to her.

"In fact, I already have. Five thousand words yesterday."

He tapped the edge of a closed laptop that was tucked between the seat cushion and arm of his chair.

The chair was an antique wingback, small and short for that style, with dark carved wood framing pink velvet upholstery. The laptop was grey and bulky and only one of the things he'd jammed into the seat. The most obvious was a notebook with a pen sticking out of the top. An ink stain on the side of the chair near the pen spoke of the spilled blood of pens gone before.

I also spotted a small bottle of Coke and a pack of Fun Dip. His body was blocking the right half of the chair, but for all I knew, he had twenty issues of *Hellblazer* and a Batman Bobblehead on the other side.

"And you're backing your work up this time?" Jess said. "What if it gets stolen again?"

Charlie eyed him. "I know you from somewhere."

Jess got that a lot and usually said nothing. I'd also seen him do everything from putting on a fake accent to pretending to be Jack Lowe's cousin to simply admitting who he was, but he seemed to like silence best.

"Oh! Are you Jack Lowe?"

I was a little impressed the guy had worked it out so fast. Then again, the folk festival was on, so there were famous people around, and Denny had sent us.

It wasn't as random as running into Jess at a Drum-heller ice cream shop on a Wednesday afternoon.

"Offstage I'm Jesse," Jess told him and offered a hand to shake. Charlie leaned forward and shook it.

That sounds like Jess was trying to show me up, going in for a handshake after I got stiffed, but he wasn't. His years of glad-handing made it a reflex.

"I know people steal things off the internet," Jess went on, "but you can make it pretty secure, and it's better than having to redo your work. I've lost record-ings before, and it was a pain in the ass to start over. I can't even imagine rewriting a book."

"Nothing is safe on the internet," Charlie said. "The internet isn't what you think it is."

Jess smiled a little. "I'm not sure what I think it is," he said.

"I've got my own backup system," Charlie told him. He flicked his index finger off the flash drive plugged into his laptop.

"I thought your drive got stolen along with your computer," I said.

"I solved that." Charlie pointed at a black box a few feet from his chair. It had to have been new since there were only a few books piled on top of it. "That's a fireproof safe. If the drive's not with me, it's in the safe."

It was one of those small household units you could get off Amazon, light enough to steal unless you bolted them to the floor. Without opening it, or trying to move it, it was impossible to tell whether Charlie had used the bolts. You got what you got when you ordered a safe online, and spending more did not guarantee high quality. You had to do your research. Some safes were waterproof and fireproof and some weren't. Some were tough nuts to crack and others caved if you waved a sledgehammer in their direction.

If nothing else, though, a safe would increase the difficulty level of walking away with Charlie's book.

"It's something, anyway," I said. I crouched for a closer inspection. "Digital code. Any biometrics?"

"I don't need someone using my dead fingerprint to get into my safe."

"That doesn't work," Jesse said. "Does it? I saw something about that on YouTube."

"You need a fresh finger," I said. "If you kill someone right next to the scanner and press their finger against the scanner, you're in. You could give them a good beating if you preferred that. Drag them over to the safe while they're on the floor. Or you march the person up to the scanner at gunpoint. I'd say it's a little easier than getting a code out of someone, but all of those things require interacting with the victim, which a lot of thieves would rather avoid."

"You think you could break in?" Charlie asked. He seemed genuinely curious.

"Tough to say just from looking at it," I said. "I'm going to assume I've gotten into your house while you're away or upstairs. First thing I'd try is to leave with this safe and break in at my leisure. If it's bolted down, I'd try some factory passwords. One, two, three, four. Four zeroes. A lot of people never reset the code. Speaking of which, some of these safes can be reset with a paperclip, so I'd check for a reset hole in the back. Next thing, I'd look for the code written somewhere around that chair you're in. If your safe has a delay after an incorrect code entry, I might decide to do that first. I can't spend forever hunting for the code, though, so the last shot is to use a tool. Since that will be loud, it has to be fast. I'd go after the door with a sledgehammer and hope it's not made well."

Jess was giving me raised brows.

"What?" I said.

"I know you're a detective," he said, "but you have spent too much time thinking about breaking into safes."

"It's come up before," I told him. I turned to Charlie. "You know the expression 'kill the money'? It's harder to break in if you care about the contents. If you want to destroy the contents, that's different."

"They want to know what I know," Charlie said. "They want to read it. Then they'll want to delete it."

"You sound like you know who took your book," Jess observed.

"I do."

The redhead made a huffing sound and left the room, fast enough that Jess and I both had to jump out of her way. I didn't turn, but I could hear her sandals on the stairs.

"You do," I repeated.

"Yes. That's why I know you can't get it back. No offense. I remember reading about you now. You seemed pretty smart, but the media likes to puff people up."

"If you know who the thief was, we could go talk to whomever took it," Jesse said. Whomever. You could take the boy out of fancy expat private schools, but the boy was still going to talk like a jackass sometimes.

"Not as a thug," I added. "I don't do that. But we could suggest they give it back."

"It wouldn't work," Charlie said. "Denny meant well when he sent you here, but can you tell him I don't need a detective?"

"Did you even call the police?" Jess asked.

"What could they do?"

Jess looked at me like he expected me to talk sense into this guy. Denny had obviously had a similar conversation with Charlie and had also sent me to talk sense into him. Everybody was mistaking me for a therapist, or a magician.

"I think this man has asked us to leave," I told Jess. "He just said it nicely."

Jess and I said some polite and meaningless things, including an offer to extend Charlie's gratitude to Denny, then saw ourselves out. The redhead was still wherever she'd gone. Neither of us said anything until we were back on the sidewalk and nearing my car.

"They make safes with reset holes in the back?" Jess said. "You can open them with a paperclip?"

I smiled. "Do you have a cheap safe you're reconsidering?"

"It's not that cheap."

"Forward me the specs and I'll let you know."

He took the passenger side, leaving me both to drive and to decide where we were going. Since I didn't have a case, it was hard to say.

"Lunch?" I offered.

"Yes. Are you going to call Denny? I can do it while you drive if you want."

I could phone and drive at the same time, and Jess knew it. I wasn't sure why he was offering to break the news to Denny, aside from the sheer joy of telling the prince of pap that he couldn't have something he wanted. In fact that might have been the entire reason. Jess wasn't above petty.

"It's my case," I reminded him. "You're just my—"

"Agent?" Jess said, grinning.

"Acolyte," I said.

"Minion."

"Gunsel."

Jess side-eyed me, took out his phone and started typing. Possibly looking up gunsel. Or texting his label babysitter, Gia, to ask for Denny's number so he could go around me. Typical gunsel.

"You'd better be checking restaurant reviews," I told him.

"I'm not going to call Denny. Unless you change your mind."

I glanced at Jess. "Is there some reason you live to disappoint that guy?"

He gave me a one-shoulder shrug. "Ran into him at the Grammys one year. He asked who I was with."

"Like you were a plus-one?" I asked. "You weren't dating Matt at the time, were you?"

"No, and I've got a fucking Grammy."

"I know. It's on the page."

It was one of our running jokes, that everything I knew about Jess was from his Wikipedia entry. He did not smile. Normally I'd have said something about the Alternative category being fake, like the Nobel for Economics, or how he could get more Grammys by trading in Junos at the standard ten-to-one exchange rate, but I was a sensitive guy and could tell this was not the time.

Chapter FOUR

I DROVE RANDOMLY, following people who seemed to know where they were going, and wound up on a street lined with small restaurants, art galleries that probably weren't making rent, and pot shops that probably were. If there was a practical limit to the number of cannabis dealers a given community could support, the towns and cities of Alberta had yet to find it and seemed determined to keep pushing until they got there.

It didn't take Jesse long to pick a lunch spot. A burger bar was advertising bourbon shots in their shakes for qualified customers.

"Not that I want one," he said as he held the door open for me and three college kids who went in on my heels. "But I like their style."

It was a bare-bones place in terms of decor, reminiscent of a small-town Chinese restaurant, but the food was interesting, and to Jesse's delight, they were offering something called a Ben Burger.

"They saw you coming," he said.

"No, they saw you coming and put hard alcohol into their milkshakes. This burger is a coincidence."

"Will you coincidentally order it?"

I did. We both passed on the boozy milkshakes. Once we were settled in with our orders given and a couple of small-batch sodas from Canmore in front of us, I addressed the obvious.

"Guess I don't have a case."

"You still have a client," Jess said.

"You're kidding, right? You think I can work a case when the actual victim of the crime doesn't want me to? I'm making a rule right now—I do not take cases by proxy. You can't hire me to perform for someone else. I am not a stripper for bachelorette parties."

A slow grin moved across Jess' face. "You'd do really well."

"I don't want a side hustle. Seriously, I shouldn't have taken this case in the first place. And I'm not looking for the Brasher Doubloon."

"The what now?"

"It's a rare coin. A real one. I forget how many are left in the world, but they're worth millions."

Jess was moving the pull tab on his pop can back and forth. It would snap any second.

"So," he said.

"Go on."

Snap. Jess set the tab on the table.

"The Brasher Doubloon seems like the case of a lifetime. I don't understand why you wouldn't take it."

"There's a Philip Marlowe movie where an old woman has a Brasher Doubloon, and it gets stolen. So she hires him to find it. She says she knows who the thief is, but she won't tell him who, and she doesn't want the police involved."

"I bet Marlowe took the case."

"If I recall correctly, he takes it and quits it a few times. It's been a while since I've seen it."

"Right." Having finished with his pull tab, Jess had moved on to tormenting a napkin. "I get it. I'm not a detective or anything—"

"Hang on," I said, getting my phone out. "One more time and louder."

"Ha. You're saying that if you walk into a case and everyone involved is being cagey and even the client knows relevant stuff they're not telling you, you don't want the job."

"That's about it. Yes."

"Isn't that every case, though? Isn't it like being a lawyer or a PR person, where you have to assume your clients are hiding things they don't think you need to know?"

I put my phone away. "There are limits, Jess. Everyone sets their own, and some people are more patient than I am. If I think someone is going to be uncooperative or even obstructive the whole time, I'm out."

"I get that. Even *I* think this seems like it's inter-personal bullshit between Charlie and, I don't know, someone he's close to. I see why you don't want to get involved in it."

"But also I'm not invited to be in it," I reminded him. "Denny doesn't get to issue that invitation. He can hire someone to find somebody else's laptop, I guess, but he can't give me the right to search Charlie's house or question whoever lives there."

Jess barked out a laugh before he could get a hand over his mouth to stop it. "Oh my God. I'm sorry. Searching Charlie's house. My first thought when I saw that living room was, yeah, I bet you can't find your laptop. Can you imagine trying to search that place?"

Our food arrived, and I kept my thoughts to myself until the server had left.

"It's organized, though," I said as I took my half of the fries. "Kind of. He prioritized efficient use of space over everything else, so I doubt it's categorized or al-phabetized or whatever. But it's not a hundred empty pizza boxes. I went into a few hoarding situations when I was a cop. It's a different scene. And the places smell bad. That house didn't smell bad."

"That did seem weird to me," Jess said. "Even a used bookstore with that much stuff in it would be musty."

"Someone's cleaning it. The hallway was clear. Stairs were clear. That's not what you usually see. The floor of that room had a few piles of books, but mostly things were on shelves. And nothing on the shelves looked like trash." Before Jess could say anything, I waved a hand. "I know, I know, but it wasn't old flyers and crushed pop cans. If you can call this guy a hoarder, he's the first one I've seen that only kept things with some objective value, threw actual trash away, and didn't spill his collection into the hallways."

"If he's not a hoarder, what is he?"

"I don't know. A collector who likes to have all of his things in sight? In terms of loss prevention in a store, you could do worse than putting everything on shelves that are visible from the centre of the room and sticking the till there."

"Except it's a house, not a store. Do you think he's that worried about theft?"

"Do you think I know where that guy's head is at?"

Jess laughed. "Fair. But it doesn't do him much good if someone can walk into that room and steal his laptop."

I shrugged and put my Ben Burger down. It might have been good or it might have been pressed sawdust. I'd forgotten to taste it.

"We don't know it was stolen from that room. Maybe he slept with it under his pillow and the tooth fairy took it."

"Mm." Jess nodded thoughtfully. "No one gets anything back from the tooth fairy."

"The tooth fairy is a tough customer. That's why Charlie figured I couldn't do the job. Anyway, I'll call Denny, tell him his buddy doesn't want me on the case, and we'll be free to go."

Jess pushed his half-cleared plate away. Not far, because the table was small and a good shove would have sent it into my lap.

"Yeah, makes sense. I can cancel the hotel if you want to drive back today."

"You don't seem eager to go," I said. "Has Calgary done something to offend you?"

"The Stampede," he said automatically. I could have asked him that in the middle of the night and he'd probably have said it in his sleep. Other things he'd called the Stampede included the Fringed Shirt Festival and the Publicly-Funded Horse Murder Spectacular.

"That was last month. It won't happen again for a year."

"Yeah, I know. I'm not avoiding Calgary."

Great talk we were having. I'd interrogated criminals who'd been more forthcoming.

"If you want to stay up here for a few days," I told him, "I don't mind. Luna already told me she was good to keep watching Frank. Or we could go to Jasper. Or there's... whatever's north of here."

"Do you mean more than half the province?" he asked with a grin. "More than half of the province you grew up in? Is that the north of here you know nothing about?"

"Oh, because you're the king of northern Ontario."

"I've played Tuk," he said, which was neither Ontario nor relevant. He'd been flown in and out. And a guy didn't become the next Mackenzie because he'd one time worn sequins next to the Arctic Ocean.

"We have the hotel here tonight anyway," I said. "Anywhere you want to go in town? Rent a canoe for the river? Go to that fancy instrument store Reiss was talking about? Go to West Ed and throw hot dogs at sea lions?"

Jess pulled his plate back and picked up a fry. "That hot dog thing might be an ejectable offense. Or even a banned-from-the-mall offense. Is this what you and your high school friends got up to when you went to Edmonton?"

"We were busy watching girls at the waterpark," I said. "I was definitely watching the girls."

"Absolutely. Boys are icky. You know, I've never been to West Ed."

West Ed, more formally the West Edmonton Mall, had once been the largest mall in North America and was still, in my mind, the tackiest. But it also had something for everyone, if you divided the world into people who liked penguins, people who liked oxygen bars, and people who liked to target shoot next to a Bubba Gump's.

"You should see it at least once," I said. "So you know better the next time someone offers to take you there."

"Then let's go."

I called Denny on the way to the mall, putting the call through my car and signaling Jess to stay quiet.

"Ben! How did it go with Charlie?"

"Not well. He doesn't want me on the case."

"He doesn't want…. Would he prefer someone else?"

The lane I was in disappeared without warning, and I took a second to swerve before answering. "I think he'd prefer to be left alone. He says it's not possible to get it back, and he's started rewriting it. He's bought a safe to keep his flash drive in."

"That's ridiculous," Denny said. Jess made a "that's what *I* said" gesture at the stereo.

"He also says he knows who took it."

The silence on the other end was long enough that I thought the call might have dropped.

"You still there?" I asked.

"Who did he say it was?"

"He didn't."

"Oh, for the love of Pete. He probably thinks it was the government. Or aliens, like you said before."

"I was kidding before," I said, ignoring Jesse's raised eyebrows. "But you and Charlie and the aliens are on your own, because he doesn't want to work with me."

"He's not the one paying you," Denny said.

"Neither of you is paying me. He wasn't rude, but he was clear. I don't think I'd be let in the house again."

"Give me some time to talk to him."

I had to weave through construction and took that time to think. I knew it was a no-go, but arguing with Denny would only prolong the call.

"Fine," I said, "I'm here until tomorrow morning. If Charlie changes his mind before then, let me know. Otherwise, I'll send back your retainer and wish Charlie all the best."

"I'll talk to him," Denny said again.

"Okay."

"If he changes his mind, I'll let you know."

Jess waited until the stereo switched back to the radio before saying,

"Aliens?"

"I said aliens as a joke, because he said Charlie was a sci-fi author. Science fiction author. Denny said Charlie would rip my head off if I called it sci-fi."

"Hard to picture Charlie ripping anyone's head off."

"That's a good point. He'd send me a Roy Lichtenstein postcard expressing his disappointment."

"Maybe he's sent one to the aliens. Dear aliens: shame on you for taking my manuscript to Beta Reticuli."

"Maybe he did."

We left it at that and wandered the mall for a few hours. The place was largely unchanged from my last visit. The Deep Sea Adventure area still smelled of cinnamon and chlorine, and the amusement park was still a noisy maze where all the rides looked like they were about to collide. As ever, teenagers in long coats were selling shrooms in the haunted house. As ever, the mall wasn't obviously grimy but gave off an aura of not having been properly cleaned in a long time.

As I should have predicted, Jess found the place adorable and hilarious. He lived it up like a big kid and cheerfully agreed to selfies and autographs for everyone. He even had me take shots of him with an Edmonton Oiler that I wouldn't have thought he'd know from a hole in the ground.

I let him buy me a couple of shirts, and he let me buy him a pass to see the penguins. I managed to hustle him out the door before he crossed a line by suggesting laser tag or getting elephant ears.

"Did you ever do drugs in the haunted house?" he asked on the way to the car.

"That was for losers," I told him. "Cool kids did drugs an hour before going to the haunted house. You wanted to be good and—huh?"

That *huh* was for my phone, which had rung while I was talking and was now showing me a number I didn't recognize. Whoever it was had a 604 area code. Lower Mainland BC. Not that area codes meant anything these days. Jess was still using his Toronto number.

"Yes?" I told my phone. There was a long pause.

"Is this Ben Ames?"

Oh. Right. I'd forwarded my business number to my personal number before leaving Calgary. I kept doing that, then forgetting I'd done that and answering my phone the personal way instead of with "Ben Ames Investigations." This was why I'd never be Calgary's small businessperson of the year.

"Yes, that's me."

"I… this is Barbara Ga—…. Barbara Gudzyak. Charlie's sister. We met this afternoon."

So that had been his sister.

"I remember," I said.

"You gave me your card." Her voice sounded strange. Thick in the middle. "I didn't know…. I know he didn't hire you. But I didn't know who to call."

"That's fine," I said. "What can I do for you?"

Jess was mouthing "Who?" at me. I turned away.

"Charlie's… I think he's dead."

The pitch of her voice rose at the end. She wasn't panicking, but she was open to it. I kept my voice calm.

"You're not sure?"

"He wasn't breathing and… I think he's dead."

"Have you called an ambulance?"

Jess had circled me to be in my face again. Now he was mouthing "What?"

"I called 911. The fire department came. I don't know why."

"They often arrive first," I said. "They can do CPR. It's normal. Are the police there?"

"No. No. Will they… should they be? Should I call them?"

"Don't worry about that. When the EMTs get there, talk to them and do whatever they say. I'll be there in…." Hell. In Calgary I knew this kind of thing. How long from here to there at this time and with or without construction. In Edmonton, I could only guess. "Twenty minutes."

"What's going on?" Jess said, aloud this time. I held up a shush finger and he pressed his lips together, hard. He was annoyed. He could be as annoyed as he wanted. Some people had real problems.

"Okay," Barbara said. "I'll do that. Thank you."

"I'll be there soon."

I hung up and turned to Jess. "Charlie's dead. Apparently. We're going to the house."

"Holy shit. What happened?"

"No idea." I was already heading for the car, and Jess fell in beside me. "The EMTs are on their way. We might be able to catch them if we hurry."

"Did someone kill him? Holy *shit*. Is his laptop missing?"

"I have," I said again, "no idea. You know what I do. Except that the redhead is his sister and her name is Barbara. Now you're all caught up."

We got in the car, and Jess played navigator, using two apps and keeping an eye out for detours. Part of my brain was imagining scenarios. Charlie going upstairs for a nap and not coming back down. The redhead going into the living room to find Charlie dead under a pile of overturned bookshelves, VHS tapes, and Marvel figurines. This was pointless because I didn't know enough for useful speculation.

The other part of my brain was imagining the fire department and ambulance circling the block like Jess and I had done, trying to find the house. What would happen in case of a fire? This was also pointless, but it was better than cluttering my head with false ideas about Charlie's death, so I let it run.

Jess got us there in less than twenty minutes, despite sending me north and through an industrial area. Two ambulances were parked near the footpath to Charlie's house. I'd seen ambulances hop over meridians, power through ditches, and come to a screaming stop on immaculate lawns. If these EMTs hadn't found a way to get their vehicles onto Charlie's property, no one could.

There were no cop cars in sight so far. The fire truck that Barbara had mentioned was already gone. Or fire trucks. Probably trucks. I'd never seen a fire department send one truck when five would do.

Around us, the neighbours were keeping eyes on the scene with varying degrees of subtlety. Some were peeking out from behind curtains or blinds, others were busy with yard work, and a few were simply standing in their yards and staring at the ambulance. Most of those spectators had glasses of iced tea or lemonade in their hands, which was a little classier than popcorn.

From the speed at which Jess got out of the car, I felt lucky he'd waited for me to stop. I had to hurry to catch up. I could feel the neighbours' eyes following us, silently and in concert, like they were robots in a 1950s horror movie.

There were no cops in the yard. The front door was open, and the porch light was on, barely visible in the summer daylight.

I knocked on the open door and called a hello inside. I could hear voices from the living room. Barbara was likely too busy to buttle, so I showed myself in, only to have to jump from the hall to the stairs to avoid the EMTs.

They were hustling a stretcher out the door, two moving the cart and one standing on the stretcher's frame to give chest compressions for the road. A fourth was carrying out gear. I could have offered to help, but they seemed organized, and I suspected I'd be in the way.

I didn't have much time to assess Charlie's condition, but my glimpse told me Barbara was likely right. His swollen face was red and white in patches, and his half-open eyes were glazed and unmoving. There was also a tell-tale smell as the stretcher whisked by—the bodily fluids released at death.

The man had looked scrawny in life and, if anything, scrawnier now. Barbara, watching red-eyed from the end of the hall, seemed substantial in comparison. She was holding a Kleenex and a phone in one hand and had a tight grip on a stair baluster with the other. From my position on the stairs, I could see grey roots beginning in her hair.

I realized as the stretcher cleared the front door that Jess hadn't followed me inside. No point worrying about that until later.

Barbara let go of the stairs and took a few uncertain steps forward.

"Did they say where they were going?" I asked. She startled, as if she hadn't noticed me arrive, but didn't turn around.

"The Alex. But they said… one of them said there's no reason I should go. And the other ones kept hitting his chest. It's not dignified."

"They have to keep trying," I told her. "I know it can be—"

"Violent," she said and pressed her lips together. Her nostrils flared as she breathed deeply despite the smell.

"Violent," I agreed. "I can take you to the hospital anyway, if you want to go. Is the Alex—"

"The Royal Alexandra," she said. "I forgot you weren't from here. I don't need to go."

"I can take you somewhere else if you want," I said. "If you'd like to get out of the house."

"No. But I want to ask you some things. If I can."

Jess appeared at the front door as she spoke. I waved him inside and he entered, pulling the front door shut behind him. He threw the deadbolt for good measure.

"No one's in the yard," he said. "Your neighbours are pretty curious, so I took a walk around in case they were, uh, encroaching."

She regarded him, her head tilted slightly.

"You'd be used to that," she said. "People following you around."

He nodded. "It's not like being an author. It sounds like Charlie got to be anonymous when he wanted."

"Charlie never sold well here," she said. A faint smile moved over her lips. "But even I can go out in public without being noticed, most of the time."

Even I? Jess and I exchanged glances. If he had any better idea than I had who Barbara was meant to be, his face didn't show it.

"You wouldn't know," Barbara said. "I'm Barbara Gable."

I could see it as soon as she said it. A name in frilly print at the top of drugstore paperbacks, an illustration of a forgettable couple below. Half-dressed and invariably surrounded by autumn leaves. I almost could hear Jesse, with his fine arts degree, pointing out the obvious. Leaves, nakedness, fall. Innocence to experience. Madam, I'm Adam.

"You write romance" was all I said. She nodded once, crisp as a baking apple.

"Guilty as charged. Both of us turned out to be writers."

Two authors, neither using their real names.

She turned over the phone in her hand to glance at the screen. Checking the time or for calls. For someone making it official.

It reminded me that a call of that kind was coming, and it would be safer to have Barbara off her feet when it did.

"Is there somewhere we could sit and talk?"

"Yes. Yes, of course."

She led us down the hall to the closed door at the end and opened it to show a spacious kitchen. It was the old farmhouse style, everything against the walls and a wooden table and chairs to one side in case you wanted to sit while chopping vegetables or committing some other deadly sin. My mother had always insisted on standing, on the theory that legs were a use them or lose them kind of thing. For some reason, sitting while shelling peas or snapping the ends off green beans was okay.

The kitchen was tidy and a match for the house's old-fashioned style, with canisters and a bread box on the counter and floral china on display in the glass-fronted cupboards. A door at the back led to the yard.

"Right through here," Barbara said and swung us around a tight curve, through a full but neat pantry, to a dining room even larger than the kitchen. It had an old buffet at the back, under a window covered by lace curtains, and a closed door on the east wall. The middle of the room was filled by six high-backed chairs with velvet seats, the dining-set version of the wingback Charlie had used in the living room, and a heavy wooden table with a split in the middle for a leaf.

"There are doors from the living room," she said, indicating a pair of French doors on the west side, "but the bookshelves block them."

If I hadn't known that from seeing the living room, I'd have figured it out from the bookshelf backs visible through the door panes. Kit-built by the looks of them, likely ordered from a department store. The backs were thin panels, decorative more than anything and attached with a staple gun.

"Is there anyone else in the house?" I asked as we sat. Barbara shook her head.

"Only Charlie and I live here. And there's a maid who comes."

I'd meant, was anyone else in the house at the moment, but I never turned down extra information.

"Do you want tea or anything?" Jess said suddenly. "Water?"

If Barbara found it odd for a stranger to offer her a drink in her own house, she didn't show it.

"No, thank you. I'm fine."

"You said you had questions," I said.

She set her phone on the table, face up. The wadded tissue stayed in her hand. "I don't know what happens when someone... when they pass away at home. My parents were both in care when they went."

"It depends on a few things," I told her. "Was Charlie ill?"

Her back stiffened. "What? Why do you ask that?"

It seemed obvious to me. Charlie wasn't a twenty-year-old, but neither was he ninety-five and frail. His death would be considered "unexpected" unless, for some reason, it wasn't. One of those heart conditions, say, where you could go at any time. A history of aneurysms. The medical examiner would still be likely to get involved even then, but it was a certainty if Charlie had died with nothing terminally wrong.

A normal question in other words, but Barbara was regarding me as if I'd come from the *Enquirer* to root through her brother's underwear drawer.

"He's asking if Charlie had a heart condition or something like that," Jesse said. "Did he have a condition or an illness that could have made him pass away suddenly?"

Barbara took a deep breath. She seemed relieved. "Oh no. Nothing like that. He has high blood pressure, I think? There are pills in the bathroom, and I think they're for that. He's a man. He doesn't like to talk about his health, and he hardly ever goes to the doctor. Once every few years if I push him."

So Charlie could have had a stroke or a heart attack. He could even have been in the late stages of some other disease if he really did avoid doctors like Barbara said. But mights and maybes weren't enough to avoid an investigation.

"And are you named as his health-care agent? Does he have a green sleeve?"

Jess gave me a puzzled look, probably wondering why I was bringing up "Greensleeves" at a time like this. He'd figure it out soon enough.

"No. I suggested it when our parents got theirs, that he might want one, too, but he thought that was… premature, you could say. He said it was buying trouble, and he said some rude things…. It doesn't matter. He was being Charlie." She paused. "I am his next of kin."

"As long as he hasn't had a recent live-in partner, anything like that, they'll probably treat you as the decision-maker," I told her.

She nearly laughed before catching herself. "Oh Lord no. I don't think he's dated anyone in a very long time. It's not his forte. Romance. It's never been for him.'

"Then it's probably you," I said again. "If he has died—I know you feel that he has, but people can surprise you. If he has died, there'll be an investigation. Not police, necessarily, but the medical examiner will investigate. If they find it was a stroke or an aneurysm, something like that, it'll be similar to when your parents passed away."

She swallowed hard enough that I could see her throat move. "And if it was… something else?"

"If they suspect foul play, the police will be involved. If the cause is undetermined, the police will hear about it and ask some questions. I think the missing manuscript may be notable enough that they'll continue investigating."

"I saw a mark on his neck," she said. "Red. About as wide as a shoelace. I don't know. His head was down. Maybe it was a crease from being bent like that?"

"It could be," I told her. "That's the kind of thing they'll examine."

You'd hope, anyway. I'd seen victims with finger marks on their necks come back as "undetermined." But that didn't seem like a helpful thing to say to Barbara Gable.

"Is the computer gone?" I asked. Barbara blinked in surprise.

"I don't know." She pushed her chair back and started to stand. "I didn't think to check."

"I can check," I said. "If that's okay. There are some things I'd like to see."

She accepted that and sat down again. Jess stayed with her as I went to the living room. The ex-police officer living in my head was bawling me out for messing with a crime scene, but I told him to put a sock in it. We didn't know there'd been a crime. There might not be a corpse.

As a nod to the ex-cop, I trod carefully and touched nothing. I paused in the doorway for a moment to take in the scene.

Something about the change in light, or the absence of Charlie, had altered the room. The empty chair in the middle of the shelves seemed like a throne surrounded by sentries, or devotees.

I shook that nonsense off and examined the space around the chair. It was tight. The biggest empty space was between the door I'd entered and the chair. It was possible to walk around the chair, but there wasn't room behind it to do much other than stand once you got there.

When Barbara had mentioned that red mark, she'd been thinking he might have been strangled. She hadn't said it but didn't have to.

Strangulation didn't always leave a mark, but it could, especially if someone used what the cops called a ligature—a rope or a scarf or piano wire if you preferred the classics.

Could that have been done from behind the chair? It was possible if someone was strong and knew what they were doing. Cutting off air would lead to a struggle, the kind of thing that might knock over some shelves in a room like this, but cutting off blood flow—that could have been quick.

The chair wasn't that tall. Would it have been possible to sneak up behind Charlie and get something around his neck before he knew what was happening? If you were someone he knew and you tricked him somehow? Close your eyes. It's a surprise.

Would there have been noise from the struggle? Maybe not if it went fast.

It could have happened. But plenty of other things could have happened too.

I looked at the chair itself. A dent in the seat showed where Charlie should have been. The Coke bottle was tucked between the cushion and arm, as it had been, though everything was a little disordered, like it had been gone through in a hurry or pushed around in a struggle. Or it was the same, and I was imagining things I expected to see.

There were other things I hadn't noticed. A remote for the lights. Empty wrappers from chocolate bars. And a flip phone. I used the bottom of my shirt to protect any prints as I picked it up.

It couldn't have been a true flip phone from the olden days. I didn't think it was possible to keep those things limping along. But there were still companies that made simple phones for people who either didn't like checking Instagram or liked it too much, and that seemed to be what I had in my hand. I tried to turn it on and was faced with a lock screen. No chance a guy like Charlie would have failed to change the factory password. I put it back.

The notebook was gone, and the pen was on the ground beside the chair, along with another chocolate bar wrapper. Probably dislodged when the notebook was pulled out.

The laptop was nowhere in sight.

The laptop should have been by Charlie's chair. He was rewriting a book. He was paranoid to start with, if Denny was to be believed, and he'd already had the manuscript stolen once. The idea of him leaving it somewhere didn't track. I was willing to bet he'd been taking it, or at least the flash drive, with him to the bathroom.

It wasn't on the chair or beside it or under or behind it. I couldn't see a flash drive either. The drive would have fit into the safe, but not the computer.

I checked the underside of the chair, where a pocket could have been attached or even cut into the fabric that covered the springs. It wouldn't be the first time I'd found something stuffed into a chair.

Admittedly, the flash drive could have been anywhere, including inside the safe where the laptop wouldn't fit.

The safe. I turned around.

It was gone too.

I was almost willing to believe it was possible that Charlie had mislaid not one but two laptops and become so paranoid and worked up about it that he'd had a stroke or a heart attack. I wouldn't have considered it the most likely possibility, but I'd have entertained it.

I wasn't willing to buy that he'd misplaced his safe.

I RETURNED TO the dining room but took my time. I'll admit I checked the fridge. And the oven. Not for laptops or safes, just to see what I could see. I found nothing unusual in either, though the fridge and freezer might as well have had a line painted down the middle. Pizza Pops and Cheez Whiz on one side, brie and salad mixes on the other. Being a great detective, I had ideas about who owned which.

Jess and Barbara were talking when I entered, as I'd expected. He liked digging around in people's lives. For songwriting materials or because he was always gazing down the road not taken. Or because interviewers and fans had gotten so far up in his business that he enjoyed the table turn.

"…in Vancouver, mainly," Barbara was saying. I took the chair next to Jess without speaking so Barbara could keep going, but she stopped and eyed me.

"Did you find… was the computer there?"

"No. His safe is gone too."

I didn't ask whether the hospital had called. The atmosphere would be different if that call had come in. Until it did, I'd talk about Charlie as if he were alive. Whatever Barbara believed, it would be less jarring for her.

"Does he take the laptop places with him?" I asked. "I know he probably didn't move the safe."

"Maybe he did, though," Jess said. "You went on a whole tear this morning about how cheap safes aren't that safe. Maybe he hid it."

I hadn't thought of that.

"Okay. It could be in the house somewhere. We could try to find it." I turned to Barbara again. "If he did move the safe, and if he maybe left his laptop somewhere, do you have any idea where?"

Barbara looked confused. Outside the window, a red-wing bawled out the neighbourhood. The lace curtains and the branches of trees resting against the panes made a "can you spot the blackbird" puzzle that was too tough for me to solve.

"Not really. It would definitely be in the house because he really never goes anywhere. And he leaves his computer next to his chair when he's not using it. I don't know how he can write like that. It's terrible for his back. I don't understand not having a proper writing desk."

"What if he was writing and he wanted to get something from the kitchen?" I suggested.

She considered it. "He will do that if he's on a hot streak. He calls it a hot streak. You'll see him walking with his computer in one hand, typing with the other."

"You said no one else was in the house right now," I said, "but has anyone else been in the house today? Aside from Jess and me?"

"And I," she said absently. I didn't say anything. It took a certain type to correct people and be wrong, and Barbara was apparently it.

"Denny came by this afternoon," she said. "Late afternoon. He wanted to talk to Charlie. I don't know what about. I let him in, but I had to take a business call upstairs, so I left them to it."

"Do you remember the time?" I asked.

"Sorry, no."

"Is it on your phone?" Jess asked.

Her eyes widened. "Oh! It would be! That didn't cross my mind. You must think differently to be a detective."

I could feel Jess's eyes on me while Barbara checked her phone. I didn't look at him.

"Three," Barbara said. "About three. I'm not sure how long he stayed. He was gone when I came down for a drink at four thirty. Oh! Did I offer you something to drink?"

"You did," Jess assured her, though it had been the other way around, "and we're fine."

So Denny, after the call from me, had decided to talk to Charlie in person. I wondered how that had gone.

"Did you see Charlie when you came downstairs at four thirty?"

"I… don't know."

One thing I'd learned over the years was that there was no such thing as a universally straightforward question. People dealt in complexity. Some more than others.

"What do you mean?"

"Well, I didn't speak to him. I came downstairs and went to the kitchen, so of course I went past the living room. I would have seen him. But it would be like seeing a tree or a house. No, I'm saying this badly. Now I sound terrible. What I mean is that it was usual to see him there, so I wouldn't have noticed him. I'm sure I saw him from the corner of my eye, but I don't remember it. I think I would have noticed if he hadn't been there."

Maybe or maybe not. People often saw what they expected to see. They could even remember seeing the expected thing, clearly and in detail, when it had never happened. I did not say this to Barbara.

"So you think he was in his chair," I said, "but you don't know whether he was… well?"

"No, but—"

She stopped. Her hands were holding the edge of the table, like claws. She gazed down at them, a mindless inspection.

"What were you going to say?" Jess asked gently.

"Denny wouldn't have done anything. He's good to Charlie. We've been friends since we were children."

"I wasn't suggesting anything," I told her. "You said you weren't sure when Denny left. It's possible someone came into the house after he was gone."

"You have a doorbell camera," Jess pointed out. "Can we see the footage?"

"I don't know how," Barbara said. "Charlie set that up. I think one of his friends from work might have helped him."

"Are you and Charlie the only ones with keys to the house?" I asked. "You mentioned there was a maid?"

"Yes, but Charlie lets her in, or I do. He's not one to give out keys."

"Seems like he wouldn't be," I said. I had other questions, but they'd have called for speculation. Like, would Denny have locked the door behind him? Even her best guess wouldn't be the same as knowing for sure.

What I was going to ask was whether Charlie had been secretive for a long time or whether he'd become this private more recently. Before I could, though, her phone rang. She jumped in her chair and took a moment before turning it over to see who was calling. Then she pressed her lips together, took the phone, and left the room. So much for getting her into a chair before the bad news came.

"Would it be the hospital so soon?" Jess asked.

"I'm surprised it took this long," I told him. "They probably called it as soon as he got there. Maybe it took a while to get someone to sign off."

"Are cops on the way here?"

"You sound worried. Are you holding?"

"Hilarious. I was thinking it might complicate things if the cops showed up and found us here."

"Things are complicated anyway," I said. "And the cops will find us regardless if they decide to investigate. But you're right—it would annoy them to find us here tonight."

"So maybe we should—"

He didn't get to finish that thought because Barbara had returned. Her eyes were red and her makeup was smeared. Not just below her eyes, all over, like she'd splashed the tears and mascara off her face but not scrubbed enough to get her foundation off.

"He…. Charlie was declared dead at the hospital," she told us. Jess started to get up, but she waved him back into his seat. "I'm fine. I don't know. I might be in shock. My parents and now Charlie."

"I'm so sorry," Jess said. I nodded, to second that.

"Yes." Barbara took the seat she had been in earlier and put the phone on the table. "I believed it from the moment I found him, but I still don't believe it. I know that makes no sense."

"It doesn't have to," I said.

"He's always been… he's just always been."

We considered, in silence, the eternal nature of Charlie Gudzyak. After a few minutes of that, I said, "What did they say on the call? Did they give a cause of death?"

"They did," Barbara said. "They said it was probably a stroke."

"A stroke," I repeated.

"Yes. But they also mentioned the mark on his neck and that they were concerned. They said they need to do… ah, an… autopsy." Her voice shook on that word. The idea of her brother, now a body, something to be cut up and emptied and weighed bit by bit. Jess put a hand on her arm. She allowed that for a moment before drawing away.

"Did they say anything else?"

She shook her head. "Only that they'll let me know… for the arrangements. They'll let me know when they'll be, ah, releasing him. He didn't want a funeral. He read some book, and he's been against them ever since. But I should do something, shouldn't I? My mother always said funerals were for the living."

"You don't have to decide anything tonight," I told her.

"It's cremation of course. I offered to buy him a plot next to our parents, and he said… oh, something rude. That book he read, honestly. Will there…? There won't be police, then? Since it was natural causes? I told him the way he ate, and he never got any exercise, he was going to have trouble." Her eyes welled, and she looked at me intently, insisting I understand. "I did tell him. You can't make someone be different."

"It rarely works," I agreed. "There will only be police if they find something at the autopsy."

"I may have called you for nothing," she said. Half apology and half a musing to herself.

"Or you might not have. Either way, I'm glad we were able to be here."

"Do you have a friend you can call?" Jess asked. "Someone who can stay with you? Or you might want to stay with them instead."

Barbara was thinking something over, but whatever it was, she packed it away before she spoke.

"Yes, thank you. That's a good idea."

She stepped out of the room again to make the call. Jess raised his eyebrows at me, and I shrugged. Communication was a vital part of a strong relationship.

"A stroke?" he said.

"If you stop blood flow when you're strangling someone, you can easily cause a stroke. It is technically the cause of death, brought on by strangulation."

"So you think that's what happened."

"I don't have to think anything. It's not my case. If he was strangled, they'll find it at autopsy. The cops will investigate, and presumably they'll find the killer—if there was one."

"Your confidence has sold me."

"Well, it's definitely not my case."

Barbara appeared in the doorway as I finished those words.

"My friend Candace will be by in a few minutes to pick me up. I'm going to go upstairs and pack a few things. You don't have to wait. I've taken so much of your evening already."

"We don't mind," I said. "We can walk you out."

"That's very kind."

She disappeared again. A moment later, I heard her on the stairs.

"Should we be watching her pack?" Jess asked. "In case she sneaks something out?"

"Like a laptop?" I said "Or a garotte?"

"Both. Either."

"She had time to do that before she called me. I don't think we need to hover over her while she packs her unmentionables."

"Should we search the house for the safe?"

"The police will search the house, if they get involved," I said. "I was willing to take a careful pass of the living room, but tossing this place would be a bridge too far."

That didn't mean I couldn't take a hands-free mini-tour.

I'd seen most of the ground floor, it turned out. The closed door leading off the dining room went into a small room lined with shelves. The shelves were filled half with books and half with cardboard boxes full of comics.

I should say it was only a guess that the boxes were full of comics. I based my assumption on having seen long boxes before, in the bedroom of a high school friend who'd been into all things Batman.

In the middle of the room was a square wooden table with four chairs pulled up to it, all the same vintage as the rest of the furniture but plainer. *Dungeons and Dragons* books were sitting in front of one chair, next to a purple velvet bag that I was willing to bet was full of dice.

Jess snuck past me into the room, eyed the bookshelves, and shook his head. "How much of this stuff do you think he had?"

"No idea. There's a second floor. There could be an attic. And the basement."

Going upstairs would have meant explaining to Barbara why we were going through the bedrooms, so I went downstairs instead.

It was all one room, with a crumbling concrete floor and the sour smell that old basements took on. Hot water heater, furnace, washer and dryer. Boxes piled up at one end. The floor had patches of residual dampness that showed where water seeped in, and someone had been wise enough to pile up the cardboard packing boxes well away from that. A few large lumps covered in tarps were likely the furniture that had been in the living room before Charlie's personal bookstore had taken over.

The only lighting came from a few bare bulbs and a small window toward the back of the house.

Jess stayed on the stairs while I looked around, either keeping an eye out for Barbara or saving the soles of his fancy boots from the concrete crumbles. A pair of clogs sat near the bottom of the stairs, and I was willing to bet they had been put there for the same reason.

I turned off the light, and we went back to the dining room. We were seated as if we'd never left when Barbara returned, trailing a dark blue spinner. She was wearing a slouchy suede purse across her body, and it might have cost a hundred dollars, or it might have cost more than my car. Judging from the racks of Barbara Gable books in every supermarket, she could afford it either way.

"My friend is out front," she told us, "at the street."

I took the spinner, and we walked her out. I had to remind her to lock the front door, which made sense if she was used to Charlie always being there. The doorbell camera watched us go, sending our pictures to God—and Charlie—knew where.

On the street, a silver Cayenne was waiting next to the path with a woman Barbara's age behind the wheel. Her thick grey curls were barely controlled by a floral print headband, and she had wire-framed glasses over blue eyes. She gave us a sunny smile and waved. Barbara waved back before turning to me.

"Don't they say it's important with a crime that you investigate in the first few days?"

"It helps," I allowed. Some people specialized in cases that were decades old, but those people were climbing a steep hill.

"Then I'd like…. I know they said it was a stroke, but just in case… I was thinking as I was packing, should the autopsy show…. Maybe I should hire you to investigate. As if this were a crime. In case it is one and I find out too late."

"I understand what you're saying," I told her, "but this is another decision you don't have to make tonight. We're staying in town at least until tomorrow. Think about it, sleep on it. Talk with your friend."

"All right. Thank you. I will."

We shook hands, and I put her spinner into the back of her friend's Porsche. Jess and I waved as they drove away. Jess put an arm around my waist, and I put an arm around his shoulders, like we were parents watching our kids go off to college.

"They grow up so fast," I said, and he laughed.

"I miss them already. Do you want to get something to eat or can you wait?"

"I can wait," I said. "But if you're hungry…."

"No. I want a walk."

CHAPTER FIVE

IT WAS good walking weather. Not too hot. Not too many mosquitoes. Combing the block that morning, we'd found a few paths that seemed to go to the river, so we took one of those. It was wide and paved, but the sun was scattered by leaves and the air smelled boreal, like the woods outside Jasper. The trees were tall enough to hide the city's buildings and thick enough to muffle the traffic noise. Above the bird song, mixing with the high notes, someone's radio was playing frostbitten reggae from a Toronto band.

"It would be nice to live next to this," Jess said. "I like living harbourfront, too, but you don't get this kind of forest experience. It's like we've left the city."

Harbourfront was where his Toronto condo was. He did not say anything about my Calgary house, which was not convenient to a forest or a harbour. It was quite close to both a Walmart and an IKEA.

"This town is three hours away from the mountains," I reminded him.

He laughed again. "My God. The Edmonton-Calgary rivalry runs deep. What will you do when they put in a bullet train and it all turns into one big city?"

"Rag on Toronto," I assured him, "as we have always done."

We linked hands, not something we did often, but it felt right somehow.

"Why did you tell Barbara not to make a decision on hiring you tonight?" he asked. "She doesn't seem uncooperative. She has money. As your agent, I've noticed you turn down a lot of good work."

"I don't want people to regret hiring me. She might feel different when she wakes up tomorrow. Maybe she'll want to leave this to the police and get on with planning the funeral. Or planning to not have a funeral, in Charlie's honour."

Jess smiled. "I bet it was *The American Way of Death*. What do you think?"

"What?"

"The book. The one that turned him off funerals. I read it at an aunt's house when I was a kid. It's a screed. I'm not saying it's unfair."

I'd never asked him about funerals or cremation or any of those things. He'd never asked me. Or maybe we had talked about it, drunk, in university, and both forgotten. This could have been an excuse to open the topic, if I'd had it in me.

I didn't.

Besides, his label would have a plan in a file somewhere, a media release and key messages and a strategy to monetize the nostalgia with re-releases.

I switched to putting an arm around him.

"What exactly was wrong with you as a child," I said, "that you picked up that book?"

"I was bored," he said, as if it were a full explanation for anything he had ever done.

"Are you bored now?"

"Hell no. I'm on a case."

"I meant in general. Do you want to tell me why you don't want to go back to Calgary?"

"It's not Calgary. And it's not you."

He leaned into me. I brushed a stray lock of hair over his shoulder. It was getting long.

"Now," I said, "we're getting somewhere. Not Calgary. Not me. We just have to go through the million other things it isn't."

"I don't want to talk about it."

"I have been picking up on that."

"Is there some other reason you didn't want to take the case?" he asked. "Besides not wanting her to regret it? What if she calls tomorrow and says she still wants to hire you? Or what if Denny calls and tries to hire you again?"

I sighed. "When I invited you to ride along on this, I thought it would be harmless. I was trying to cheer you up."

"You were trying to cheer me up with a snipe hunt?"

"Close enough. I didn't think the manuscript was fictional, but I did think there was no way in hell I would ever be able to find it."

"But you took that case. Does that mean you were planning to take Denny's money for nothing? I don't object. He has more than enough money. But I thought you were against that kind of thing."

A small path to our left led to a bench and a lookout over the valley. We took the path and the bench and settled in for a view of the city's lights slowly coming out. It was early yet, but the lights seemed set to a year-round schedule to cover the short winter days. That or they were alert to the first hint of dusk.

"I turned the case down at first," I admitted. "When Denny asked me at the party, I told him it was impossible, and I turned it down. I only told you I had the case because I thought you needed a distraction from whatever is bothering you. And then I had to call Denny and tell him I'd take his case after all."

"You lied to me about having a case," Jess said. "And then you called Denny and walked back your statement that the case was impossible, even though you still thought it was impossible."

"Yep."

"My God. The mendacity. All so we could waste Denny's money together."

I dropped a kiss to the top of his head. "Is it a waste if it makes you feel better?"

He smiled. "Yes."

An older couple, grey-haired and holding tight to their walking sticks, came up the path to the lookout. They started to back away as soon as they saw us, to give us our privacy or because we were the devil's sodomites. It was hard to tell these days.

I stood and pulled Jess to his feet, then offered the bench to the couple with a wave of my arm. They smiled and accepted, so either they were fine with sodomites or they were too weary to care.

"Anyway, you can probably find the murderer," Jesse said once we were back on the main trail. "A murderer is way bigger than a manuscript."

"There might not be a murderer," I reminded him. "And there's no guarantee I'd find them."

"Pfft. You catch everyone. You caught the last two."

"I also don't want to drag you around while I hunt down a murderer."

He kicked a small rock off the path, like the world's gothest pre-schooler.

"I'm not being dragged," he said. "What if I'd rather you didn't hunt down a murderer on your own?"

"How about neither of us does it? If you need a distraction for some reason, that's not a problem. We can go wherever you want. Doesn't even have to be around here. Anywhere that we won't be threatening the freedom of a killer would be fine."

The trail ended at the top of a bank, not to the river but to a ravine. People below were going to and from the river along a paved trail, the same dog walkers and cyclists I'd seen downtown, with a rollerblader gliding through them all like a ghost from the nineties.

"It feels worthwhile," Jess said. "Catching someone or keeping the police from getting the wrong person. I don't want to go lie on a beach somewhere. And don't suggest volunteering, because I can't do it. It turns into a publicity thing."

I let him go and turned to face him. He seemed as imaginary as the rollerblader, with the fading sun on his face and his hair caught by the breeze.

"You suddenly feel like you need to do something worthwhile? You haven't let that bother you before now."

"If you think you're joking, you're hilarious. If not, that's hurtful, and I wish I didn't agree."

For the first time in days—or weeks—I was suddenly realizing—he was being both miserable and completely present with me. Someone on the river shouted, and their excitement carried without the words.

"I don't understand the problem," I told him. "I keep telling you, you have money. Do whatever you want. You don't like the gig, quit the gig. You want to keep doing it, keep doing it. You want to record an album of Bulgarian choral music, do that, but please bring me along when you turn it in to the label because I want to see their faces."

He smiled a little. It wasn't happy. He said, "I know you don't understand the problem."

"I don't know why you think my job is the answer."

He turned to look down the ravine at the ordinary lives below. Really those people could have been anything from scientific geniuses to serial cannibals. The soft focus of distance made them one bland and untroubled thing.

"I know it's not. I just want to do it for a little while. I know I'm not a detective. I do actually know that. But I want to feel like I'm doing a real thing."

By pretending to do my job, I didn't say.

"We can't find someone's lost dog instead?"

"Do you know of one?" He turned to me again. "This is the case you've got. If you'll take it. This is where you've been asked to help. And you can stop someone who's done something genuinely bad instead of helping someone get the summer house in the divorce settlement."

He had me there. Divorce photos weren't what I'd gone into criminology for. Insurance fraud, though a crime, wasn't it either. I'd had an idea that I could change up the game a little, rising through the police ranks, putting the focus on real bad guys, not people who'd boosted a wrapped sandwich from a gas station or slept in the wrong doorway. When that had failed, I'd opened my own agency with the idea that I could do good work on my own.

Since then I had done a few good things but had mostly, in exchange for money, wasted my time.

"Okay," I said. "If she wants to hire me tomorrow, and if it sounds like Charlie was murdered, I will take the case."

"If she doesn't hire you," Jess said, "I cou—"

I held up a hand. "Nope. I'm barely willing to work with—no. Not with you. Near you. But I'm not working for you. The last time we tried that, I didn't tell you to fuck off often enough and you almost died."

He cocked his head. "That is not how I remember it."

"If you are going to follow me around on a murder investigation, you need to do exactly what I tell you to do."

Now he had the nerve to look amused. "That *is* how I remember it."

"You kept testing the fences, you little raptor. I'm not putting up with that this time."

He rolled his eyes. "Fine."

"Good." I held out my hand. "Do you want to eat something now? Where do you want to go?"

He took my hand. "What do raptors eat?"

"They were scavengers," I told him. "I'll find you a dumpster."

Instead, after a leisurely walk back to the car, we found a Moroccan place that the internet spoke well of. It was small and dim inside, with rows of red leather booths and a candle in a lantern at every table. We grabbed a booth at the back and put away iced tea while we waited for our food. For a while we said nothing, just sat and watched the leaves of potted ivies being tousled by fans.

When the food came, Jesse regarded it cooly. It wasn't the fault of the food. He hadn't finished lunch either.

"I forgot to tell you before," he said as he turned bits of tagine over and over with his fork. "I talked to Barbara while you were in the living room. She told me about the house and Charlie's stuff. Do you want to hear it?"

"I'm curious," I said. "What did she say?"

"That they grew up there. When their parents got older, they moved into assisted living and gave her and Charlie the house. She said it was an estate-taxes thing."

I nodded. "Yeah, gifts aren't taxed. I guess, if they had enough money to live without selling the house, giving it to the kids might have made sense. Did you ask how long ago that happened?"

"No. She was nervous talking. I thought she'd stop if I interrupted her."

I reached across and speared a piece of meat from the stew on his plate. "So she moved in with her spinner bag and Charlie moved in with a bookstore?"

Jess smiled a little. "No. Charlie was already there. He either never moved out or he wasn't gone very long. It wasn't clear. Barbara was in Vancouver. She still has her own place in Van. But she didn't want him filling every room with bobblehead dolls, so they negotiated a way to share the house."

"The living room is yours but keep your crap out of the dining room?"

Jess nodded and ate a little of his food. "He has rooms and she has rooms and the common areas are kept clear. She also hired the maid. Now she lives in Van, mostly, but she comes back a few times a year to visit…"

"…and to make sure there's no comic creep."

"She didn't say that, but yeah," Jess said. "She never said that Charlie needed supervision, but she seemed to think he needed check-ins. And she was there for most of that year when their parents died. The parents died a few months apart. It didn't sound like there was anything strange about that."

"Older people do that a lot," I said. "Going one after the other."

"Yeah. So they passed away. And then there were two."

"And then there was one."

Jess nodded. "I wonder if she'll inherit all those comics. She won't know what to do with them."

"Cleansing fire?" I suggested. Before he could say anything, I shook my head. "I'm kidding. For all I know, he's got a million-dollar comic in one of those boxes."

"Do comics still sell for a million bucks?" Jess asked. "I heard comic collecting was over."

"Even if he's got, I don't know, a few twenty- and fifty-dollar books in each of those boxes, that was a lot of boxes. And he had a lot of collectibles in packaging. You'd need an expert to go through them. Or you could put it all on eBay and let the invisible hand of the market sort it out."

"Hmm." Jess was eating steadily now, if slowly. "Probably not worth it to Barbara Gable."

"Maybe she'll have an estate sale and make some Edmonton nerds very happy."

"This is assuming she's in his will," Jess said. "She must be, though. There's no girlfriend."

"Or boyfriend," I agreed. "There might not even be a will."

"Did you ever see a murder over a will, when you were a cop? It's always the thing in, like, Agatha Christie."

"I keep telling you, we almost never got whodunnits."

The server returned with more iced tea, which we accepted, and a bowl of mint leaves. Jess put a leaf into his drink. It might have been for that, or for the food. Or decoration. I never knew and was always scared to guess.

"It is insurance sometimes," I said. "If you're talking about your garden-variety middle-class murder for profit, there's at least as much money in insurance as in the estate. Especially if they don't have a lot of equity in the home. Sometimes the property being underwater is part of the financial pressure."

"I wonder whether there's one of those business life-insurance policies on Charlie. The label has one on me."

"That's nightmarish," I told him. "I hate your label."

He nodded and put a dried apricot onto my plate. He had a thing about peaches and apricots both, the little hairs, though you couldn't even feel them when the fruit was dried.

"At least it's not worth it to the label to kill me for the money."

"I don't think insurance murders are only for the money," I said. "Not most of the time. I didn't write a thesis on this or anything, so I could be wrong, but I feel like you don't kill someone for their money unless you're comfortable living without them."

"Well, I wouldn't do it to you," Jess said. "I don't think. I've never been underwater on a house."

"Please. You own a condo. You'll never see that money again."

He smiled and did not disagree.

"I wonder if the word's out in China," he said instead, reaching for his phone. "Would it make the English-language media?"

"You're asking me?"

"I'll set up some alerts and see what I get."

I could have done the same and arguably should have, but the news aggregator Jesse paid for was better than mine.

"I wonder if Barbara will call Denny," I said.

"And then he'll call his manager," Jess predicted. "Who will call his lawyer. And then he'll call you."

I nearly pointed out, as I did at least once a week, that Jess needed to get a manager. He'd fired the last one for an understandable reason, so I'd mostly kept shtum about it. But he wasn't operating an indie band out of his dad's garage. Sooner or later, he needed to staff up.

This didn't feel like the time to mention it, so we talked about other things. Jesse's trip to Morocco as a kid, about which he only remembered a lot of blue-tiled buildings and a ride on a camel. My mother, who had been making edibles for her arthritis and wanted to know if it was okay to send us butter in the mail. Toronto's new mayor and what Jess had made of her when they'd met. I was getting drowsy from the food and the day and thought I'd probably dream about it all, something about Barbara and my mother and Olivia Chow eating pot brownies in Marrakesh.

"What does your mom think of me?" Jess asked suddenly. They still hadn't met, though I'd told her Jess was living with me because, if I hadn't given her that update, the rest of the world would have done it for me.

"She thinks she doesn't know you," I said. "We can go see her sometime."

"Kelowna," Jess said, screwing up his nose.

"Kelowna," I agreed.

"I could fly us all to Morocco," Jess counter-offered. "Or whatever. I said that because we were talking about it, but I meant to anywhere. Do you know if there's anywhere she wants to go?"

Like many of his counter-offers, he both did and didn't mean it. Would he pursue it himself? No. Would he pony up for the plane tickets if I booked them? Yes.

But we both knew it was a dodge to avoid Kelowna, which was in itself a dodge to avoid meeting my mother. Not because he had anything against her personally but because, in Jesse's experience, a mother was kind of mean. To him in particular.

I'd half-expected to hear from Denny before the bill came, or at least before we got back to the hotel, but my phone remained silent. Jess stayed close through the parkade and in the elevator to the room, like he was hoping I'd catch him if he fell asleep on his feet. The joke would be on him if I fell asleep first.

"This place seems abandoned—" He yawned as I swiped our key card. "—now that the festival people are gone."

"Do you still want to stay in the castle?" I asked him. "The Macdonald? We can move over there tomorrow. If Barbara still wants to hire me."

"Maybe," he said. His eyes were nearly closed.

We got ready for bed like sleepwalkers, with clumsy showers and clothes dropped to the floor, and fell into Jesse's bed. On top of the duvet, not bothering to get up and pull it down. The city lights were glittering through the open window. I didn't care enough to draw the curtain.

"We're exciting people," Jess said as he nuzzled into my shoulder. I put an arm around his back and yawned.

I wanted to say that Denny had probably gone to bed at eight, with a cup of Metamucil in his hand, but I was asleep before I could put the words together.

CHAPTER SIX

I WOKE UP first the next day because my phone was ringing. Jess was right next to me, but sometime during his years on the road, he'd developed a talent for sleeping through every ringtone but his own. I envied it.

"Ben Ames Investigations," I said, like a professional with a job.

"It's Barbara Gudzyak."

Both names, because it might have been one of the dozen other Barbaras who'd be calling at this hour. Whatever hour it was. If I'd been a brilliant movie detective, I'd have known from the height of the sun in the hazy sky.

"Hello, Barbara," I said. "How are you?"

"I'm not so well. The police called. They do feel that Charlie may have been... ah, they said ligature strangulation. A stroke, yes, but it was brought on. They said. They said his hands, too, they were... like he'd tried to pull something away from his—"

She stopped.

"I'm sorry," I told her. "That must have been hard to hear."

"Yes. They want me to meet them at the house. The police. I have to show them things, places. Where I was. Is this usual?"

I got up and started getting dressed, awkwardly, with the phone held to my ear. I could have put it on speaker, but I hated to do that when something private might be overheard, and I wasn't sure how thin the hotel walls were.

"There isn't really a usual. Did you agree to go?"

"Yes," she said. Her voice was even but a little higher pitched than normal. "I said I would meet them at eleven. Should I have? Should I call them back? Do I have to go?"

Eleven? I looked at my phone. Eight minutes past nine.

"There are legal questions," I told her. "Do you have a lawyer? Even if it's a contract lawyer or an estate lawyer. They can connect you with someone in criminal law. I recommend having a lawyer meet you there, if you can arrange that."

A pause. Then, "Will they think it was me who did it?"

"You'll be a suspect," I said. "That happens when someone you live with dies this way. They have to investigate you."

"Won't they be more suspicious of me, though? If I call a lawyer?"

Car keys. Car keys. They had to be in the room somewhere.

"You're well-off and famous. They should expect it."

"I would still like to hire you," she said. "To find out what happened to my brother. Unless—I forgot, you were working for Denny to begin with, weren't you? Will this be part of that, ah, that case? Have you spoken to Denny about it?"

"I quit working for Denny yesterday, after I talked to Charlie and he told me to pound sand. I'm sorry. That was a little blunt."

"No," Barbara said quickly. "He did say that. Not in those words, but more or less. Charlie was blunt."

"Anyway, I'm free to take your case. I'll text you my fees and an email where you can Interac the retainer."

Jess was up on his elbows in the bed, regarding me through half-closed eyes. His hair looked like he'd stuck it in one of those shopping-mall wind tunnels. He hadn't got all the product out in the shower, most likely, and then he'd gone to bed with it wet.

"All right. Thank you. Did you… will you meet us at the house? I told the police about yesterday, and they said they would need to see you."

Of course they had.

It was dicey to chat with cops when you were one of the last few people who'd seen a murder victim alive. Sure, Jess and I were mere bystanders at this crime, but that didn't mean we couldn't misspeak, or be misunderstood, in a way that made trouble for us.

Any lawyer would have told me to create a written statement and have a lawyer vet it before handing it over. I was pretty sure this was what Jesse would be told to do if he called his label's big-deal suits for advice.

But I was a detective trying to work a case, and the best way to make a cop friend was to be a cop's friend, or at least not actively obstructive when they asked you things.

I must have taken longer than I'd thought to mull that over, because Barbara filled the silence with hurried words. "Denny will be there. I called him and he said he'd come."

"Does he know the police will be at your house?"

"Yes. I asked him if he thought I should talk to them. He said what you said. And he said he would be calling his own lawyer."

The cops weren't the only ones who'd need a word with Denny. I had things I wanted to ask, and I wanted to see his face when I asked them.

"I'll be there," I told Barbara.

"Oh, good. That's good. Thank you."

Once she'd hung up, I set my phone on the table by the door and got serious about getting dressed. Jesse went into the washroom, saw himself in the mirror and swore, with feeling.

"Do you want me to shave it all off for you?" I asked.

"Was that Barbara?" he said, for some reason ignoring me.

"Yeah. The cops think Charlie was strangled. Ligature strangulation, specifically. She's meeting them at the house at eleven. I'm surprised they haven't called me yet."

He came back into the room with me. "Do you get marks on your hands from strangling someone?" he asked. "Should we be looking at people's hands?"

"It's pretty easy to avoid that. If you see something, let me know, but it's not that likely."

He checked his phone. "Oh, it's not much past nine. I thought it was later. Are we going to the house?"

"Yes. And the cops will probably want to interview us there, or invite us downtown, so don't be surprised. You can give them a written statement or talk to them or freeze them out. Whatever floats your boat."

"You told me never to talk to cops." He'd dropped his phone on the bed and was now trying to pull a wide-toothed comb through his hair, wincing with every millimetre of progress. I held out my hand, flat, like I was offering sugar to a horse. He put the comb across my palm and sat on the bed with his back to me, waiting for me to work some kind of miracle.

"We're not suspects," I told him as I eased apart a snarl at his crown. "But a written statement might be the way to go. You'll know exactly what's in it, in case someone leaks it. You can work on it with a lawyer. Or a lawyer and a PR person if you prefer."

"I know this is a murder, but that sounds way more serious than I was expecting after you said we weren't suspects."

There was product in his hair, as I'd suspected. Jess had been so tired last night, he might have forgotten to use shampoo. Even as I combed the strands out, I could feel them wanting to twine up again.

"The difference between you and me," I told him, "is that you get nothing out of this. I'm trying to establish a working relationship. And I want to know where their heads are at, which I can figure out based on what they ask me. So I'm going to talk to them. If I were you and I didn't need them to like me, and I was worried about my personal business hitting the internet, I would be putting a statement together already."

"Okay. What do I put in this statement?"

"Give them the basics of why you went to the house yesterday. What times. When you left. Who you saw when you were there. If they have more questions, they can send them to your lawyer."

"We didn't do this before. In Calgary. Almost everyone talked to the detective."

I shrugged, accidentally pulling at his hair. He yelped and I petted the top of his head like he was a fretful Maltese. He swatted my hand away.

"Everyone in Calgary was under pressure. A lot of you probably should have handed in statements then, too, but we were essentially trapped in there with a murderer. That changed people's priorities." I handed his comb back to him. "You can think about what to say while you wash this gunk out of your hair and start over."

As soon as Jess was back in the bathroom, my phone rang again. I grabbed it and saw a call coming from an undisclosed number.

"Hello?"

"Ben? Do you know how I woke up this morning?"

Denny. His voice was louder than necessary and all sharp edges. VH-1 wouldn't have recognized him.

"You got a call from Barbara Gudzyak?" I suggested. "Or the police?"

"My friend Barbara called me," he said, as if I hadn't spoken. "Charlie's sister, Barbara. She told me Charlie had passed away. Last night. And that you were there."

"Is that how she put it?" I said. "She called us after she found him. The EMTs were taking him away when we got there."

"You knew about this last night and you didn't call me."

I took a deep breath.

"I'm not working for you. And it wasn't my place to call you. It was Barbara's news to share, or not. I'm sorry about your friend."

Jess stuck his head around the corner of the washroom and mouthed "Denny?" at me. I nodded.

"Well, she decided to wait until this morning to tell me that my oldest friend—not just that he's *dead*, as if that wasn't bad enough. She said… do you know what happened to him, Ben?"

"He seems to have been murdered. Suspected stroke to begin with, but they found signs of what's called ligature strangulation. That means whoever did it used—"

"I know what it means. You are impressively well-informed about this."

"If you're upset that Barbara called me instead of you, that sounds like something you can take up with her. Or you could consider that both of you have suffered a loss and let this go."

"You knew Charlie and I were close. Not so much lately. I should have…. Anyway, you knew this would be impactful to me, and you didn't bother to make a simple phone call. As a human being."

"As a human being, I think this is a hard loss. Murders are more complicated than natural deaths. Take a minute."

He was silent for a while. I heard voices in the background. A television or his phone, delivering the day's news. Sounded like CBC. I didn't hear anything about Charlie.

Denny cleared his throat. I waited.

"I'm sorry. You're right. I'm… this has thrown me. You can't imagine."

"Murder is hard," I repeated. "Barbara says you're meeting her at the house today?"

"She shouldn't be alone with this. She asked, and of course I said yes."

"Were you and Barbara friends too?" I asked. "Growing up?"

"Off and on. You know how it is. Mmm. You may not. But at first you're all children, around the same age, in the same sandbox. On the same swing set. At some point it comes to you that boys are boys and girls are girls. That's not the fashion now, but it's how it was. In the teenage years, you find one another again."

Somewhere in the cut-rate John Hiatt of all that, I caught a hint that he and Barbara might have found each other in the backseat of a car or under the high school bleachers. Wherever kids had made out in Denny's day. But this wasn't the time to ask.

"I'll see you at the house, then," I told him.

"Oh, you'll… did Barbara ask you to come to the house?"

"Yes."

I didn't know if Barbara had told Denny that I was working for her. Probably not, or he'd have said something about it. That he had dibs somehow, or that his money was as good as hers.

"The police must want to see you too," Denny said. "Since you were at the house yesterday. They— the police—made Barbara write out a list of everyone who'd been there."

"That makes sense. They need to put a timeline together."

"Well, I didn't…. My God, the idea of it. Or Barbara. It's insane."

I had to clamp my mouth shut and take a moment to keep from asking him who he thought might have done it. Whether he thought it was about the manuscript. For good measure, what time he'd arrived at the house, when he'd left, and what he and Charlie had said to each other. I'd be able to ask him all of that and more, soon enough.

"Are you planning to speak to the police?" he said suddenly. "I've got my lawyer working on a statement. I have to recommend that you do the same, and I'd be happy to have my lawyer review it for you."

"I appreciate that."

"So you'll do it?" he asked.

"No. I need to speak to the police directly. Think of it as a professional courtesy."

There was another long silence. The news had moved on to sports. I couldn't make out words, but the excited patter of play-by-play announcers was unmistakable.

"You're right," he said finally. "You're a detective, and you would be expected to talk to the police. As Charlie's friend, I want you to. I want us all to do everything we can to find justice for Charlie. But I need to be certain you understand that you can't tell police, or reporters, or anyone, the things I said about Charlie. I said some candid things because I wanted you to clearly see the situation. I said these things in confidence. You'll tell the police you can't share anything we talked about, won't you?"

My head was starting to ache. Too long between waking up and having my morning coffee. I sat on the floor, where the light from the window wasn't as strong.

"This happens sometimes," I told him. "I think it's confusion about the retainer. Lawyers ask for retainers, and they have protected conversations. I ask for a retainer, and people think I do too. But I don't. There's only my discretion. I won't tell them anything that isn't relevant."

"Ben."

"Denny."

"I brought you in on this because I thought you understood. Unflattering things I've said about a friend, especially now that he's dead. I can't expect the public to put that in context or understand that I spoke from a

caring place. I'll come off as callous. You can't be dating Jack Lowe and not understand how these things go."

I did not ask what he meant by that. Maybe just
that I knew how it was with celebrities, that people
jumped down their necks without knowing all the facts.
But he could also have meant that I knew what it was
like for a celebrity to look bad because Jack was such
an endless disaster, and obviously I couldn't pursue that
topic because I didn't want to have to sock Denny in his
Roman nose. Not in front of the police.

"I'm planning to be reasonably forthcoming. I'm
not planning to sell a transcript to Buzzfeed."

"Well… be mindful."

"You bet."

We hung up. I saw a glint under the bed and bent
down further. Goddamn. I'd kicked my keys under
there somehow. I grabbed them and stood, feeling a
twinge in my back as I did. However I'd slept the night
before, it hadn't done my back any favours.

I could hear the shower. I considered joining Jesse
in there, but experience had taught me that very few
shower environments made for a good two-person experience. This one, with a standard bathtub and a relatively low showerhead, would not make the list.

Instead I went out into the world to get us breakfast. The day was a copy of the day before, bright and
hot and dry. People in shorts and T-shirts were relaxing
in the civic mall while others, in summer business casual, were rushing up and down the sidewalks around it. A
guy with a mic and a portable amp was telling everyone
in earshot that the rapture was nigh.

I picked up breakfast at a café in the downtown
mall and grabbed a few pairs of overpriced socks and
underwear at the Bay while I was there. When I got

back to the hotel, Jess was in a chair by the window, dressed and casually perfect. His hair was damp and in a ponytail. He held up his phone as a greeting.

"I'm getting the statement printed in the office centre," he said. "All I have to do is sign it and it's good to go."

"I bought socks and underwear," I told him. "And breakfast."

"We've been productive. We should toast that with coffee."

We did and ate and decided we had barely enough time to mess up Jesse's hair again before getting his statement and heading to the crime scene. It was close, but we were efficient. Thank God we'd had the foresight to not make the bed.

WE WEREN'T late, but we cut it close, and the police had beat us to the party. When we got to Barbara's house, all the parking space around the walkway was being used by patrol cars, a forensics van, and a white Impala that couldn't have been a more obvious ghost car if it had been wearing a sheet and trick-or-treating.

"Is there a rule that cops have to use certain models for unmarked cars?" Jess asked as I pulled in behind it.

"No, they're free to use any Impala or Crown Vic they want," I told him.

He grinned. "I have no idea whether you're kidding."

I could feel the eyes on us as we walked past the Edmonton Police motor pool to the walkway. Who were we? More cops? Reporters? Criminals? Had we come to steal their mosaic glass birdbaths and dragon-fly solar lights? Eventually they'd find out a murder had happened in their little slice of heaven, and either they'd double down on the staring or they'd all go inside and stay there.

The police themselves weren't visible until we were through the walkway and on the front lawn of the house. The ones I could see were milling around like bees circling a hive, and there had to be more inside.

A uniformed officer was inspecting the doorbell camera while a tall woman with French-braided brown hair talked to Barbara a few feet away. The tall woman was wearing a coffee-coloured summer-weight suit over a white dress shirt, and I could see the outline of her gun under the jacket. She was not wearing a sandwich board that said Homicide Detective, but might as well have been.

"Do you know her?" Jess asked softly.

I shook my head. "I don't know any cops up here."

I didn't see a lawyer, but as we approached, I could see that Barbara was holding her cell phone between herself and the detective like it was a third person in the conversation. It made sense, since her lawyer was probably in Vancouver. Or New York for all I knew.

The detective noticed us and turned. She was about to say something, maybe to ask who we were or to kick us off the property, when Barbara greeted us with a shaky smile and a wave. Now that she was facing us, I could see the red eyes and puffy, pale skin of a woman who'd had a rough night and a worse morning. Her voice was surprisingly clear as she said, "Oh good— you're here. Detective Broz just got here."

As we crossed the lawn, I saw a second uniformed officer around the corner of the house. On the hunt for broken glass, footprints, more bodies, or a signed confession.

"This is Ben Ames and… oh dear, I'm sorry, I've forgotten your real name."

"Ben Ames and Jack Lowe," Detective Broz said with a wry twist to her mouth. Her lips were thin and coloured brick red. "Your reputation precedes you."

"Jesse Serik," Jess said, offering a hand to shake. She accepted. Her hand seemed strong, and her nails were all business, short and buffed instead of polished.

"Oh, is that your real name? I don't think I've ever heard it," she said. "I've seen you both in the news. A few times. I'm Detective Alice Broz, Edmonton homicide department."

"I've hired Ben to investigate Charlie's… how Charlie died," Barbara said. I didn't think she was actively trying to avoid the word murder. It was more that she'd walked up to it and lost her nerve, like a kid getting to the edge of a diving board and turning to go back down the ladder instead.

"Careful, you'll put me out of a job," Detective Broz said lightly as I offered my own hand to shake. She did a decent job of acting like my presence hadn't immediately tanked her day, but it was still evident to a detective such as myself.

"I don't know what your caseload is like," I told her, "but this is the only case I've got at the moment. Think of me as help that you don't need to find budget for."

She smiled a little. "I hear you used to be a cop. Can I trust that you won't be in the way?"

"I'll do my best."

With that settled, we both turned to Barbara. I could see now that her phone was set to a video call. A balding man in a blue paisley dress shirt was in view. I could see a high-rise window behind him but not enough of the skyline to be sure of what city he was in.

"Is that your attorney?" I asked Barbara.

"Oh! Yes, this is Philip Grieg. Philip, this is Ben Ames, the detective I told you about."

I gave the phone a nod, since shaking it like a hand would have been awkward.

"Ah yes, you advised Barbara to call me."

Detective Broz narrowed her eyes.

"Barbara, I'd love to have a word with Mr. Ames if I may," Grieg went on.

"Of course." She gave me her phone and stepped away.

"We've put together a statement," Grieg informed me. "Barbara and I and one of our criminal-law specialists. It's a written statement for the police, something straightforward to use as a starting point. Barbara asked me to extend the same service to you. Or I can review any statement you have. She considers this an expense to be covered under your fees."

"That's very generous," I said, with a glance around for Barbara. She had wandered to the walkway and was looking for someone. Denny, most likely. He was now officially late. "I appreciate it. But it's not necessary."

"Of course it crossed my mind that you might have your own attorney and prefer to work with them."

It was a question, disguised as an observation. Is this accurate, Mr. Ames? Do you have your own attorney? And a follow-up, have you engaged them in this matter?

"Of course," I told him. He could spend a thousand-dollar hour trying to guess what I meant by that. "Do you and Barbara have anything else you need to talk about? Or should I let you go?"

"Please hand me back to her," he said. "We've judged it prudent that I be a third party for all conversations with the police."

"Right. Will do."

I caught Jess's eye and pointed my chin at Detective Broz, who was on her phone now with her back to us. It wasn't universal sign language for "Please eavesdrop on that call," but he was a clever guy, and I trusted he'd figure it out.

I crossed the lawn to give Barbara her lawyer back. She took her phone with a nod and a fleeting smile.

"Have you given them the nickel tour already?" I asked.

"The—oh. Yes. I showed them the house. They're going through it now. I really don't know what they're looking for."

"Clues," I said. "I'm not trying to be funny or rude. You look for clues in a general way because you don't always know what they are until you see them. And the usual things too. Fibres, footprints, fingerprints. The murder weapon. It might have been left in the house."

From Barbara's sudden pallor, I guessed that thought had not occurred to her. I kept a hand by her arm in case she needed to be steadied.

"This is terrible," she said. Not with histrionics, but as a statement of fact. I nodded.

"I don't know how you feel because this is your personal grief, but I know that violence makes death harder. I recommend finding help—the professional kind, if you're open to that."

"I have someone," she said.

"Good."

Someone in a black polo shirt and cargo pants cracked the front door of the house, peeked out, and called Broz inside. Forensics. They didn't show up in plastic jumpsuits like people expected, not unless they were walking into a bloodbath. I gave Barbara an encouraging press on the arm and went back to Jess.

"Did you make the detective your new best friend?" I asked.

"I wouldn't go that far. I gave her my statement, and she asked why I wouldn't just talk to her like a normal person."

"So you explained you weren't a normal person."

"I said I was very abnormal. And that I was a brand and big companies had money on me."

"Did you get anything from her phone call?"

"She was asking someone about crime in the area for the past two weeks. She asked about burglary, and then she said 'nothing?' So either the person didn't know, or there haven't been any."

"She can't seriously think this was a burglary."

"You'd have to ask her that. Oh, by the way, word's out."

I was going to ask what he meant, but he pre-answered me by handing me his phone. His aggregator had found stories, both local and international, about the death of Wolfgang Waltz, aka Charlie Gudzyak. On the socials, not much talk yet, but it seemed he'd had at least a few devoted fans in Canada. The kind who'd taken an interest in his life, his times, and his high school yearbook. Wasn't it funny, and odd, that he'd gone to school with Denny Hill?

We both turned our heads, then, at a minor commotion where the walkway met the lawn. The man himself, Denny Hill, had arrived and announced this to the neighbourhood with a full-throated, "Boosh! I'm so sorry I'm late."

Boosh? Jess and I exchanged a glance. Our unspoken question was answered by Barbara, who went to Denny for a hug. I'd have guessed she was a Barb or a Barbie, maybe a Babs in her youth, but Boosh was a new one.

"It's fine," she told him with a quavering voice. "The police are inside. They had to look at the place where… where it happened."

He patted her back while she cried a little. It was hard to be sure from where I was, but I thought there might be a post-cry puffiness around his eyes.

Jesse and I strolled over and waited politely while Barbara sobbed and Denny comforted.

"Ben," Denny said once they'd separated. In case I'd forgotten my name.

"That's me," I confirmed. "There's a detective inside who can take your statement."

"Have they found anything? Any leads?"

I didn't have time to tell him I didn't know, because a voice came from the walkway and made him spin—first to face it, and then away.

"Denny? Denny, over here!"

"Oh shit," Jess said under his breath.

Denny was on the move, running for the house with no thought for dignity. Jess hesitated for a half second before taking off after him, with Barbara on their heels. She moved faster than I would have expected, especially in sandals.

With them out of the way, I could see what had put them on the run. The media.

I wouldn't have called them paparazzi because I'd seen the real thing, and because Denny wasn't quite at the paparazzi level of fame, but they were pushier than I was used to from local media. There were also more of them than usual, a mini mob that had to include social media types and some out of towners.

It felt undignified to run from them, but the last person standing was going to get all the questions, and I didn't want that to be me.

We'd all moved so quickly that the police weren't able to get between us and the door. I made it into the house and slammed the door shut. Barbara latched it. Jess and Denny were in the kitchen, peeping at the chaos outside from behind drawn curtains. I joined them and saw the uniformed cops trying to manage the crowd.

"At least they're keeping the cops too busy to throw us out of the house," Jess observed.

"Is there some reason you're all in the house?"

That dry voice belonged to Detective Broz, who was now standing in the hall. Two forensics people were behind her, looking like kids who'd run to the teacher about someone misusing the monkey bars.

"Our apologies," Denny said, moving forward with his hand out to shake. "The media have somehow heard about what happened here, and they've entered the yard. They seem a little aggressive. I hope you don't mind us staying inside while your colleagues manage the situation."

"Well, I do," Broz said. "I do mind. This is a crime scene."

"Is there somewhere we could sit, just for a few minutes?" Barbara asked. "I'm not prepared to speak to them about my brother."

It was the best card any of us had to play, and I could see Broz weakening.

"Do you have a room you've already cleared?" I asked. "Somewhere you've been working from?"

Broz tapped her foot a few times. The hard sole clicked on the kitchen's tile floor. "We've been using the dining room. I could clear out some things and let you stay in there until the media have been removed from the property."

"Oh, thank you," Barbara said, dabbing a tissue to her face. From where I was, I couldn't see any new tears there.

Broz herded us to the dining room and left us in the doorway while she grabbed a few spiral notebooks from the table. The rest of the detritus—used coffee cups, balled napkins, an empty doughnut box—stayed. A few fresh notebooks and a box of pens were also left behind.

"No one goes anywhere," she told us as she waved us in. We took our seats, and Barbara began clearing the mess, moving it to one side of the table.

"While I have you here," Denny said, "I might as well give you my statement."

As he pulled an envelope from his satchel, I watched Broz's face take an emotional journey. At first she was irritated to be receiving another written statement. Then resigned to it. And then something seemed to occur to her, because she froze and stood there, barely blinking, for a good ten seconds before taking a chair at the end of the table. She held her hand out for Denny's statement, and Jess took it to pass along to her. She read it over, turned it face down, and set it on the table.

"Thank you. While we wait, I may as well tidy up a few things. Ms. Gudzyak, you let Ben Ames and Jessie Serik into the house yesterday, and you've put a time for that in your statement. Eleven in the morning. But I don't see a time when they left."

"I wasn't there," she said. "Charlie must have seen them out."

"We saw ourselves out," I said. "Around eleven thirty."

"Mmm," Broz said, writing something in her notebook. "And the same question about Mr. Hill. You saw him in at three thirty. Did he also see himself out?"

"I did," Denny said. "I didn't note the time. Around four?"

"I didn't notice him leaving," Barbara said. "I'm sorry. I wasn't downstairs again until four thirty, and he was already gone. I was on the phone until then. That's in my statement."

"Mmm," Broz said again.

She had them talking in spite of the written statements. That must have been what occurred to her when she paused for thought. She might not be able to get the one-on-one interviews she wanted, where she might be able to get them to contradict each other. But she had signed statements. We could all try to make our stories match as we listened to each other, but there was only so far we could bend things because we—or three of us at least—were already committed to a version of the truth.

"Mr. Hill, your statement mentions a conversation with Mr. Gudzyak, but it doesn't say what you talked about."

"Well, I'd tried to hire Ben here to find Charlie's missing manuscript. All of that is in my statement."

"I see that."

"And Charlie didn't want Ben on the case, which I thought was silly, so I came here to talk to him. To convince him to allow Ben to investigate."

Broz poised her pen over her notebook.

"And how did that go?"

Denny took half the room's air in through his nose. "Charlie was a different kind of cat."

Broz glanced at Barbara, who was staring at her folded hands. She'd laid them on the table, between a crushed coffee cup and a swizzle stick.

"You know he made his living as an author," Denny added.

"Barbara mentioned that earlier," Broz said.

"Incredible imagination. He always had an incredible imagination. And with genius comes eccentricity."

"So I see," Broz said, glancing at the barricaded doors to the living room. "He seems to have been interested in collectibles."

"He loved his science fiction," Barbara said. "Loved it so much."

She sounded genuinely sad, in a way I'd come to recognize. The moment when something that annoyed you about someone became a fond memory instead.

"He felt there were... let's say currents below the surface of everyday life," Denny said. "Machinations. Shadowy figures. It's not so unusual, is it? Conspiracy is a popular theme these days."

"What does this have to do with your conversation yesterday afternoon?" Broz asked.

Denny gave her a smile that he probably thought was fatherly and not patronizing. "Everything. He believed he knew who had taken his manuscript. He wouldn't say who, but I'm sure it was tied into the conspiracies he believed in. He thought a great power, even unearthly, had taken the manuscript, and there was no possibility that anyone could get it back."

"He'd started over," Barbara said. "That's how sure he was. He'd started the whole book over again."

"I see." Broz made a note, then raised her head. "Did Charlie have any mental health difficulties? Anything he might have been receiving treatment for?"

Barbara's face went hard, icier than I'd have thought she had in her. "He was imaginative," she said.

"All right," Broz said. "Let's switch gears. One of my colleagues had a look at the doorbell camera. It doesn't have an onboard memory slot. Would you be able to provide the footage for yesterday?"

A new notebook was near my hand, along with a discarded pen. I moved them closer with a casual swipe of my fingers. Might as well take notes, since Broz was doing my job for me.

Camera footage, I wrote.

Jess glanced at my writing and picked up the pen nearest him.

Not in the cloud, he added at a slant in the margin.

Laptop? I added beneath it.

"Barbara mentioned that Charlie had a lot of readers," Broz said. "Did any of them ever reach out?"

"Oh, his agent took care of that," Barbara said. "I can't think of anyone who ever came to the house, at least not when I was here. Charlie really did not engage with his fans at all. He preferred not to go online if he could avoid it, and he didn't take calls unless he knew who they were from. He barely used his phone. Hardly anyone had the number."

"We've taken his phone," Broz said. "We'll provide a list of things we've removed from the house. They'll be returned as soon as the investigation is complete."

That was true, or at least it was protocol, but she wasn't saying when. Things could stay in evidence boxes for years. Decades. Like Charlie's manuscript, the things in police custody might never be seen again.

"This house has a landline as well," Broz observed.

"Yes, it's always been here," Barbara said. "We never thought to cancel it. It has the same number as when we were children."

"Were you worried about break-ins?" Broz asked. She gestured with a pen, drawing an imaginary circle around an invisible house. "This house is set off from the street, and you've got access from the goat paths in back. You must have to deal with unwanted visitors sometimes."

Jess quickly drew a cartoon of the house, with brush behind it. Through the brush, he drew a narrow path and an arrow pointing toward it. *Goat path.* He'd have seen that the night before on his expedition around the yard.

"We keep everything locked," Barbara said. "There's only the front door and the back. The windows are latched. We have air conditioning for the hottest days. And Charlie was home most of the time. I really think that's discouraging to people who want to cause trouble. There are so many houses around here where no one is home during the day."

"So the kitchen door and the front door were both locked yesterday evening? Did you lock up after Mr. Hill left? When you came down at four thirty?"

"No," Barbara said. "But Charlie must have because I had to unlock the front door for the ambulance men."

"He did not see me to the door," Denny said. "He was irritated with me. But he may well have locked up after I was gone."

"Was this a heated argument?" Broz asked, disappointing me a little. She'd been good so far, even smooth, but that was clunky. Denny's shoulders went back, and his chin rose.

"Of course not," Denny said. "He understood that I was trying to help. Charlie was a private person, and I knew he wouldn't hire an investigator by himself, but I felt like I had to do something to help him find his manuscript. Can you imagine having an entire manuscript stolen from you?"

"I can't," Broz said simply. "Can you tell me more about this manuscript? Was it one of his science fiction novels?"

Barbara and Denny glanced at each other.

"No," Denny said. "No, it was different."

"Yes," Barbara said. "It was something quite different for him. I called him from Vancouver—that's where I live most of the time—I called him from there about six months ago to see how he was doing, and he said he was writing his memoir. Which I thought was strange because he has never had an interest in that kind of thing. He doesn't read biography. And to be honest, he hasn't had much experience or… oh, there's no way to say this that doesn't sound terrible."

"I think what Barbara means is that Charlie's life was bigger on the inside than the outside. He told incredible stories. But his life here—he spent most of it right in this house. He grew up here. He worked at a comic bookstore for most of his youth, until his books started to sell. And then he stayed here and wrote. What would his memoir be about?"

"What would it be about?" Broz asked. "Did you ask him?"

Denny smiled. You don't get it, his smile said. You don't understand.

"He said to wait and see. Charlie never liked to talk about anything he was writing."

Why a memoir? I wrote.

Six months ago, Jess added beneath it.

"So he was writing a book about his life and someone stole it? Do you mean they've pirated a copy?"

"Sadly, no," Denny said. "And I'll be honest, I don't think there would have been any market for a pirated copy of this book. If it had been another book in his series, that might have been different."

"It was taken," Barbara said. "His laptop was taken last Thursday, in the afternoon. He was writing in the living room, and he went upstairs to use the bathroom. We've only got the one bathroom, unfortunately. He was there for a few minutes and came back downstairs, and it was gone. It had the only copy of his manuscript on it."

"What do you mean, only copy?" Broz asked. "He didn't have a backup saved online?"

"He didn't like the idea of saving things to the cloud," Denny said. "He felt it wasn't secure."

"More secure than his laptop," Broz muttered, then cleared her throat. "Ah, sorry. Ms. Gudzyak, you say someone stole his laptop from the living room. Was anyone in the house other than the two of you?"

"It was only Charlie," Barbara said. "I was at an afternoon concert. I'm afraid it's my fault someone was able to take the laptop because Charlie found the front door open. I must not have locked it when I went out."

"Is that the only possibility?" Broz asked. "Does anyone else have access to this house?"

"Only the maid," Barbara said. "And we let her in. She doesn't have a key. She comes on Fridays."

"Is it possible," Broz said, "that someone stole the laptop incidentally? If the front door was left open, there would have been an opportunity. Especially with the lack of street visibility for the house. Was anything else taken?"

"Nothing," Barbara said. "I suppose it's possible. They might have heard Charlie come downstairs and run away before they could take anything but the laptop."

I kept my mouth shut and prepared to give Jess a kick if he opened his. It was a ridiculous suggestion that someone might have noticed a briefly unlocked front door and stolen nothing but the laptop. But running ridiculous ideas up a flagpole was part of the job when you were a cop. Or a detective. You could learn a lot from the ways people reacted to them.

"That does not make sense," Denny said. "Barbara, I'm sorry, but think about it. What time was your concert on Thursday?"

"Two."

"And you left here when? One o'clock?"

"Mmm... maybe one fifteen?"

"And Charlie told me his laptop was stolen around two thirty. You'd have to be the luckiest burglar in the world to stumble by here that hour, just over an hour, that the house was unlocked. It doesn't make sense.

Someone had to be watching the house, Barbara. Waiting for you to leave. You do have a habit of leaving the house unlocked."

I picked up my pen, but Jess was ahead of me, putting the times into the notebook.

"Did anyone report this theft to the police?" Broz asked.

"Don't you know that already?" Denny asked. "It would be in your records if they'd reported it."

"Charlie didn't want to," Barbara said. "He said he knew who took it, and there was nothing the police could do."

"He said the same thing to me," I confirmed. "Yesterday, when I met with him."

"And who was this person?" Broz asked, looking from me to Denny to Barbara. "Did he say?"

Barbara stared at her hands again. Denny scratched at a mosquito bite on his arm.

"He didn't say," I said. "Not to me."

"He said the book was gone," Barbara said. "He wouldn't talk about it. He just started over."

"About that," Broz said, "Wasn't he concerned the new manuscript would be stolen as well?"

"He used to back up his manuscript to a flash drive," Barbara said. "That was taken along with his laptop, so when he got a new laptop and a new flash drive, he got a safe as well. One of those little ones. He put it on the floor of the living room and said he was going to put his flash drive into it every night."

Broz raised her eyebrows. "Did he?"

"I don't know. I never saw inside it. I didn't have the combination. And it was taken last night, along with his laptop. It's all gone. I'm sorry, did I forget to put down the safe?" Barbara looked at me. "They asked for a list of anything that had been taken."

I nodded. "When I was here yesterday evening, I noticed that the laptop and safe were gone."

"And you all think he was killed because of the book."

Barbara was rubbing her folded hands together. Trying to soothe herself.

"I don't know," she said. "I don't know why any-one would have done that to Charlie. He stayed home, and he wrote his stories."

"It must have been the book," Denny said. "His book was stolen a few days ago and again last night, the safe and everything. If it wasn't about the book, then… what? Someone came in and killed him for no reason? I mean, Barbara is right. He was a harmless man. And then someone else came and took the book? That's ridiculous."

"There's no other reason?" Broz said. "No one had any kind of grudge against him? Or something they wanted? I don't understand this whole collectibles business, but I understand there can be money in it."

"I don't know about the collectibles," Barbara said. "Denny, do you?"

"It was never my thing either," Denny said. "I couldn't say if he had anything worthwhile. But this is a waste of time, Detective. He's had these collectibles for years. Once he started to make real money, he made a deal with his old boss for, I don't know. Everything he'd ever wanted. He bought most of it at once. Why would someone suddenly kill him for any of this?"

"There'd be a record of what should be here," Broz said, "if he bought it all at once. Who was his boss?"

"Nick something?" Barbara said. "I wasn't here much back then. My parents were still in the house."

"I left town when I was seventeen," Denny said. "Graduated, got on my dad's old Vincent, and I was gone. Went to Toronto, didn't come back west for almost ten years. And later, for that whole part of Charlie's life, I was on the road so much I didn't see him that often. I don't recall us ever talking about his job."

"Where did he work?" I asked Barbara. "Do you remember the name?"

"I really don't. Myles might know. Myles would have to know."

"Who's Myles?" I asked.

Denny sat up straight. "That's an excellent idea. You should talk to Myles."

"Who is Myles?" Broz asked, pen poised to write.

"Myles Murati," Barbara said. "He and the boys met in high school. Myles and Charlie still see each other. Myles works at Greenfields, the conference centre on Calgary Trail. He does sales and marketing for them."

"Is he still editing that magazine of his?" Denny asked.

"Oh yes. It's more of a hobby really. I can't think it makes any money. The conventions might make money for him. I know Greenfields gives him a good rate."

"Conventions?" I asked.

"Myles hosts a science fiction convention every year," Denny said. "They moved online for COVID, but I'm sure they were back at the convention centre this spring. Same name as the magazine, I think. Science... Scientist...?"

"Mad Science," Barbara said. "The Mad Science Convention. Charlie has all the issues of that magazine around here somewhere. Don't ask me where. Myles used to publish him before Charlie signed his publishing deal. He published Charlie's short stories."

I wrote Myles's name down, along with the name of the magazine. I saw Broz doing the same.

"And did Charlie have any enemies that you know of?" Broz asked. "Did he mention anything about being threatened? Did he seem nervous? I know you say he was a conspiracy theorist, but did he ever talk about more personal, specific threats?"

"No," Barbara and Denny said, together and too quickly. Broz breathed too loudly but said nothing. She put her notebook into the crossbody bag she was wearing.

"I've been told the media have left the property," she said, "so you're all free to go. Mr. Hill, are you planning to be around Edmonton for a while?"

"I'll be here for as long as Barbara needs me," Denny said, giving a squeeze to Barbara's hands.

"Good. I may have more questions. Here's my card in case any of you think of anything you'd like to share. Ms. Gudzyak, I'm hoping to release your home to you later today, as soon as forensics have cleared it."

"Thank you," Barbara said. "Thank you so much. There's so much to do. I'll need to find his will and his agent's number. His agent hasn't even been told, and it's already on the news, isn't it? It must be, with all the media outside. Oh, and the funeral. Not a funeral. He didn't want that. But a celebration of life. I need to plan that. I don't even know where to start."

"I'm here to help," Denny told her. "We'll get it done."

We all took Broz's cards, and she walked us to the front door. Forensics had already packed up and gone, leaving behind a bright yellow ribbon across the living room doors. Jess was on his phone as we walked, probably checking for whatever his new aggregator had turned up. Or reading angry texts from his contact at the label, asking why he was involved in a murder again.

"Jess and I are going to head out," I told Barbara. "You've got my number if you need anything. Otherwise, I'll check back this evening."

She nodded. And Denny nodded, as if I'd included him. I steered Jess toward the walkway, and not looking up from his screen, he let me lead him back to my car.

Chapter Seven

"Where are we going?"

Jess had waited to ask until we were on a bridge halfway to the south side of the city. He'd been busy with his phone until then, checking the news and finding himself all over it, along with me and Denny. Then talking to Gia, his label person, and working out a management plan because everything in Jesse's life required some kind of high-level plan. I'd once asked him if he checked with Gia before using the bathroom, and he'd said there was no need because they had an established bathroom protocol. I had chosen to believe he was kidding.

"We're trying to get to Myles…"

Jess opened the notebook he'd somehow filched from me. "Murati."

"…Murati before the cops do."

Jess grinned at me. It was not my favourite grin.

"What?"

"Didn't you once tell me," he said, "that you can't outrun the radio? What if she sends a patrol car to pick him up?"

"I'm hoping that she intends to be polite and talk to him somewhere less uncomfortable than headquarters," I said. "And that she'll want to talk to him herself. What are people saying on the socials?"

"There's a lot of information out there. I don't know how. They know he died, that the police are investigating, that he was Wolfgang Waltz, that he went to school with

Denny, and that his sister is Barbara Gable. It's funny because his Wikipedia article doesn't mention her at all."

"It will," I predicted.

"Yeah, true. I guess the media found out about her
from the socials. A few people have tagged Myles, but
he hasn't responded yet."

We took a wide swing between the university and
the river before coming back east to Calgary Trail. It
was a one-way main drag with endless big-box stores
on either side. The lanes merged and split again without
warning, and I knew from experience that you had to
stay sharp or you'd fly past your destination and have to
backtrack by crawling across a parking lot to the north-
bound one-way drag on the other side.

"Any comments about Denny?"

"Nothing notable. Reddit has a thread dedicated to
this murder already. Someone mentioned that she went
to school with him and Denny. Says she used to date
Denny, and Charlie would tag along."

"Is the RBI on the case?" I asked.

Jess laughed. He was not unfamiliar with my
thoughts on the Reddit Bureau of Investigation. "They
haven't opened a file on him yet, but give them time."

"Five, maybe ten minutes," I predicted.

Was that the convention centre up ahead? I started
to ease into the next lane. The driver behind me sped up
to block me. There was a free lane on the other side of
him, and he had to change his speed to catch up to me,
so I wasn't interfering with his life in any way, but that
was Edmonton for you. Every driver wanted a fight.

Greenfields Convention Centre was a large rectangle
that straddled the space between the two one-way streets.
The parking lot was generous and about a third full.
Scraggly trees were planted in islands around the lot in a

nod to the centre's name. They'd be dead before the year was out, replaced with more scraggly trees next spring.

"It's hard to imagine people needing this much convention space," Jess said as I pulled in close to the main doors. "Didn't I see a convention centre downtown too?"

"I'm surprised you're surprised," I told him. "With your big-deal business dad."

"He prefers private meetings in windowless rooms," Jess said. "Where he can speak without fear of prosecution."

"I don't know why all criminals don't do white-collar crime. You can do it inside from a nice chair. You have an executive assistant to tell the police you're too busy to talk to them. The coffee is good. And you can steal from a million people at one time."

"You should tell street criminals that," Jess said. "I bet it would clean up this town."

The lobby of Greenfields was trying hard to sell itself as a tropical oasis. The first thing we encountered as we went through the doors was a grove of ficus trees, with a burbling brook crossed by a tiny bridge. LED fairy lights lit the way through the neither deep nor dark woods. The chlorine smell of an artificial pond hung in the humid air.

The front desk was to the right of the doors, a plain brown afterthought. A girl—young woman—about Izzy's age was looking as serious as she could, with her hair slicked back in a tight ponytail and her name pin perfectly straight on her black blazer. Your conference was safe in her hands.

I went up to the desk with Jess a step behind me, and she did her best to pay attention to me as I spoke, though her eyes kept going to him. A fan. Not a super-fan, because those people knew me now too.

"Hi. I'm looking for Myles Murati."

Her eyes hardened. I wondered how many reporters had called asking for Myles. They might even have had calls from the RBI.

"Of course. Can I give him your name?"

I put my business card on the desk in front of her.

"Tell him Barbara Gudzyak sent me."

She rolled her lips a little, smearing the thick pink-tinged gloss. Was this some kind of trick? Was I really a detective? Would Myles want to talk to a detective? I watched as she decided this was all above her pay grade. She picked up the phone.

"Myles? There's a private investigator at the front desk. He says Barbara Gudzyak sent him?"

She listened and nodded. Picked up my card and flipped it over in her fingers a few times. She was wearing a claddagh ring. Left hand, heart pointing out. I couldn't remember what that stood for. I suspected she didn't know either.

"All right, I'll send him up."

She tore a map from the pad of convention centre maps in front of her and began to add lines and circles to it.

"You want to take the elevators here up to the third floor. Myles's office will be at the end of the hall."

I took the map, since I couldn't think of a way not to, and we headed for the elevators. We passed another small forest on the way, this one boasting a koi pond surrounded by indoor palms and dragon trees. I'd had a dragon tree for years, until my boyfriend and my former cop partner had decided to play fetch with my dog inside the house and Frank had gone flying into it with his entire eighty pounds of fluff and knees.

I pointed in that direction, about to ask if Jess remembered my tree, but he cut me off. "I said I was sorry, and I offered to buy you a new one."

"I liked the one I had."

"Then I guess you're SOL."

In the elevator, he said, "Would you like a koi pond?"

"My landlord might not be into it."

"Too bad we're renting." In the hall on the third floor, he added, "I saw a listing in Edmonton for a house with a two-storey tree growing up through the middle of it."

"I saw a goat ride a horse once. What are we talking about, Jess?"

"Apparently nothing."

Myles Murati, Director, Sales and Marketing, had his door closed. I knocked and was surprised when he answered himself. I would have expected the director to have a secretary, or some gofers at least.

"Hello. You must be Ben. And?"

"Jesse Serik," Jess said, extending a hand. If Myles recognized Jess by any other name, his face did not show it.

"Come on in. Watch the boxes."

Myles was a little guy, not much taller or broader than Jess. His hair was a thick and glossy brown, styled like he was a fifties dad in a Sears catalogue, and he had carried the style through with thick black-rimmed glasses and single-creased black dress pants. His shirt was up to date and more daring, a burgundy paisley print with contrasting floral cuffs.

"I reached out to Barbara when I heard about Charlie, and she asked me to please help you in any way I could," he continued as he walked back to his desk. The office was small, with a chunky wooden desk at the back and a pair of leather-and-metal chairs facing it for guests. The boxes to which Myles had referred were plain cardboard, about a foot and a half wide and deep and a foot tall, with a printer's return address on the side. Three of them were stacked crookedly by the door, like a late-stage Jenga tower.

Myles waited until Jesse and I were safely seated before sitting and putting his spread hands onto the desk before him.

"So. How can I help you?"

"First," I said, "my condolences about your friend. I understand you'd known him a long time."

"Since high school," Myles said. "And I still saw him every two weeks at least for our D&D game. It's hard to believe. Who would want to hurt someone like Charlie?"

"That's the big question," I said. "As unlikely as it seems, someone did."

"I guess I can't argue with that. But Charlie was a good guy. He was a little strange, but who isn't?"

"Do you know of anyone who had a grudge or some kind of issue with him?" I asked.

Myles frowned. "Really, no. Are they sure—are the police sure it wasn't some kind of robbery? Or a home invasion? I don't think of this as a place where home invasions happen, but then no one does, do they? Until they've got one next door."

"I don't think they've ruled anything out," I said, "but I understand his laptop was taken last week, with the only copy of his memoir on it. The new laptop disappeared yesterday. How much do you know about the book Charlie was writing?"

"It was the story of his life," Myles said. "From childhood to now. I never saw any of it because Charlie never let anyone read anything before it was done.

Before he got his publishing deal, I published him a few times in the magazine. Short stories. A novella. Did Barbara mention my magazine? I edit *Mad Science*. That's the latest issue in those boxes by the door."

"She did mention it," I said. "Not a lot of print magazines around these days."

"Not much of a market for them. We scrape by. Grants, proceeds from the convention. Some ad sales. And those issues with Charlie's early work in them, they're collector's items for those in the know. So I do some business in back issues."

Like so many things, would the value of those back issues increase now that the artist was dead? It couldn't be enough money to incentivize a murder, regardless.

"When was the last time you saw Charlie?" Jess asked.

"Easy. Friday night."

"As in this past weekend," Jess said.

"Yes. We had our regular game. Charlie called me Thursday night, all upset about losing his manuscript, and he was talking about canceling game night, but I talked him into going ahead. I didn't think it would be good for him to sit alone and stew."

"Why did he call you?" Jesse asked.

Myles shrugged. "To bitch. I don't blame him. I've never had a whole manuscript stolen, but I lost an issue of the magazine once, back before you could keep things online. I've told him a hundred times to suck it up and put his books into some kind of off-site backup, but he wasn't hearing it. I may have said I told him so."

"How'd he take that?" Jess asked.

"Not as bad as you'd think. I said it at the game the next night, and he was like, oh well, guess I'll rewrite the whole thing. Since I'm never getting the first copy back. He'd already decided on that."

"Did he say who he thought might have taken the book?" I asked.

Myles huffed out a laugh. "Sure. He said it was the aliens. I mean, it was more complicated than that. There's aliens and there's people possessed by aliens and there's aliens who look like people and there's government people who aren't aliens but they work for the aliens.... One thing you could never accuse Charlie of was a lack of creativity. Or maybe you could accuse him of that, because his alien shit was pretty standard. What do the Brits call it? Bog standard?"

"Did he see these aliens?" I asked. "Did he describe them?"

"Was I listening?" Myles answered. "I don't mean to sound like an insensitive asshole, but you spent enough time with Charlie and you learned to stop listening to the alien talk. He's been on this kick since high school. It only got worse after he started hanging around with those whack jobs in the UFO cult."

Jess, who had been taking notes, stopped and stared at Myles. "UFO cult? Like what? Like Heaven's Gate or something?"

"No. Oh my God, the thought of these guys killing themselves. They would never deprive the world of their genius. Sorry, I'm sounding like an asshole again. They just get on my nerves. They're very, very sure they've got the whole world figured out and the rest of us are deluded. I put up with Jeremy because he was okay to game with, but I didn't get into conversations with him if I could avoid it. I was not there to be recruited into UFOUND."

"UFOUND is Jeremy's group?" I asked.

Myles nodded. "Yep. Hey, I'm sorry. I haven't asked if I can get you anything. Coffee? Tea? I can have it brought up from downstairs. Or I've got some pop here in the fridge." He nodded at a bar fridge that was jammed under a printer table at the side of his desk. Like everything else in his office, it looked like it had done long and honourable service in a meeting room somewhere before being decommissioned and given to Myles to use. It didn't create the aura of assured opulence sales guys liked to project, but this was a conference centre, and he would have had his pick of fancy rooms in which to meet his customers. This was more of a secret lair.

"We're good, thanks," I told him.

"You and Jeremy and Charlie were in the D&D game," Jess said, scanning his notes. "Do you have Jeremy's number?"

"No, but you can find him. He's on all the socials, and he's got a website for UFOUND. Last name's Gustafsen. He lives up in St. Paul."

"Was anyone else at the game?" I asked.

"Eddie. He's an old work friend of Charlie's. He works over at Capes—you know, the comic bookstore? There's three in town. I think one in Calgary, too, and a couple in Saskatoon. Eddie works at the one off Whyte. It was me, Eddie, Charlie, and Jeremy. Barbara was at the folk festival. I don't usually see her on game nights anyway. D&D is not her thing."

"Did Charlie have anything worth stealing that Barbara might not have noticed?" Jess asked. "He had a lot of collectibles."

"He sure did," Myles said. "I'll be honest—I don't know if Charlie could have told you what all he had and whether any of it was missing. He loved that stuff, but there was too much for anyone to keep track of."

"And was it worth anything?" I asked. Myles rocked his head from side to side. Yes and no. "To who? That's the question with collectibles. You can say it's worth this or it's worth that, but at the end of the day, it's worth what someone will pay for it. Some of those back issues I've got with Charlie's stories in them, I couldn't get cover price for them around here. Used bookstores wouldn't take 'em for trade. But in China it's a whole other story. So if they're toilet paper here and gold in China, what are they worth?"

"But it's not that simple," Jess said. "People love the Beatles, but there's always going to be a difference between an album that was produced in the millions and a test pressing. You need a mismatch between how many people desperately want something and how many copies there are."

"I knew you looked familiar!" Myles said, pointing at Jess. "You're different without the makeup. Aren't you Jack Lowe?"

"It's Jesse offstage," Jess said. "Today I'm just tagging along with Ben."

"Oh yeah! That murder in Calgary"—he pointed at me—"and you're that detective! I should have put it together as soon as Barbara mentioned your name. Do you know Denny? Did he introduce you to her?"

"Something like that," I said. "You and Denny go back a long way too."

"We do. I stayed a lot closer to Charlie over the years. Denny cleared out of town as soon as they put his high school diploma in his hand. He comes back and visits, and he did that musical here one time, but Charlie's always been a local guy. Like me. Sorry, I think I got us off track. We were talking about the bobbleheads."

"Surely not the bobbleheads," Jess said. It was a nod to our friend Luna, who used those words when she not only thought something was not true but felt that the world would be irredeemable if it were. *Surely you're not wearing a hockey jersey in public, Ben. Surely this restaurant didn't just put ranch dressing on a caesar wrap. It simply cannot be.*

Myles didn't know Luna, but he laughed anyway.

"No, not the bobbleheads. Some of the figurines, maybe. The porcelain ones, ten inches and up? Those weren't cheap to begin with. And he had some things that started out slow and took off later. He's got the first issue of *Nightwing*, from before everyone got obsessed with Nightwing's ass."

"It is a truly exceptional ass," Jess observed.

Myles laughed again. "I guess you would know. Charlie had a lot of first issues. If a character got their own title, the first issue, he'd pick that up. If he liked it, he might buy more. And sometimes with those first issues, you can get lucky and they go from nothing to having a movie or a TV show. But you ask me what those gems were, and then you ask me where Charlie kept them? I mean, a team of professional geeks could probably shake that house down for a month and not find everything. No offense. I am a geek myself."

I wasn't sure who he was worried about offending… other than himself.

"Do you think anyone might have been worried about what Charlie would put in a memoir?" I asked. "It can be embarrassing when you know someone well and they decide to write about their life."

"Do people kill each other over embarrassment?" Myles asked. I said nothing. He raised his eyebrows. "Wow. I don't know. I'm sure Barbara wasn't delighted. She likes her image, and her readers see her a certain way. Maybe having a conspiracy-theory nut for a brother would be bad for Barbara Gable's business. But is she going to kill him over that? Does she seem the type?"

"It's not as easy as people think," I told him, "to know who's the type. You don't think it's like her?"

"She doesn't like fuss. And she loved her brother in her way. Like he loved her in his way. These were strange ways. I don't mean that like they had something sexy going on." Myles coughed. "Sorry. Just saying that, I threw up in my throat a little. I mean they were weird kids and weird adults and totally different people, but they got on okay. I think they were fond of each other."

"And you can't think of anyone else who'd be worried about the contents?"

"His publisher, maybe? If he seemed too crazy it might hurt sales. But it might also help sales. Who knows. That's science fiction for you. Other than that, I can't see anyone taking anything Charlie wrote all that seriously."

"Denny seemed uncertain about what Charlie would have to write about in a memoir," I said. "It sounds like Charlie lived around here, worked for a comic book shop, and sold a lot of novels overseas. I'm sure that's an interesting life if you're living it, but it might not be a great read."

"Are you asking me why Charlie got it in his head to write a memoir?" Myles said. "Because search me. I can tell you, Charlie's idea of what his life has been like and everyone else's idea—those might be different. Not might. They will be different. Charlie thinks he's tapped into this big conspiracy. If he thought he needed to write a memoir, that's what it was really about."

"Barbara says Charlie first mentioned the memoir to her six months ago," Jess said. "Do you remember anything unusual happening six months ago?"

"Real things?" Myles asked. It sounded like he was riffing on the line from *Big Trouble in Little China*. Given that I was sitting next to a tower of science fiction magazines, he probably was.

"Anything you were aware of," I said.

Myles sighed. "Not… no. Christ, the guy always thought the boogeyman was under the bed. Who listened?"

"So Charlie did feel threatened," Jesse said.

Myles took on an odd stillness, unexpected from someone who had been animated since we'd arrived. It was like the stare of an intelligent bird.

"He always felt threatened. I think he liked it." Myles blinked a few times, then smiled. "Why else would you convince yourself that Will Smith and Tommy Lee Jones were coming for you?"

"Brains are funny things," Jess said.

He looked at me, and I nodded. "I think that's everything for now." I put one of my cards on his desk. "If you think of anything that might help, call anytime."

"Will do. Did Barbara say when the wake was going to be? Or the celebration of life or whatever. I know Charlie was death on funerals. No pun intended."

"She has a lot of things to do," Jess said. "She did mention that was one of them."

"She might not mind some help," I said, "from someone in the event planning business."

"Right," Myles said. "That's a good thought. I'll give her a call. Do you need me to walk you out?"

"We'll be okay," I said, pulling the desk clerk's directions from my back pocket. "We've got a map."

Chapter EIGHT

"DUNGEONS AND Dragons," Jess said as we got into the car.

"You say those words like someone who never played D&D," I said. "And I don't think I believe that."

"I never did," Jess said. "Not D&D. When I was in that boarding school in England, one of the guys ran a horror game, and I thought he was intellectually fascinating, so I joined up."

"What did you find the most intellectually fascinating about him?" I asked. "Did he have a sophisticated ass?"

"I'm shocked by what you're insinuating. We were fifteen. And his ass was a genius."

"But nothing compared to Nightwing's."

"That standard is impossibly high. Where are we going next?"

"I'm torn," I said. "I want to talk to both of the other D&D players, and I wouldn't mind talking to Charlie's agent, if I knew who that was. I'm also interested in this UFO cult."

"I have an idea."

"About which of those things?"

"All of them? You're running around trying to get to people before Detective Broz tells them not to talk to you or drags them down to the station or something. Yes?"

"Correct."

"But you need time to do research. Which I could do, but I'm also taking notes for you in these interviews, and I know you don't think you need that—"

"I didn't say that. It seems helpful. I haven't had anyone to do it before."

"So we need a third person."

"You're suggesting we call TaskRabbit?" I asked. "Look up junior private investigators on Kijiji?"

"I'm suggesting Izzy."

I hadn't started the car yet since I hadn't had a destination in mind. His words sat in the furnace-temperature silence.

"Izzy," I said finally.

"Yes, and please turn on the goddamned AC if nothing else."

"She's not a detective," I said as I turned the key.

"She was helpful the last time, and you know she needs money, and she already sort of knows about the case. She won't be obnoxious to any of the famous people. She won't sell anything to a gossip site. You could do worse."

"Okay. All right."

I found the address for Capes Off Whyte and checked the route. Simple enough without getting directions. I handed my phone to Jess.

"Put her on speaker while I drive to that comic book place. We'll see what she says."

She answered on the second ring with a bored-sounding, "Yello."

That didn't mean she was bored, because I thought she might use the same tone to tell me her hair was on fire, but her answering so quickly did suggest that she might be at loose ends.

"Izzy. It's your not-real dads."

"Hey, not-real dads. Can I borrow the car tonight?"

"No, but you can make some fast money if you're interested."

"It's a good thing you're gay," she said. "Otherwise that would be a super creepy thing for you to say to a girl my age."

"I'm on a case right now, and it's not the mystery of why you're unemployed. I'm investigating Charlie Gudzyak's murder."

"Yeah, that's what the internet says. I don't get it."

"What don't you get?"

"Denny asked me about hiring you on, like, Saturday night. And the socials say he knew this Charlie guy, so obviously it's the same case. But this Charlie guy didn't get killed until yesterday. Did he hire you to solve a murder that hadn't happened yet? Because I think I know who did it."

Jess smiled. Of course he did. It was the kind of thing he would say.

"The case evolved," I said. "Denny hired me to find something of Charlie's that had gone missing. And then Charlie was murdered."

"His whole life went missing," Izzy said. "Man. You realize that there's a history here where you know a guy for, like, a day, and he drops dead."

"Yes, Izzy. I'm the Jessica Fletcher of Alberta. Would you be willing to do some research for me? I can pay you… I don't know. Whatever researchers make. You can research that too."

Izzy snorted. "Why do I feel like you won't be emailing me a contract?"

"If I had time for that, I'd have time to do my own research. Do you want the job?"

"I'm broke and have nothing better to do, so yes."

"Your enthusiasm is appreciated. I need you to find out everything you can about a group called UFOUND. They're into UFOs."

"On it. Anything else?"

"I'd like to know who Charlie Gudzyak's agent was and how to get in touch. Charlie wrote under the name Wolfgang Waltz."

"Yeah, I know. Remember, I've been following this shit?" Izzy said. "It's kind of all the talk today. Oh, you want me to keep an eye on the socials for you?"

"Sure. Jesse's blood pressure will thank you."

"I do what I can to help the olds."

I found a parking spot about two blocks from Capes, which wasn't bad for the neighbourhood. Whyte Avenue was generally busy—in the day with people rushing from fair-trade gift shop to vegetarian café, and by night with people stumbling from faux-Irish pubs to cowboy bars.

Capes was, like a lot of smaller shops, about a block off the street itself, in this case facing onto a paved alley and nestled between a corset shop and a health-supplement store.

Myles had been right when he said there was a Capes in Calgary. I'd only been in there once, with a friend who was getting a birthday present for a nephew. Or so he'd said—for all I knew, he'd wanted the Superman action figure for himself. It had been a single open and drafty space, with bins of comics and vinyl records across the middle, bookshelves at the back, and collectibles along the sides. The place had smelled like a cross between a pulp mill and a pigeon coop, and every piece of shop furniture had looked like it had been kicked down a long flight of stairs.

This place was a significant step up. It was a two-storey building, the front glass was clean, and no one had thrown up on the doormat.

The merchandise was new and split into sections—board and role-playing games to one side, collectibles by the till, comics and books on the second floor. There were customers milling, not a huge crowd, but respectable for a summer weekday afternoon. At a table in the back, a few long-haired guys in black were flipping cards and squabbling over the rules of whatever game it was. Did people still play Magic? I had no idea.

Behind the till, a twenty-something girl with a half-shaved head and a *WandaVision* tee shirt was putting dice into Lucite holders. She glanced up when we entered, with wariness instead of a bright customer-service smile.

I gave a smile anyway, along with one of my cards. "I'm looking for someone who works here—a guy named Eddie. Is he here today?"

Her eyes flicked from me to Jess and back, and then to my card. I saw her put it together. Jesse's face. My name. Private investigator. She knew about the Calgary thing. She knew exactly who we were.

"It's you," she said before she could get her mouth under control. Her cheeks flushed red under her ivory makeup.

"This is about a friend of Eddie's," I said, to give us both the relief of a different topic. "Don't worry. Eddie isn't in any trouble."

"He's in the basement. It's not a public area."

"I'm not really the public," I told her. This was not true in any legal sense, but it was also not, in any legal sense, against the law to pretend I had a special status of some kind. As long as I didn't claim to be a cop or use a fake ID, I was golden.

"I'll stay up here while you talk to him," Jess said. The girl stared at him. She seemed to have forgotten how to stop. Her cheeks were bright again.

"Is that the basement door there?" I asked, pointing to a door a few feet behind her. She glanced where I was pointing, then tried on a smile.

"I guess it's okay. Since you're an investigator."

I went around the desk and through the door before she could change her mind.

I found a flight of stairs in front of me, leading to the basement. They were plywood, painted battleship grey, nothing like the shiny dark wood in the public-facing part of the store. The lights were on, a few bare ceiling bulbs. Shipping boxes and flats of Coke Zero were stacked along the side of the staircase. There were a few doors at the north end of the room.

Grey metal shelves took up the rest of the open space. They were as unfussy as shelves could be, bolted together to form long rows. More shipping boxes and piles of unpacked merchandise covered the shelves, like Charlie's living room on a grand scale. Except Charlie had only had one of everything, and this place had, at a glance, enough Marvel's *Eternals* T-shirts to clothe a small nation.

I couldn't see anyone from where I was. I went down the stairs, started for the first row between the shelves, and stopped.

I don't know whether I saw it because of some ingrained habit to look for that kind of thing, or whether I'd been lucky to glance in the right direction. On the shelf in front of me, at eye level. Blood.

I stepped closer. Other things could appear to be blood, but few of them set the way blood did. And it was hard to imagine someone getting paint on the corner of a metal shelving unit, at head height, with some dripping to the shelf below and down the edge of the unit to the floor but nowhere else. With a dent in the shelf corner where the stain was. And with nothing else that same colour anywhere around.

Someone could have tripped and fallen into the corner of the shelf. Accidents happened. But people who tripped usually fell down, and anyone who'd fallen down onto something that was at my eye level ought to have been playing professional basketball, not hanging around the basement of a comic shop.

I was so busy considering the blood and its possible implications that I was startled by the soft voice from the next row.

"I'm sorry," the voice said. "This isn't a public space."

It was a gentler tone than the clerk upstairs had used. I stepped back to see the next row and found a beatific figure with curly light brown hair and a matching beard, both a few inches past his shoulder. He was about my height and easily double my weight, though the overall effect was more of an amiable mountain than an overweight man. I put his age in the thirties, at a guess, but it was hard to be sure.

He raised a pudgy pink hand and smiled.

"This is the storeroom," he said. "You're not supposed to be down here."

"I'm not a customer," I said. "Are you Eddie Shiner?"

He blinked in surprise but not alarm. Whatever some stranger had come down to the off-limits basement to discuss with him, it couldn't possibly mean trouble. He said simply, "I am."

"I'm Ben Ames. I'm a private investigator. Barbara Gudzyak has hired me."

"Oh." His smile drooped. "Oh no. Poor Charlie."

I nodded. "I'm sorry about your friend."

"Thank you. I don't really believe it yet. I do believe it—I saw it online, and then I talked to Barbara. But I feel like I'll go over there and Charlie will be there like always. Does that make any sense?"

"It does," I assured him. "You might feel that way for a while."

"She said someone… strangled him?" He shuddered at the thought. He wasn't wrong. It was an ugly way to go.

"It seems that way," I said. "I'm sorry to do this so soon after your loss, but I have to ask some questions. The sooner I ask questions, the better my chances of finding out who did it."

"Right. Right. Someone did it. That's crazy. Was it a burglar?"

You'd think Edmonton had a fatal burglary every second day from the way everyone was jumping to that conclusion. I couldn't have sworn that wasn't the case since I hadn't looked up the stats, but it seemed unlikely.

"Tough to say," I said. "A few things were missing. Can you tell me when the last time was that you saw Charlie?"

"Friday night. For D&D. I'm in—I was in—his D&D game. Every second week. I've been in that game for years."

"You, Myles Murati, and Jeremy Gustafsen. Is that right?"

"Yes."

"And you were all there Friday night?"

"Yes. Is it okay if… I'm supposed to be unpacking some things. Can I do that while we talk?"

"Sure."

He led me down the row to an open cardboard box, large enough to take up an entire shelf. He put one big pink hand into the box and pulled out a clear plastic box containing a rubber duck in an Iron Man costume. He did not seem surprised by this. Casually, he picked up a pricing gun, stuck a tag on the bottom of the box, and set it on the next shelf.

"Did anyone arrive late or leave early?"

He pursed his lips. "No. Jeremy was early, but he always is. He comes into town for the game. You're always more on time when you come from farther away."

"Was there anything unusual about the evening?"

"Barbara wasn't home. But she isn't always home on Fridays. I think she went to the folk festival. They knew Denny Hill—oh, you already know that."

"I do. Was there anything else?"

"Charlie was upset about his book. It took a long time to start the game because he wanted to talk about that. Do you know about that? His book?"

"I heard his manuscript had been taken. What did he say to you about it?"

Eddie pulled out a pair of Hulk Ducks, priced them, and placed them next to Iron Man Duck. From my angle, I couldn't see whether one duck was more valuable than the other.

"He said… I want to get this right. It was his memoir. He'd been writing that for a few months. I guess he finally got it finished on Wednesday. I was sort of curious to read it and see if I was in it. Does that sound bad?"

"It sounds normal," I said. "Did you have any idea what he wrote about in his memoirs?"

Eddie shrugged. His halo of hair bounced lightly, a few strands flying upward and taking their time to come back down.

"His life, I guess. He never talked much about his life, so I don't know. I know he worked here for a long time. We overlapped for, like, a year. I started, and then his books started to sell and he made all that money, and he quit. But we got along, so he asked me to be in his game. And I went to visit him sometimes. Sorry, that's not what you asked me."

"I would have gotten to it eventually," I assured him. "Had he let anyone see the book? After he finished it?"

"Not yet. He was going to send it to his agent, and that would have been the first person to see it."

"Do you know his agent's name?"

Eddie priced an Ant Duck and paused to think, turning it over in his hands before shaking his head and putting the duck on the shelf. "Sorry. He might have said, but I don't remember."

"And he told you the book had been stolen."

"Yeah. The laptop and the flash drive. He went upstairs to use the bathroom, and it was gone when he came back down. Barbara forgot to lock the door, which is pretty usual. I thought he'd be mad at her about that, but he said it didn't matter and that it was capital-T Them who took it. To keep the truth from getting out. Um, now that I'm saying this, it sounds really bad, like Charlie was way more messed up than he was. He was just a funny guy sometimes. It wasn't a big deal."

"Funny like he was joking?" I said.

Eddie took out a few more ducks. "No. He had ideas. Like he thought that aliens and the government and I forget who else all had this conspiracy—Jeremy could tell you. He believes in all that stuff too. But it wasn't like… I mean, if he went to the fridge and there wasn't any milk left, he blamed Barbara. He didn't think it was aliens. He thought they were watching him and all that, but he didn't think they were doing stuff to him most of the time. This thing with the book, where he said they came right into his house and took it? That was new."

"Did he say he saw them take it?"

"I don't think so? He said he knew it was them because of everything he wrote about them and how they couldn't let him tell the world."

"I don't suppose it ever occurred to him to tell the world on social media?"

"Jeremy does," Eddie said. "And he has a podcast. The world doesn't seem too interested. But maybe Charlie's fans would have taken it seriously. I don't know."

"Did he say anything else about the manuscript?" I asked.

Eddie pulled more ducks, priced them and placed them, and repeated it a few times before speaking again. "Nothing about what was in it. He said he was going to rewrite it. He said he had a system for keeping them from stealing it this time."

"Can you think of anyone else who might be worried about what Charlie had put in his memoir?" I asked. "Other than aliens or the Bilderbergers?"

Eddie's eyes widened. "Oh, he did say the Bilderbergers! He and Jeremy mentioned them sometimes. I tried not to get to the game early because they had their talks before the game, and I kind of didn't want to hear it, but sometimes my bus connections were going to be either a little early or really late. They keep changing the bus routes around there."

"But the memoir," I said. "Do you think anyone else might have been worried about what was in there?"

"I really don't know. Barbara didn't like the idea of him writing a memoir, like, in general. She doesn't—I mean, she loved Charlie? I'm sure she did. But also if no one ever knew he was her brother, that was okay. She never talked about him in interviews or mentioned him in her author blurbs. I got a few of her books from the library after Charlie told me she was his sister. They weren't for me. But the author blurbs were all about Vancouver, like she never even lived here."

"Was she embarrassed about something in particular?" I asked. "Did you get the sense there was something in their past she wanted to keep hidden?"

Eddie shook his head. "There could have been but Charlie never said, and Barbara never would have said. Myles might know. Or Denny Hill, I guess. I've never met Denny, but I know they were all close when they were kids."

"Did you see any tension between them?"

Eddie huffed out a gentle laugh.

Apparently I'd missed a joke. "What's funny?"

"You're talking like Barbara might have—it's not her. I don't know who it would have been. It's creepy. I guess I thought of a robbery or something first because otherwise it might be someone I know. That's so creepy."

"It is," I agreed. "If it had to be someone you knew, is there anybody—I'm not asking you to make an accusation, but do you have a sense about anyone?"

He pulled the box of ducks toward him and peered inside. Apparently satisfied, he pushed it back onto the shelf.

"Not Barbara. She'd lie about him being her brother, and she totally hired that maid to spy on him. Not spy-spy, but I bet she called Barbara when the house started to get out of hand because Barbara would mysteriously come back to town. That's Barbara. Not killing someone. Especially not Charlie."

"If not her, then who?"

"Who took the cookie from the cookie jar," Eddie sing-songed. "Nobody."

"It was somebody," I said.

Eddie sighed. "I know. It's sad his books didn't protect him."

"What's that?"

Eddie moved down the shelf and opened another box. This one had stuffed toys in it, in bright colours and covered in tentacles and extra eyes.

"He thought his comics and books, all the stuff on the shelves in the living room, would block out the thoughts the aliens were trying to put into his head. He said the thought waves would hit the ideas in the books and comics and disperse."

I leaned against the shelves, careful not to knock anything over or get blood on my shirt.

"That is a pretty out-there idea," I said.

Eddie's sad brown eyes got sadder. "I think he should have seen a doctor or something. When you think someone's trying to put their thoughts in your brain, that's bad news. But he didn't think he was sick at all, and Barbara didn't…. I don't think she wanted anyone to know. She could maybe have gotten him to see a doctor, but she wouldn't. So I don't think he ever did."

I didn't know what to say to that. Eddie and I looked at each other in sadness. I gave that a few beats, then moved on.

"What about his collection? Was it valuable? Will it go to Barbara? I understand she'll be getting his half of the house."

He nodded.

"She has money anyway. But she'll get the house. She might sell it. I don't know. I think she only came back here for Charlie. To make sure he was okay."

"And the collection?"

Eddie's shoulder twitched. He seemed, for the first time, uncomfortable in his skin. "He said he was leaving it to me. I don't know whether he did. He and I talked about comics and science fiction all the time. He wanted... the thing about Charlie, he likes what he... what he liked, sorry. He had a bunch of Peter Milligan's early Vertigo runs because he liked them, but I don't think they were worth much. He had tons of Gold Key because he liked them, and they're all over the map. The money wasn't the point. And he knew I was the same. He said I was supposed to take what I wanted and sell the rest and give the money to Jeremy. For his organization. The UFO thing."

"How much money are we talking about?" I asked.

Eddie shook his head. "I really don't know. Those prices go up and down. And I'm not the kind of expert you'd have to be to price what Charlie had. You'd really need a bunch of experts. He liked all the old pulp magazines. The real kind from a hundred years ago. You'd need someone who was into that. I don't know anything about, like, *Black Mask*. I'm not a detective fiction guy. No offense."

I had no idea why that was supposed to offend me, but I gave him a reassuring smile. "None taken."

"So he had all that stuff. And he liked TV and movie novelizations from the sixties. I don't even know who specializes in that. Somebody somewhere, I guess. There's somebody for everything."

"Did Jeremy know about this plan?"

"Sure. Charlie told us at a game one night. It was a long time ago—like a year or more? It was sort of funny because he wasn't leaving anything to Myles. That was Charlie. He wouldn't have thought that he might hurt Myles's feelings."

"Did he?" I asked. "Hurt Myles's feelings?"

Eddie stared at the ducks he'd put in a row. He had a distant expression, like he was seeing through them. To another duck pond in another town.

"No," he said. "I don't think so."

We both turned our heads then, because the basement door had opened. Detective Broz was at the top of the stairs. I thought I could see Jess behind her and got confirmation when Broz headed down the stairs with Jess a few steps behind her. Upstairs, someone closed the door.

Broz came directly to the row we were in without seeming to notice the blood.

"Detective," she said.

"Detective," I returned. "How's the investigation going?"

"It goes," she said and turned to Eddie. "They tell me your boss is down here."

I looked at Jess, who shrugged. *No, Ben, I also don't know why she wants to talk to Eddie's boss and not Eddie.*

"He's in his office," Eddie said, pointing to one of the doors at the back.

"Thanks."

Broz headed that way and I followed. Jess was hanging back between us and the stairs. When Broz got about halfway to the office door, it opened and a man walked out. He was an older guy, maybe seventy, with a widow's peak and a fighter's beat-up nose. Despite his age and the arthritic way he moved, he had an air of violent competence that would have made most people hesitant to test him.

Broz didn't seem intimidated, but she did stop and square her shoulders.

"Mr. Antonis," she said.

"Detective Broz. We met last year. I don't know if you remember."

"I remember," she said. She did not sound like the memory was fond. "Do you know why I'm here?"

Antonis smiled and spread his hands. They were large, with knobby knuckles that had broken and not healed right. "I would not presume to guess."

He was one of those guys. I'd met a dozen or more, working in Calgary. Small-time thugs with a little money who spent their evenings watching *The Sopranos* and taking notes on how to talk tough. He was smart enough, though, not to take the line she'd cast.

"It could be so many things," Broz said, then gave him a mean little smile. "I'm joking of course."

"Of course."

"One of your former employees died last night."

"I heard. Terrible. I've sent flowers to his sister."

"I'm sure she'll appreciate them," Broz said. She took a step forward. Antonis rolled his head to the side, making a crack so loud that Jesse jumped. Broz took another step, and Antonis smiled like he was hoping she'd try it, whatever it might be.

"Charlie Gudzyak was murdered."

"I know," Antonis said. "I know. It's all over the news."

Jess was crossing the room behind me, toward Eddie. What was he doing?

"He'd just finished writing a memoir," Broz said. "Did you know about that?"

Antonis shrugged. "Maybe. Maybe not. I hear things and I forget. I'm an old man."

The classic "I'm an old man" bit. *I don't remember. I couldn't kill anyone. I'm not currently sticking a knife into you. I'm an old man.*

Jess had stopped by the second row of shelves, the same place where I'd stopped to look at—oh. Dammit. He'd noticed the blood. Antonis glanced in Jesse's direction, and his eyes narrowed. I didn't care for it and was relieved when Broz's voice caught his attention again.

"Mr. Gudzyak worked here a long time. You'd have to think that would feature in a memoir. That book probably has some things to say about you."

Antonis laughed, bringing up a rolling smoker's cough. "Charlie? Writing about me? When he could be writing about little green men? I haven't seen this book, but if we sold it here, I have a feeling we'd shelve it under fiction. Science fiction. That's all Charlie ever wrote."

Broz took out her notebook. "I've come all the way down here, and my boss won't be too happy if I don't ask. Would you mind telling me where you were yesterday between four and six in the afternoon?"

I caught Jesse's eye and shook my head. Stop staring at the crime scene in front of the criminal, Jesse. I don't think he likes it. Fortunately, Jess caught on and went back to his place near the stairs.

"I was here. I was here from ten in the morning to after seven. Eddie over there can tell you. He was here. And my granddaughter, Hailey, upstairs. The one with the—" He waved a hand by the side of his head. "—the hair. I'm sure they will both be happy to vouch for me."

Of course they would. Even if they didn't, so what? A guy like Antonis had people to do things for him.

At least it sorted out Eddie's alibi. If Eddie was Antonis's alibi, however unconvincing that might be, Antonis was his.

"Since you remember me," Broz said, "I'm sure you'll have no trouble getting hold of me if you think of anything that might help my investigation."

"Of course. I wish you success."

We left—me and Jess and Broz, with Jess up the stairs first and Broz last. The clerk gave Jess a sheepish glance, like she might find her grandfather a little embarrassing. Possibly as embarrassing as Barbara had found her brother.

"It was good talking to you," Jess told the clerk, and she smiled.

"Can I buy you gentlemen some coffee?" Broz asked.

"Absolutely," I said.

CHAPTER NINE

"THAT MAN," Broz said, "is a thug."

We were in a park a block north of Whyte with takeout coffees and a giant pretzel that Jess and Broz had cut a deal to share.

"About that," Jess said. "I saw something in the basement."

Broz snorted. "Sorry. I'm not trying to be rude. I'm sure you did. What was it? American cigarettes? A box of parachute knives?"

"Blood," Jess said. "On the shelves."

"I saw it too," I told her. "Someone got their head introduced to the corner."

Broz nodded and chewed pretzel. Once it was down, she said, "That's probably what happened. Antonis likes that store. It's his showpiece. He thinks it makes him seem legit. But he's not above having someone roughed up in the storeroom."

"So the store is a front?" Jess said. "Or all the stores? Does he own all of them?"

"He owns stores here, in Calgary, Saskatoon, I think maybe Regina and Winnipeg too. That's just Capes. He owns some other things. Bars, pool halls."

"I doubt it's a front, exactly," I said.

"Mmm." Broz brushed pretzel crumbs off her lap. She'd put down a napkin, but the wind had taken it away. "He's serious about his stores."

"So what exactly is he?" Jess said. "Why does a comic bookstore owner need to beat people up in his basement?"

"He has them beat up," Broz said. "Didn't you hear him? He's an old man. He has people for that."

"He probably does a few things," I told Jess. I looked at Broz. "Can I guess?"

"Give it a try."

"Loan sharking?"

She tapped an invisible bell in the air with her finger. "Ding."

"Moving illegal goods? You mentioned cigarettes and parachute knives."

"Ding."

"Fencing stolen goods? He buys and sells used products anyway, so it would be a natural adjunct."

"Ding, ding, ding. I think he also dabbles in criminal arson, but we haven't been able to prove it."

Jess frowned. His half of the pretzel was still in his hand, forgotten. "You say the stores aren't a front, but he's using them to do multiple illegal things. Isn't that what a front is?"

"The difference is that he also wants the stores to do well," I said. "If he's anything like the guys I ran into in Calgary, it's all business, and it's all the same to him. Selling comics and loan sharking are both ways to make money."

"It's one thing," Broz said, nodding. "The businesses provide cover for everything else he does, but he also uses his other activities to prop up the businesses when they need cash. Neither would work as well without the other."

Jess considered that while he started on his pretzel. Behind us, two buskers argued over their right to a patch of grass beside a parking lot.

"Charlie would have known," he said. "They'd all have to know."

"Oh, absolutely," Broz said. "None of them will talk, but they all know. Most of them aren't involved, per se, but they see what goes on."

"Okay, I don't get that," Jesse said. "If you're not in on the crime, why would you work for a guy you knew was a criminal?"

I shrugged. "A lot of people work for crooks. Some would say most people do. Who owns your label, again?"

Broz leaned back and sipped coffee like she was relaxing into her seat at the theatre.

"I was thinking of a more direct path between criminal and employee than just participating in capitalism," Jess said. "If I worked somewhere and I saw some guy with a broken nose stumbling out of the basement, I'd be worried about what would happen if the cops showed up. Or what would happen the next time I pissed off my boss."

One of the buskers, carrying a miniature harp and an amp, stormed off. Battle lost to the guitarist, who opened a velvet-lined case and a folding stool and sat down to play "I've Just Seen a Face" for all those people who, as Jess had noted earlier, liked the Beatles.

"Some people are not thrown by casual violence," I said. "For whatever reason. If you grew up around violence or your social circle had a lot of physical fights, and then you got a job you liked working for a guy who occasionally roughed somebody up, you might not be that worried about it."

"Or you figure your boss has a line between his crimes and his legitimate businesses," Broz said. "He doesn't, but you don't know that. You think you're safe."

"As long as you don't betray your boss," I said. "They would all know better than to turn on that guy."

"You say he might have killed people," Jess said to Broz. "Do you think he'd have killed Charlie on spec? Because he thought Charlie might have told on him?"

"It wouldn't have been on spec," I said. "Remember, the book got taken on Thursday, and Charlie was killed last night. We have to assume whoever took it read it."

"And they could have deleted it," Jess said, "if they didn't like what they read. There would still be the risk that Charlie could put the secret on social media or buy a billboard or something."

"But that wasn't his style," I said. "And he never did it before."

"If they knew he'd started to rewrite it, though…."

Broz looked at Jess. "Hold up. Are you saying whoever did this must have known he was rewriting the book?"

"I might be," Jess said. "Lemme think."

He drummed on his legs and gazed at the ground for a half minute or so. Then he raised his head. "Yeah. It's not a hundred per cent, but if you got your hands on the book and you knew it was the only copy—and you were pretty sure Charlie wasn't going to spill your secrets any other way, because he never had before—at that point, you think your problems are over. There's no reason to take the risk of going into his house and killing him. Unless you knew he'd started to rewrite the book."

"And about the safe," I said. "They might think they could keep stealing the book until Charlie gave up, but if they knew he'd started using a safe, they'd know that wouldn't work."

"They took the safe," Jess said. "They knew it existed."

"That's who we're after," I said. "The people who knew he was rewriting the book and knew about the safe."

"But what about Eddie's boss?"

"Maybe Eddie was working with him?"

"Slow down, boys," Broz said. She held up her hands, one still gripping her coffee cup. "We haven't even determined that this wasn't a home invasion. There's a lot of work to be done before we can rule anything—what are you grinning about, Ames?"

"You know it wasn't a home invasion. Come off it. Your theory is that someone walked into the home of a guy as paranoid as Charlie Gudzyak and he sat in his chair while they went around behind him? Unless you're hearing that he was strangled elsewhere and put in his chair, this was somebody he knew."

Broz scowled at me. She brushed bits of pretzel off her lap again, though in fact they were already gone.

"Fine," she said, her jaw tight. "It was someone he knew. But I need to be thorough."

"Tell you what," I said. "This is a benefit of having a private investigator on the case. You can pursue everything according to protocol while we go off chasing a theory. If we're wrong, it's not your problem. If we're right, we'll hand you a win."

Broz crumpled her empty cup and threw it into a nearby garbage can. There was a nice arc to the throw, like she was tossing a slow-pitch over the plate.

"All right. You do your thing and I'll do mine. But keep me in the loop so I can find your bodies if you get yourselves killed."

Jess eyed me.

I ignored him and offered Broz a handshake. "That's a deal."

"WHAT NOW?" Jess asked once we were back in the car.

"The hotel?" I said. "I'll check in with Izzy, see if we can meet with the last D&D player tonight."

"They sat around that table with him every two weeks."

I glanced at him. I wanted to take a longer look, but it was early rush hour, stop and start, and a glance was as long as I could safely give him.

"What, the suspects?"

"Yeah. You'd think you'd know if someone you sat across the table from for years had it in them to kill you."

"Having it in you isn't as rare as you think, Jess."

"Casual violence." He drummed on the dashboard, along with the radio. Barenaked Ladies, calling out to Brian Wilson's psychologist, or anyone, for help.

"I'm starting to wonder if this case is the pick-me-up I was hoping it would be for you."

"Beats the alternative."

He did not say what the alternative was.

When we got up to the hotel room, there were parcels on the bed. This did not seem to surprise Jess. In fact, he was so unsurprised as to say, "Good," when he saw them.

"Someone left random parcels in our room and you say good?"

He grinned. "I asked the front desk to have my deliveries brought up to the room. There's stuff in there for you too."

"Hotels will bring your parcels up to the room?"

He was already opening boxes and didn't bother to respond. Obviously they would if you threw enough money at them. Or maybe if you simply asked. I might have been doing the hotel thing wrong all my life.

I settled myself in the chair by the window and called Izzy. This time it took four rings to get an answer.

"Little busy right now, Grandpa."

"With what?" I asked.

"Your bullshit," she said. "I am hard at work on it."

Jess's phone rang. He looked at it, raised his brows, and took it into the bathroom. For quiet, I assumed, and not to film something he'd have to apologize to the planet for when it got leaked in a year or two.

"Do you have anything for me?"

"Ben Ames, what I have for you is a date with a total freakin' nut job."

I smiled. "I'm flattered, Izzy, but you're too young and too female for me."

"It's your money you're wasting with this banter."

I put my feet up on the coffee table and stared out the window. "It's not wasted if I enjoy it. Who's the nut job?"

"Jeremy Gustafsen. Founder of UFOUND, the premier UFO research and documentation association of Edmonton and northern Alberta."

"How about that," I said. "When and where is this date?"

"Tonight, midnight, at the dark sky preserve."

"The what?"

"Dark sky preserve. Are you telling me you have never watched for extraterrestrial visitors at a dark sky preserve?"

My text alert went off, and I flipped screens to find a message from Jess.

Reiss still in town wants to meet for dinner

I sent back a thumbs-up. After a second, I added, *Might bring a guest*

k I'll tell Reiss

"You still alive over there?" Izzy asked. "You'd better have left my money in your will."

"You're getting my comic book collection," I said.

"The hell?"

"Nothing. It's been a day. We're meeting Reiss for dinner. Did you want to come?"

"Oh my God, a murder reunion? I wouldn't miss it!"

"Great. I'll send you the details."

"Cool. I've got the agent's number too. I keep leaving him messages. Do you want the number, or do you want me to keep trying?"

"You might as well keep trying," I said. "He's not any more likely to talk to me."

We hung up and I went to knock on the bathroom door. "Izzy will be joining us," I said.

Jess opened the door. "Nice. He'll be happy to see her."

"She got us an appointment with Jeremy Gustafsen. Midnight tonight."

Jess went past me into the room and got back to his work sorting clothes into Ben and Jesse piles. A can of mosquito repellant came out of a cloth supermarket bag. He set it firmly on top of my clothes.

"I don't know why they love you so much," he said.

"Don't you?" I said with what I hoped was a rakish smile. He put his hands on my shoulders and kissed me.

"There is a certain charisma," he admitted. "Why does this guy want to meet at midnight? Is he a reverse Cinderella?"

"He wants us to hunt aliens with him."

Jess looked at the ceiling like he'd hear a xenomorph in the vents.

I laughed. "Not like that. He's going to something called a dark sky preserve to watch for UFOs."

"Oh really? I went to one of those in Wales. You'll like it. It's a place where there's no light pollution so you can see all the stars. On a clear night, anyway." He went to the window. "Pretty clear right now. Toss me my phone."

I grabbed it from the bed and threw it to him. He caught it with his usual grace. He had an unfair amount of it for someone who'd never gotten into sports.

"There's one really close by. That's probably the one he means. It's about forty minutes east of here. If we're lucky, we'll get northern lights."

"If we're extra lucky, we'll get Martians."

"Anything could go." His phone bleeped, and he checked it. "Reiss sent the restaurant. I'll forward to Izzy. He's thinking six."

That gave us some time to ourselves, which Jess used in his usual way of late. He shoved the clothes to one side of the bed and went to sleep. I sank into my chair and stared at my phone. Read through Barbara Gable's website and watched an interview on YouTube. Texted Luna to update her on our situation and make sure she was okay to keep watching Frank. Flipped through an online issue of *Mad Science*. I didn't learn much, except that Luna would keep Frank for as long as we needed. When we got home, she'd consider giving him back.

I woke Jess after an hour, and he stumbled to the bathroom to make himself presentable. I thought about asking why he was so tired and whether he needed to see a doctor or something. It seemed like a better conversation for later, when we weren't chasing ETs and a murderer. I tacked the thought to an empty space in the back of my mind.

Reiss had picked an Asian fusion place in the back of an old warehouse, close enough to our hotel that Jess and I chose to walk. Izzy was at the front door when Jess and I got there, digging in her purse like she was hoping to find something different in there. Like a richer person's purse.

Jess bumped her arm with his. "It's on me, kid."

She rolled her eyes. "Absentee fathers always think they can buy your love."

Reiss was waiting inside. He'd put on a dressier shirt than I'd seen him wear before, and his hair was tied back in a loose ponytail. The style suited him, but I had yet to see one that didn't.

He greeted Izzy with a huge grin and a hug. "They said they were bringing a guest, but they didn't say it was you."

"Surprise!" she said. "I didn't get to tell you on Sunday, but I thought your workshop was really good. And your show on Saturday. Except I kept getting pulled away for stupid shit. I missed, like, half of it."

"Catch us next time. We'll be back. We're always back." He looked at me and Jess. We got a smile but no hugs. "I booked us a spot in the speakeasy. I thought you might appreciate the privacy."

"Are they unaware that prohibition is over?" Izzy asked.

"Are they unaware that we never had it up here?" I said.

"I didn't ask," Reiss said. "Follow me."

He led us past the line of hopeful diners, through an atmospheric space full of long plank tables and red lanterns, to a cabinet that seemed like the end of the line until a nearby server swung it open to let us through.

"Don't," Jess said, pointing a warning finger at me.

"Don't what?"

"Whatever you were going to say. Especially if it rhymes with phipsters."

I nudged Izzy. "You see what I put up with."

"I do. I'll call the Hague."

Reiss had reserved a booth at the back, a large half moon around a gleaming hardwood table. We piled in and picked up menus, which were one-third food and two-thirds fancy booze. Fortunately, what food there was looked good.

"How did you know about this place?" Jess asked Reiss.

"A promoter took us here last year. You don't find the good places in this town unless someone shows you."

"I never stayed long enough," Jess said. "It was always do the show, get on the bus to Calgary."

"Or the other way around," Reiss agreed. "What are we doing with our lives?"

They put a pin in that topic because a server had arrived for drink and starter orders. Jess got a whiskey he liked, and I felt my shoulders relax. I hadn't even known they'd been tensed. Jess had money, sure, but even he didn't order top-shelf whiskey if he was planning to get blackout drunk.

Reiss and I had beers, and Izzy ordered some monstrosity with about eight kinds of liquor in it.

"That thing will show up with three cocktail umbrellas and a slice of pineapple on a real sword," Jess predicted.

"Good. This can be a rough neighbourhood at night."

Everyone batted jokes around for a while as we waited for the drinks and appetizers to come. Even in the dim light, I could see that Reiss was tired. Not unhappy but not completely plugged in.

"You doing all right?" I asked him.

"Yeah. I get road sick. I need to go home and stay there for… ever. No. Not forever. For a while, though."

"I didn't even make it through my last tour," Jess said, as if anyone at the table didn't know.

"Oh, you poor guys," Izzy said. "With your success and your sales and people wanting to see you. It's tragic."

Reiss and Jess exchanged a look that I couldn't read.

"I heard your band broke up," Jess said to Izzy. "I'm sorry. I thought you were good."

"Yeah, well, good isn't everything. I guess."

"This job isn't everything either," Jess told her. "The music thing. If it's what you really want, get another band and keep going. But other things are okay too."

I stared at him.

"What?' he said.

"The hypocrisy," I said. "I keep telling you to quit, and you keep not quitting."

"That's different," Jess said.

"What, because you're already successful?" Izzy said.

"No."

That was all he said, and silence followed. Reiss broke it.

"It's not good as a subsistence life," he told Izzy. "You have to love it so much you can't imagine anything else. Otherwise you're touring and writing and recording and touring, and you don't get to stop because it's the only way you can make rent on the apartment you never see. Most people don't make as much money as Jesse. They don't even make as much money as the Twist is making now."

Izzy looked from Reiss to Jesse and back. "What is this, an intervention?"

Jesse sighed. "It's not. It's really not."

She turned to me. "Why do you keep telling Jesse to quit?"

"Because Jack Lowe is a self-destructive asshole."

The food and drinks arrived, saving me from expanding on that. The server took our food order at the same time, and we hashed it out quickly—one or two of a lot of things and all of it meant to share. As soon as the server left, Jess downed half his whiskey in one swallow. He might be less concerned about the economics of a top-shelf bender than I'd thought.

"Since we're meeting this UFO guy tonight," I said to Izzy, "You might as well fill us in about his club."

Reiss coughed on the beer he'd been trying to swallow. "What? What was any of that? What are you doing?"

"I'm on a case," I told him. "Jess and Izzy are helping. It sounds weirder than it is."

"It doesn't," Jess said.

"No," I conceded. "I guess not."

"Good thing I brought my notes." Izzy pulled out a notebook with pink fun fur on the cover and a pen shaped like a candy cane sticking out of the top. "I'll start with history."

She delivered a respectable precis, covering the formation of UFOUND by Jeremy Gustafsen in 2005 with the stated intention of studying unexplained flying objects in northern Alberta, moving on to its slow growth among interested Albertans in the 2000s, and its much faster growth online as Jeremy started his podcast in the 2010s. With the growth and the attention came a branching out into the more esoteric realms of alien possession, abductions, governments in the pockets of Big Betelgeuse, and the owls not being what they seemed. Iz didn't know when Charlie had joined, but I thought I could guess.

"Some people are crazy," Reiss observed dryly. He'd finished his beer and moved on to water, a pattern I'd noticed the day we'd met. Whatever his medication mix was, it seemed to allow him one drink only.

"Jeremy lives in St. Paul," Izzy said with a grin.

"Should that mean something?" Jess asked.

"They're sort of famous for having a UFO landing pad," Izzy told him.

"I thought that was in Vulcan," Reiss said

"No," I told him. "Vulcan has the starship."

"What goes on in rural Alberta?" Jess asked. "Do I even want to know?"

"There's a giant Ukrainian easter egg," Reiss told her.

"There's a giant bee," Izzy said. "And a giant dragonfly."

"Mundare has a giant sausage," I said. Jesse grinned.

"Mundare started that rumour."

"My favourite thing," Izzy said, "is that they closed the UFO landing pad during COVID. I guess so we wouldn't give COVID to aliens and start an intergalactic incident."

"Does Jeremy live under it?" I asked. Izzy shrugged.

"Couldn't get an address. He's a cagey one. You're lucky he agreed to meet you at all,"

"At the dark sky preserve," I said.

"Oh yeah," Izzy said. "I almost forgot. You're gonna need some stuff. I pulled it together for you. It's in my car. I mean, my mom's car."

"What stuff do I need for a dark sky preserve?" I asked. "Martian antennae?"

"Lawn chairs and citronella wrist bands?" Jesse suggested.

"You need to prepare your car. You have to black out all the lights you can and put red gels over the other ones. Don't worry, I grabbed everything you need. And I printed out the list of instructions."

"There's a whole list?" Jess said.

"And you have to wait until you're off the highway to black stuff out," Izzy added. "It's illegal to be on the highway with your lights covered like that. Make sure you do this on a deserted country road."

I narrowed my eyes at her. "I feel like you're enjoying this."

"Why would I enjoy the thought of you having to stop on a dirt road in the middle of the night to dress up your car like it's a float in the Santa Claus parade?"

"If you hadn't set me up to meet with Denny," I said, "none of this would be happening right now."

Izzy nodded and took a healthy swig from her drink, which had not come with a sword but did have something moist and green floating in it that I couldn't identify.

"You're welcome," she said.

"Now," Reiss said, "you have to tell me about this case."

I didn't have to, but I did anyway. He knew about the summoning by Denny, since Brennan had filled him in, and I didn't feel like getting into any of the interpersonal stuff with Jess, but aside from that I gave him a high level of the story. When I was done, he stuck a chopstick into a dumpling in the bad-luck, funereal way and shook his head.

"You're telling me someone got that worked up over something a guy with psychosis wrote in a memoir about an alien invasion. Are you sure it wasn't aliens who took the book?"

Jess smiled a little and took a sip of his second whiskey. I wasn't sure what that smile meant, specifically, here. But in general it meant he was amused by something he thought I would never understand.

"You think Charlie was psychotic?" I asked Reiss. "That sounds a little strong. He was eccentric."

"He thought aliens were trying to project thoughts into his head," Reiss said. "I bet he heard voices too. Look, I never knew this guy, and I probably shouldn't be sitting here playing guess-the-diagnosis, because I hate it when people do that to me. But speaking as a guy with psychosis, it sounds like he was one of my kind."

"Schizophrenia?" Jess asked.

"Or bipolar disorder. You can even have psychosis if you're really depressed, but was that a fit for Charlie?"

"Not if he was going to write a whole book twice," Jess said. His voice was flat, and he seemed tired again, only a few hours after his nap.

"How are you doing?" Izzy asked Reiss suddenly. "You said you were tired before. Unless I shouldn't ask."

"No, you can. I know, by the way. I know I dropped a bomb in Calgary when I just blurted out that I had schizophrenia without any, uh, context. I'm relatively lucky. My mom is a psychologist. Funny story, kind of. She went into psychology because her brother—my uncle—got schizophrenia as a teenager. Jump forward, I'm a teenager, and I've got all the same signs. Well, not all of them. It was mostly prodromal stuff. She caught it early. I don't know if I'd be as functional as I am if I hadn't gotten treatment early."

"So you're mostly good?" Izzy asked.

Reiss smiled. "I'm mostly low key. I slow down. I have trouble thinking clearly. I don't want to do anything or see anyone or talk to anyone. I don't mean that like I would want to do those things except I'm too sad or anxious or tired. There's an absence of wanting. There's no reason for anything. It's like there's a hole in me." He shook his head. "I don't know how to say it."

"But no voices?" Izzy said.

"I get those. I see things. That mostly happens when I push too far. Like it's the end of the tour and I should have gone home a week ago."

"Are you seeing things now?" Izzy asked. "Or hearing voices? Is that okay to ask? I know, I'm snoopy."

"It's not a great thing to ask," Reiss said. "I'm not embarrassed—well, okay, I am. A little. I know I shouldn't be, but those things are the ones that people get really shitty about. Uh. Where was I?" He shook his head. "Sorry. It's not great to ask because it does not help me if I tell you I see—okay, I'm making this up, but say I told you I saw Mickey Mouse sitting next to you."

Izzy turned her head where Reiss was pointing.

Reiss slapped a hand on the table. "Exactly. What you did there. You act like it's real. That is the last thing I need."

"Got it," Izzy said. "Sorry."

"I'm usually okay, but stress isn't great for me. I hit a wall where I need to go home. If I don't notice it myself, the guys will definitely let me know."

"You have a point," Jess said. "Even what you said there, about people telling you whether you're ill and when you need to go home. I'm not saying it's not right for them to do that but… it's that whole thing where people get used to yeah-yeahing you or not caring what you think because you're not… I don't know. Capable. Responsible. Credible. Why would someone be so worried about what Charlie had to say?"

"Right?" Reiss said. "The guys in the band, my family, I'm really fortunate with how good everyone is about my disease, but how many arguments do you think I win when me and Bren remember something different ways? Or when I think my sister's boyfriend is an asshole and everyone else thinks he's the greatest? It is possible to be both mentally ill and correct, but Jesus, try getting people to believe that."

Jess nodded. "If I think something's going to go badly or I don't want to do something, oh, Jack's depressed. Jesse's being negative."

"You are depressed right now," Reiss said, looking Jess in the eye. "You know that."

Jess made a face. "It's more complicated than that."

"Okay, but people can also be fucking insane," Izzy said. The words came out of her under pressure, like she'd been unable to hold them back. "How much fucking nonsense am I expected to entertain? I'm supposed to pretend she's not unhinged?"

Reiss eyed me and Jess. I didn't have a lot of help for him. He knew as much as I did, which was that the leader of Izzy's band had been what Reiss called "mentally original" and that the band had broken up. Were those things connected? Who could say?

"We're only saying," Jess said gently, "that people with mental illness aren't automatically wrong."

Reiss nodded. "And that not everything is the disease."

"Well, that's true." Izzy stirred her second drink, something with an eight-word name that was even more colourful than her first. "My band leader wasn't just nuts. She was also a bitch."

"What do you think you'll do now?" Reiss asked.

"I dunno. The two of you seem to think I should languish in obscurity."

"We didn't say languish," Reiss said.

"Fame isn't a good reason to do anything," Jesse added.

Izzy gaped at him. "Oh my God. Are you serious? You," she said, pointing at Reiss, "got us this sweet table by calling and asking. And we're in a back room in the first place because Jack Lowe can't go anywhere without being adored. You want me to believe it sucks to be you. And you both get this for doing whatever art you want to do."

Reiss leaned across the table toward her. "Let's leave Jesse out of this. He has his own problems, but he's also an outlier. This is nothing against your talent or your drive, but you are not going to have his career."

"*I'm* barely having my career," Jess said.

Reiss flicked the side of his head. "Shh. Izzy, if you want this bad enough to spend the next ten years on the road making less than minimum wage and sleeping in a van, obviously I won't tell you not to do that. I did it. Or you could go the online route and get on the content treadmill if you think that sounds better. But it's not—you know all those bullshit movies where the guy gets the girl because he put in the work, like she's a cash prize? Success in this business is like that girl. You can't earn it. You have to work really, really hard, and it still comes down to whether you're the right person at the right time."

"With no health insurance or retirement fund," I said.

Reiss sighed. "Don't remind me."

"We're in Canada," Izzy pointed out. "I don't need health insurance."

"Sooner or later you'll need a medication that costs more than amoxicillin," Jess said.

"Or therapy," Reiss added. "Or more than six weeks of physio. Or glasses."

"Or a root canal," I said. "We're not that much older than you, Izzy. You are seeing your near future, as scary as that may be."

"You think I don't have it," Izzy said, ignoring me. And why not? I wasn't a rock star.

"Lots of people have it," Jesse said. "Whatever *it* is. I told you, I think you're talented. But I heard a busker this afternoon who had a better voice than some of the guys who played the festival this year. For all I know, he's writing and recording and doing it better than people who make a hundred times what he does. And he's not special either, Iz. No one here is special. Reiss and Brennan are really solid, evocative songwriters, but that's not why they're doing so well."

"We're not any better than we were when we were passing the hat and hoping the bar would comp our meals," Reiss said.

"No, you are," Jess told him. "Every album, you're better. And you were good to start."

"But not a thousand times better."

"And everyone levels off eventually," Jess said. "Unless they're Warren Zevon or something."

"He had his shit albums mid-career," Reiss said.

Jess nodded. "Yeah, true. I've leveled off. I think I did years ago. It would be nice to think I'm just producing shit albums mid-career."

Reiss looked at Jess like he wanted to say something, then turned to Izzy instead.

"You could do anything. Think it over. There are careers that aren't lotteries. I guess everything's a little bit of a lottery. But not like this."

Jess pushed his drink forward on the table, then crossed his arms and put his head down on them. Reiss put his hand on Jesse's back, between his shoulder blades, and rubbed his thumb against the thin fabric of Jesse's shirt.

"You'll figure it out," he said. "I know you will."

Reiss met my eyes. I had no idea what he was trying to convey, and no idea why Jess had his head down, and no idea why I was such a bad boyfriend.

"I'd give my left tit to be where you guys are," Izzy said.

"I know," Reiss said. "We know."

We talked about other things for the rest of the evening. I stepped out at one point to call Barbara and report. I left out some things, like our talk with Broz and anything that was more speculation than fact, but let her know we'd have talked to everyone in the D&D game by the end of the day.

She sounded exhausted and sad. I thought I heard Denny in the background, noodling on a guitar and singing something over and over. Goddamn, that guy made me tired. He really was trying to capture his deathless prose in a song.

"We're having the celebration of life tomorrow," Barbara told me. "At the Dice Bag—do you know it?"

"I'm still not from around here," I reminded her. I didn't give her the odds of my knowing a place called the Dice Bag regardless.

"It's one of those board-game cafes. Myles got the event room. Charlie liked it. Or he'd go there sometimes, anyway. If his friends were going. We're meeting at noon."

"We'll be there."

"Thank you. And please don't tell anyone else about this. We want to make sure the media aren't there."

I told her I understood and went back to the table, where Jess was napping against Reiss's shoulder. Izzy was telling a story about Denny's musical, something about one of the leads getting pregnant and her mom having made the costume from secondhand fabric she'd barely had enough of in the first place.

"…but he refers to her green velvet dress, I don't know, four times in the script, and the costume budget was, like, gone, so Mom said she was going to have to pull down someone's green velvet drapes like Carol

Burnett. You ever see that, where she makes a dress out of curtains but she leaves the curtain rod in? It's on YouTube."

"Were you in the play?" I asked as I slid back into my seat.

"No. My dad works for Fisheries, and he was going to be up north all summer, so my brother and I got to choose which parent we wanted to stay with for summer break. He went with Dad. I thought I was smart because Mom was going to be at the theatre all the time, and I was old enough to stay home alone, but she decided it would be better to make me sit around backstage for weeks. I bet I could do the whole play. All the parts. Like, still."

"What was it like, being backstage with Denny Hill himself?"

Izzy laughed. "Okay, I get it. He can be like that. But he was nice to me. I'd sit there and complain about my mom, and he'd listen to the whole thing even though my mom is, objectively, a saint. He told me about being a teenager back in the Stone Age. He said he stayed with his parents for way too long."

"I'm glad he was a friend for you," I told her.

"Some adult guys get along best with pre-teen girls," Reiss observed.

Izzy threw an ice cube at him. "Get off Denny."

"Is one of the things your mom had to say to you," I said.

Izzy feigned shock and went for a second ice cube, but she broke into laughter before she could throw it at me.

"That is disgusting." she said. "You're filthy. He is a million years old. That is so gross."

"Speaking of filthy," Reiss said with a smile. "It's too bad you and Jess have that midnight appointment tonight. I was thinking the two of you might like a nightcap."

I was not the best person at noticing a come-on when it was directed at me. Or at me and my sleeping boyfriend. But it was hard to interpret that any other way.

"We do have to get going," I said. It sounded good. Neutral. My voice hadn't squeaked.

"Yep. Let's settle up, and you can head out."

He shook Jesse awake, and Jess paid the outrageous bill for everyone, despite Reiss's protestations. Izzy ran to her mom's car and came back with a box filled with black garbage bags, clear red plastic, scissors, and double-sided tape.

"It looks like we're going to do a very strange murder," Jess observed. He was not wrong.

"Anything else I can do for you?" Izzy said. "I'm still leaving messages for that agent, but it's not taking up a lot of my time."

"Actually," I said, "yes. Next time you leave a message for Charlie's agent, tell him there's a celebration of life tomorrow and ask if he has any message he'd like to send. I'll text you the details."

"Will do," Izzy said. "Is that it?"

"You could see what you can find out about Barbara," I said. "I don't see her as a suspect, but technically she could have done it."

"Right. What about Denny?"

"I don't think he was in town when the first laptop was taken," I said. "I'll ask him about that tomorrow."

"Got it. Have fun with the alien hunter."

Chapter Ten

I carried the box back to the hotel. Jesse slipped his arm through mine and leaned against me for the walk.

"Should you text Detective Broz and tell her where we're going? You promised."

"You can, on the way," I said. "Or you can stay here if you're that tired. I'm not worried about getting abducted."

"No, I'm fine. I'll text, and you can drive."

I kissed the top of his head. "And you can decorate the car."

Jess had some nostalgia for the Yellowhead, since he'd taken it from Saskatoon to Edmonton enough times in his early touring days. I didn't think I'd ever been on it before, since I had not toured the country in a bus with my name on the side and mainly hopped on the Trans-Canada if I wanted to go east or west.

"There are bison up ahead," he told me. "On the north side—no, on both sides. In the national park."

Bison weren't the novelty for me that they were for Jess, but I admit I did turn my head whenever I drove by a herd. You could always tell a bison farm by the fences, sturdier than the ones put up for cattle and more than twice as tall.

I found CKUA and put it on. You never knew what you'd get. Tonight it was a slow blues set that Jess sang along to intermittently as he gazed out the passenger window.

My phone knew of the dark sky preserve, since it was tucked inside a provincial recreation area, and I was guided there without incident. I pulled onto the shoulder near the park gates, and Jess did his best with the lights, coming back twice for my bug spray. A white horse watched us from across the road.

I took it slow with the dimmed lights, and rolled almost smoothly over the Texas gate. Jess, who'd been in the province long enough to know what they were for, gave it a puzzled look.

"What are they keeping in?" he asked.

I shrugged. "No idea. Maybe they're keeping something out."

The road ended in a large round parking lot that was about half full with cars, trucks, and RVs. Each was surrounded by people in lawn chairs or lying on ground mats. One person had a camera on a tripod, aimed straight up, with a shutter device attached by a cable.

As soon as I'd parked, Jess got out and threw his head back to appreciate the sky.

"Holy shit," he whispered.

I'd seen starry skies before in the country. I knew the way the stars seemed to multiply by a hundred and how some seemed close enough to pick out of the sky. This was like that, but with more stars and a clarity that was so intense it seemed unreal.

Our star-gazing was interrupted by a man waving at us from the roof of a Winnebago. He was sitting on a folding chair, with two more set out beside him.

"You must be Ben! Come on up! Don't worry, I've reinforced this girl."

Jess hesitated for less than a second before going around the back of the camper and taking the ladder to the top. This made sense from a guy who'd once been arrested for car surfing the 401 on the roof of a limo. I followed and was relieved to see safety railings around the roof's edge. Camper roofs were more slippery than anyone thought until they found themselves unexpectedly on the ground.

This Jeremy character, it turned out, had not only reinforced the roof and added railings but had also laid down a patch of AstroTurf. He was an older guy, at least Barbara's age, with a white beard and a Tilly hat covering his scruffy white hair. Despite the lingering heat from the day, he was wearing a windbreaker over a sweatshirt and a pair of light-wash jeans.

"Nice set-up you've got here," Jesse said with seeming sincerity. He offered a handshake and introduced himself as "Ben's assistant, Jesse."

"I'm Jeremy," he told us. "The girl who called said you wanted to talk to me about Charlie. Please, sit down."

We each took a chair, and Jeremy offered us beer from the cooler at his side. Jess accepted, and I demurred. Jeremy opened a beer for himself.

"Goddamn them," he said. "Charlie was walking a dangerous path, I know, but I didn't think they'd go after him in his own home."

"Who are they? I asked. "Do you mean extraterrestrials? Or the government?"

"Either and both. Ours, theirs, who knows. It's all the same underneath. And our little friends," he added, waving his beer at the sky, "are running the whole show."

"Is there some reason the, ah, the government would have wanted to kill Charlie?" I asked.

Jeremy cocked his head at me. "Young man, there clearly was."

"What was it?"

"I don't know. And now I never will. He was putting it in that book of his. The whole thing. The whole thing opened up for him," Jeremy said, spreading his arms as wide as the sky.

"What does that mean?" I asked.

He breathed deep. "Have you ever had an alien encounter? That you're aware of?"

"No."

He looked at Jess, who was silently watching the sky. "How about you, son?"

Jess kept his eyes upward as he said, "No."

"There are many things a person can believe to be ordinary moments in their life. Or extraordinary moments but explicable ones. And these moments may feel unusual. We may have strong, strong feelings about them and not know why. Not every person has this experience, but those who do have it again and again."

"And this has to do with aliens?"

Jeremy drank beer. "Or their agents. They have agreements with most of the world leaders, and those leaders will do anything they are asked to do. Including keeping secrets. There are also devices. There are ways of reaching into a person's mind and giving that person instructions. Anyone could have carried out what was done to Charlie. They may not even remember what they did."

"That is going to make this difficult to solve," I told him. "Did the woman who called here earlier tell you that I'm a private investigator?"

"She did. She said you were working for Barbara. I've never had much use for Barbara, but I respect that she wants justice for her brother. The sad fact is that justice will be impossible to find."

"Like Charlie's manuscript," Jess said softly.

Jeremy eyed him. "What's that?"

"Charlie said there was no point looking for it because we'd never be able to get it back."

"People don't understand what they're dealing with," Jeremy said, nodding sagely. "They don't want to know."

"What opened everything up for Charlie?" Jess asked. He was still watching the stars.

"Wha—I did," Jeremy said. "In a way. Charlie did the real work, God rest his soul. But I gave him access to his memories when I hypnotized him."

"You hypnotized him," I repeated.

On the ground, I heard gasps from the crowd.

"Falling star," Jess explained. I'd missed it.

"We get a lot of meteor showers out here," Jeremy said. "Yes, I hypnotized Charlie. I helped him to see through a screen memory that had been blocking him for most of his life. That was the key for him. He told me that as soon as he could see the truth of that moment, he could see the truth of everything."

"When was this?" Jess asked.

Jeremy drank beer and thought.

"Late winter," he said. "Around Valentine's Day, I think. I remember the hearts in the stores."

Six months ago, in other words. The same time as Charlie had started his memoir.

"You said he had a screen memory?" I asked.

"A screen memory is a false memory," Jeremy explained. "The aliens implant it to keep you from remembering your true encounter with them."

That wasn't how Freud had defined "screen memory" when he'd coined the term, but a lot of people had taken it and run with it since then.

I nodded. "What was this memory?"

Jeremy smiled and slapped his leg, like he was remembering a good joke. "It was the story of the bear."

"The bear?"

"It happened when Charlie was nineteen years old. Two years out of high school, still living with his parents. Working at that comic bookstore. He was camping out by Pembina. He wasn't clear about where. He used to go camping whenever his parents would loan him the car. West of town, mostly, at all the lakes out there. Not since the bear, though. He hardly went outside in the city after that, apart from going to work."

"Was he attacked by a bear?" Jesse asked.

"Not Charlie," Jeremy said. "Not the way he remembered it. It was October, late in the season, the weekend this happened, and he was out there… well, sometimes he'd say alone and sometimes he'd say with friends. But it was cold, and there was only one other person camping there. Charlie remembered seeing a bear attack this person and drag him off into the woods. He tried to follow, but he was paralyzed with fear—note that. It's very common, this experience of paralysis."

The crowd gasped and murmured again. This time I saw the star fall from the corner of my eye.

"Charlie told me that story one time, not long after we met," Jeremy went on. "He told me he didn't like to leave the house. Well, I'd heard that before. From people who'd had encounters. This bear story was how it made sense to him. The bears could be anywhere. He knew this wasn't true, not about bears, but he felt it as truth. Interestingly, he was embarrassed to tell his story to me. Seems a lot of people told him it could never have happened."

"Because of the bear?" I said. "It's not unheard of for them to be out in October."

"The bear and other things. How he couldn't re-member where it was. How he was sometimes con-vinced his friends had been with him and sometimes certain they had not. Charlie was always regarded as a boy who told stories."

"A liar?" I said.

"Not on purpose. He was seen as confused. His parents thought he might be ill. He was in hospitals. There were medications, I believe, at one time. After the bear incident, he was in the hospital for quite some time."

"Did anyone report this to fish and wildlife?" I asked. "In case there really was a problem bear?"

"No. Everyone felt sure it wasn't real. Even Charlie, in time. They gave him medications. He stopped those once his parents were gone. With Barbara's bless-ing. She said he was creative, not ill. She never under-stood the real story either."

Barbara, who didn't want people to know her brother was odd. I wondered whether she'd been teased or ostracized over him in school.

"But he told you the real story?" I asked.

"I'd thought about that story over the years. It had the signs of a screen memory. So I offered, from time to time, to hypnotize him. He always turned me down. One day he called me, saying he'd been having terrible nightmares and he was ready to be hypnotized. I came to his home—Barbara was in Vancouver at this time—and I performed regressive hypnosis. Charlie saw the truth behind his memory. There was never a bear. The bear, the person being dragged into the woods, it was all a screen memory to cover up an abduction. His own."

"They took him to their ship?" Jess asked. He sounded like he was half dreaming over there, with un-focused eyes looking up into forever.

"He didn't tell me about that," Jeremy said. "He told me he was going to write it down because he understood it all. He saw the truth of all the little things. He was going to write the true story of his life, and everyone could read it at the same time."

"And then it disappeared," I said.

Jeremy nodded. "And when he said he would write it again, they knew there was only one way to stop him."

"Did Charlie talk about this with the D&D group at all?" I asked. "I know he talked about writing the book, but did he say anything about the bear or seeing the truth?"

"Sure," Jeremy said. "Did anyone listen, aside from me? I very much doubt it. They have no respect for our knowledge."

We sat with that under the stars. More of them fell. I thought Jess might be falling asleep again.

"Will you be at the celebration of life tomorrow?" I asked. "Did Barbara reach out to you?"

"I heard from her. Through the website. I plan to come."

"Eddie says Charlie left you an inheritance, in a way."

"The money from his collection?" Jeremy said. "I'll see to it that it keeps the group alive. In Charlie's honour."

He raised his beer and drank to Charlie. Jess, apparently awake, did the same.

"Thank you for talking to me," I said.

"Always a pleasure to share the secret world."

I let Jess enjoy the universe for a few moments more, then took his hand and got him to his feet.

"You take me to the nicest places," he said with a gleam in his eye. I had to remind myself that it would be unsafe, uncomfortable, and unpopular for us to have sex on top of a strange man's Winnebago.

In the car, on the way back into the city, he sang something about bears. Bears in the wilderness and bears across the hall.

"Did you ever believe in UFOs?" I asked.

"I must have," he said. "You believe in everything when you're a kid."

"I used to look for them sometimes," I said. "When I had to chore after dark. I don't know if I was hoping to see one or scared to."

He smiled. "Did you think they'd be little green men?"

"I thought they'd be greys. The ones with the long faces. I wasn't allowed to have a computer in my room, but I had this old black-and-white TV, and I'd watch it with headphones in the middle of the night. There was a movie… I don't think I ever knew what it was called."

"*Close Encounters*?" Jess tried. "*Communion*?"

"I was a little kid, and I was hiding under the blankets for two-thirds of it," I told him. "You think I have any idea?"

"Maybe hiding under the blankets is a screen memory for seeing the title."

"Maybe it's all a screen memory for being abducted to the mothership."

He put his hand on mine, where it rested on the gearshift. "I guess we'll have to have Jeremy hypnotize you too."

MY PHONE rang. I opened my eyes to the hotel ceiling. It felt like "I've Got You, Babe" should have been playing to welcome me to the same day as yesterday.

"Ben Ames Investigations," I told it.

"Ben Ames Investigations, this is your research department."

Izzy. I checked my phone. Almost 10:00 a.m.

"Good morning, research department. What have you got for me?"

"First, do you agree to pay my friend Lan for translating some things for me? Google Translate was not up to the job."

"Sure."

"Alrighty. Some of Charlie's fans in China found out who his sister was and read some of her stuff, and you will not believe this. It looks like she's been stealing from Charlie for, like, years."

"She… what? Has she been writing romance novels about robots or something?"

"No, just lifting stuff. Characters, settings, plots. A lot of plot stuff. I don't know, Charlie might have been helping her on purpose the whole time. Like, here, sis, have a plot for your book, and then he put it in his book too. The audiences are totally different. If these people weren't, like, disturbing superfans, no one would ever have noticed."

I nudged Jess since we had somewhere to be by noon and might want to get things done before that. He grumbled and pulled the blanket over his head.

"Are they sure it wasn't the other way around? I asked. "He could have been stealing from her."

"The superfans don't think so. I get they'd be on Charlie's side no matter what, if there even are sides here, but they have dates and examples, and some of them are pretty obvious. Like, Charlie's book comes out, and it has this storyline about a kidnapping, and the new Barbara Gable comes out two years later with the exact plot, all the same beats, except set in the real world and with bodice ripping or whatever. I don't know. I've never read her stuff."

"Some plots are pretty generic," I said. "This could be coincidental. Especially if the two of them have similar life histories."

"I'll send you this stuff," Izzy said. "It's like, beautiful twenty-five-year-old reporter gets kidnapped while on assignment in Tunisia, and she's accidentally handed off to the wrong person, who takes her to Frankfurt. I seriously doubt it's a coincidence."

"I'll take a summary, please," I said. "And I'll see what Barbara has to say about it."

"Cool. Get video of her face. I wanna see it."

"I will definitely not do that."

"Worst. Boss. Ever."

We hung up. I got up and showered, and found Jess sitting up on the side of bed when I returned.

"Bathroom's all yours," I told him.

"Thanks. Who were you talking to before?"

"Izzy. Apparently Barbara's been plagiarizing off her brother for years."

He rubbed his eyes and blinked at me. "She writes romance."

"I know. It's elements, not whole books. Izzy found some fans in China who seem to have the receipts. I was thinking we could swing by the house before the wake and see what Barbara has to say about this."

"Plagiarizing elements? Is that something you kill to keep quiet?"

"No idea. It would have to be a huge blow to her pride if it got out. And maybe financially if the publishers get into it. Izzy thinks it's possible Charlie knew and was throwing her stuff to help her out. I get that. She churns out a book a year at least."

"And it would tie her to him," Jesse said. "In public. Which she seems to not want. Do you think he'd have put it in his memoir, though?"

"What matters is whether Barbara thought he would. We'll see."

We got ourselves put together in good time, in clothes that were dark and subdued but not so obviously funereal as to be jarring. I hadn't been to a lot of wakes and didn't know what to expect. Speeches? Sobbing? Dancing? Jess voted for everyone getting rip-roaring drunk, which did seem like the safest bet.

I wasn't sure whether Barbara would be home—she might have gone for a pre-wake brunch—but we were lucky. She came to the door quickly and welcomed us with a shaky smile.

"I'm glad you're here. It's nice to have company instead of sitting with my thoughts."

I wasn't sure how glad she'd be once I started asking questions, but I accepted the welcome and a cup of coffee as gracefully as I could,

Jess spent a few minutes chatting with her about the flowers in the raised beds out front and whether they'd had much smoke from the forest fires in June. I watched her relax as they talked. I complained a lot, mostly to Jess, about the complications of having him along on cases, but there were also benefits, and this was one. After doing a thousand interviews in a thousand towns for what probably felt like a thousand years, there was no one he couldn't talk to.

Once we were settled into the dining room with caffeine and the box of scones we'd brought resting in front of us, I launched into the first thing Barbara wasn't going to like.

"We talked to Jeremy last night," I said.

"Yes, you said you were going to do that. How did that go?"

"Fine. He said a lot of what I expected. He also blames aliens."

Barbara began to tear up a napkin, not violently but in tiny pieces.

"Honestly," she said. "Those fools."

"He told us a story about a bear."

Her eyes widened. "Oh no. Why would he do that? Why would he bring that up?"

"He thinks it was an important moment in Charlie's life," I said.

Barbara tore the rest of the napkin in half. "It was a terrible moment! It was a terrible Christmas. He was in the hospital for four months. And entirely pointless. My parents didn't understand creative people, and they let Charlie's doctor convince them that he was ill. He was imaginative. No one needs to go into a… a mental hospital for four months for being imaginative!"

"I agree," I said. Her grateful expression told me she'd taken that the way I'd hoped and not how I'd actually meant it.

"Then you understand there's no benefit to bringing up that old story."

"Jeremy thinks Charlie put it in the memoir," Jesse said. "Maybe this won't lead anywhere, but we're hoping that you might have some of Charlie's drawings or notes from that time in the hospital. It might help us understand who would have wanted to stop his book."

"I can't see what good it would do," Barbara said.

"We can't know until we see it," I said. "You're probably right, but it's important to rule things out. I want to make sure I'm doing a good job for you."

"Well. If you really think…." She stood. "All of that is in the basement. Will you excuse me for a few minutes?"

"That could have gone worse," Jess said once she was gone.

"Unless she's down there getting her daddy's shotgun," I said. "But this doesn't seem like that kind of house."

"It would be her daddy's croquet mallet."

"How are you feeling today?" I asked. "I haven't seen you sleep this much since the pneumonia."

He shrugged and picked at a scone the way Barbara had torn the napkin.

"Like Reiss said. I'm depressed."

"Are you going to up your meds? What does your therapist say?"

He pushed the scone away. "Can we talk about this later?"

"Whenever you want."

We went on our phones for the rest of the time we were waiting. Checking texts, listening to missed calls. Jess showed me a photo of Frank that Luna had texted to him and not, for some reason, to me.

"This is what came home with him," Barbara said as she came back into the room. "The hospital might have more."

She was carrying a file folder, off-white and creased at the tab. Edges of white paper were sticking out. It looked both long forgotten and well thumbed. Barbara set it on the table.

"Thank you," I said, taking the folder. "We'll get this back to you."

"You don't want to read it now?" she asked.

"I might in a minute, but there's something else I have to ask you."

"You seem very serious," Barbara said with a nervous laugh.

"I'm going to read you something, if that's okay."

"Of course."

"Rochelle heard voices. German voices. How could that be? Had she been taken all the way to Germany?"

"What about it?" Barbara said.

"Can you tell me what book that's from?"

I had her. If she said it was her book, I might say it was Charlie's. If I said Charlie's, I could show her that same line from hers.

"I've written so many," she said, which was a nice feint but not good enough.

"You didn't write that one," I said. "Your brother did."

"Oh! Yes, of course—I also have a character named Rochelle in one of my books."

"And she's kidnapped," I said, "from the same place, and she's taken to the same place, by accident. It turns out some of Charlie's readers in China are your readers too."

She pressed her lips together and looked at the table.

"All right," she said finally. "It is in both of the books."

"You were borrowing things from your brother?" I asked, as gently as I could.

She raised her head. "We borrowed from each other. We shared. When we were little, we used to tell stories together with my dolls. I was better at making the dolls talk, and he was better at stories. We didn't want to write books together because we liked different things, but we would help each other sometimes." She picked up a scone, then dropped it on the table. "I probably took more than I gave. I know I did."

"You never talked about this in interviews," I said. "In your public life, there's not much connection to Charlie at all."

Tears came to her eyes, sticking to her mascara and making her blink. "Are you telling me I was a bad sister? Do you think I don't know?"

"Were you trying to keep people from making the connection?" I asked. "Between your books and his?"

"I wish that was all it was. I'm a romance writer. Do you know what romance is?"

I kicked Jess under the table, in case he felt the need to answer that.

"Tell me," I said instead.

"It's a fantasy. It's a fantasy of a perfect life for everyone, in time, if they dance the dance correctly. And I'm part of it. I know I don't have a man. That's bad enough. But to have this in my family—it runs in families. Do you know? I can't have that. I have to be ideal. I know, some other authors don't put on this image the way I do, but they don't sell the way I do either."

It was the most I'd heard Barbara say at once. Beside me, Jess was looking out the window. He wasn't being rude. I was certain he'd listened to every word.

"The public doesn't have a right to your whole life," I said.

"Maybe not. It could be, Mr. Ames, that I tell myself all of those things because it's nicer than saying I am—that I was ashamed of him."

No one said anything after that. A sparrow called from the tree outside the window. The coffee began to get cold.

"I'm going to take this," I said, putting the folder under my arm, "and go. We'll see you at the celebration of life."

She nodded, once, and said nothing. Jess and I left as quickly and quietly as we could.

In the car, Jess took the folder from me and started going through it.

"It's mostly drawings and notes. Some prescriptions… discharge notes for the parents…. I guess all the medical documentation stayed at the hospital."

"We don't need that anyway. It doesn't really matter what his diagnosis was."

"Yeah, his diagnosis seems to have been 'guy who needs to be on Thorazine,'" Jess said. "How long do we have before the wake?"

"A little under an hour. I'll park somewhere, and we can go over those in the car."

I got us within a few blocks of the Dice Bag, then went down alleys until I found a half-empty parking lot without much foot traffic. Jess went through the folder as I drove and handed it to me as soon as I'd parked.

"They must have done art therapy," he said. "Lots of drawings of a bear. He wasn't a great artist, but it's recognizable. You see the guy getting hauled off. Some of it has Charlie there with two friends, and some of it he's alone. No UFOs."

"What about the notes?" I asked.

"If you can read them, you have better eyes than I have. Oh, I put one of the drawings on top—there. That's the closest thing to aliens I could find."

It was a drawing of someone standing in the middle of a lake with water around his knees. His arms were out at his sides and he was gazing up at the sky.

"Is he walking on water?" I said.

"He's walking in water," Jess said. "But he's in the middle of the lake. Maybe there's a sandbar? It's weird. The lake has a couple of islands, so it might have sandbars too."

I flipped through the drawings. A tent, and then three tents, around a campfire. A bear, coming in like a shadow from the woods, standing in front of a man in a plaid shirt and ball cap. A radio on the ground beside the man, with jagged musical notes coming from it. Charlie wasn't a good artist, technically, but he'd had a certain talent for making the shaky lines and weird perspectives set a scene.

"That one," Jess said. "The bear is just standing there. It doesn't even seem very threatening." He picked it up again. "He did a weird thing with the guy's leg. One leg is, like, twice the size of the other."

He wasn't wrong. I hadn't noticed it the first time, since I'd been focused on the bear and since the drawings were full of misshapen things overall.

"Maybe he had that *Alice in Wonderland* thing, where things start to look really big or really small."

"Three tents. One tent. Never two tents. So he remembers being there alone or being there with two friends."

"Myles and Denny," Jesse said. "Since they were the three amigos back in the day. Except—didn't Denny say he cleared out right after high school and didn't come back for years? Charlie's bear story happened after he graduated, and Denny's a year older than him, if Wikipedia has it right."

"So maybe Charlie really was alone," I said. "Or maybe he was never even there at all. If this was right before they put him in a hospital for four months and put him on Thorazine… that's not the hallmark of a reliable witness."

"For real. Hey, you have a tablet in here somewhere, don't you?"

"Under your seat."

He pulled it out and called up a map of the area west of Edmonton. "Where did Jeremy say? Pem-something?"

"Pembina, I think. There's a river called that."

"Oh, it's a park too. That's probably what Jeremy meant." He grabbed a few of the drawings and set them out on his lap, then started to move the map around, swiping, pinching, and pulling. I watched as green and blue flew by. Finally he stopped, cocked his head, and held up one of the drawings.

"Is this the same? The shape of the shore, here? And there's a river here, and you can see a corner of something—it could be this island."

"I see it. Where's that?"

"It's called Chip Lake."

As he continued to compare back and forth, drawing to map and back, I searched for information on the lake. There were a few campsites scattered around. The one with online bookings had spots open despite the warm weather and how close the lake was to Edmonton. In October, it would probably be deserted.

A message board for fishing tips solved the mystery of why the lake wasn't busier. It was a respectable size but shallow—two or three feet deep in most places. Even the middle of the lake.

I pulled up the walking on water drawing again.

"It's shallow," I said. "Even that far out. It's a weirdly shallow lake."

Jess raised his brows at me. "What do you think?"

"I think this is the place where it happened. If it happened."

I ran the car a little to get the AC going as we searched for bear attacks in the area, the year Charlie was nineteen and a few years on either side. Nothing. Not even a sighting. For the hell of it, I checked for UFO sightings and struck out there too.

Jess seemed like he might have fallen asleep again. I put a hand on his arm.

"You awake?" I asked.

His eyes stayed closed. "Yes."

I took my hand back and went through Charlie's drawings a few more times. They were like a flip book in parts. A bear coming out of nowhere, standing next to the plaid shirt guy. And then an attack. The body dragged away. The campfire grew.

This wasn't helping. I closed the folder.

"Barbara Gable, queen of romance," I said. "Cribbing off her weird sci-fi brother."

"She explained," Jess said. "I believed her. I feel bad for her. The rate she writes at, having to come up with new ideas all the time… the pressure must be intense."

"She could farm her name out," I said. "Or do one of those collaboration things where she pretends to write half the book but actually she's on a cruise and she reads it when she gets back."

"It might be important to her that she writes them herself," Jesse said.

I looked at him. "Seriously?"

"Yes, seriously. Why not? Because you think her books are trashy?"

"Her books are objectively trashy, Jess. She doesn't write *War and Peace*. She doesn't even write *Jane Eyre*. She's the writing equivalent of a vibrator."

"So what?" Jess sat up and turned toward me. "So what if her books are what you think of as trash. She's not supposed to care about them? God forbid she's actually proud of them. What a pathetic, ridiculous person. Is that right?"

I held up my hands. "Whoa. I never said she was ridiculous. I just think her books are disposable. That has nothing to do with who she is."

"This thing she's given most of her time and effort to, you think that has nothing to do with who she is."

"You seem to be taking this personal—"

"I need a walk."

He took off before I realized what was happening. I got out of the car and yelled after him, but he was moving fast, his head down, and showed no sign of wanting to come back.

"Jesse, come on!"

He disappeared around a corner. I leaned against the car and considered. I could go after him, but he was a grown-up, and he knew where the car was. He knew where I was. He knew where I was going to be. If he wanted a walk, or to not talk to me, he had a right to both of those things.

I slammed the car door. The folder of pictures fell from my seat to the floor. A guy on a bike, with a garbage bag of empty bottles over his shoulder, stared at me as he went by.

It was nearly noon. I walked to the game café under a sun that felt like a propane torch to my neck. Barbara was waiting inside the front door.

"The room is at the back," she told me.

"I'm sorry," I told her. For her brother? For the things I'd made her think about today? For the things I'd said in the car that she hadn't even heard?

Sure. Why not all of it?

She nodded and smiled and waved me along.

The café was small and mostly taken up by shelf after shelf of games. It felt strange to be there, in a room so eerily like the one Charlie had died in.

The tables were mostly empty. A young couple was in a booth by the window, playing something elaborate and slurping affogato.

In the back room, chairs had been placed in a half circle. A table at the back had coffee and food. Sandwiches and dessert squares. Eddie was sitting in the chair farthest from the door, wearing a blue short-sleeved shirt and tan shorts. I raised a hand in greeting, and he smiled.

"Hey," he said. "Sorry things got weird yesterday."

"It's not something I have to live with," I said, taking a seat a few chairs away. "I forgot to ask you something."

"What's that?"

"There's a doorbell camera at the house, and Barbara doesn't know where the footage is stored. She said she thought Charlie had set the camera up with a friend from work."

"I am that friend," Eddie said. "Do you need to see it? I can show you."

"That would be great."

"Sure. We can go back to the house after, if it's okay with Barbara."

"Sounds good."

Denny was the next to come in. He was wearing a white linen suit and a grey silk shirt. White loafers, no socks that I could see. He sat next to the door.

"How is it going?" he asked me. "The investigation?"

"One step at a time," I told him. "I hear you're having coffee with Izzy this afternoon."

"Yes."

"Can I ask you something?"

He looked mildly surprised, either that I was conducting business at a wake or that I thought I needed permission.

"Ask away."

"I saw Jeremy last night, and he told me the story of the bear."

"That's not a question," he said, but he smiled a little. Kidding me along. "I know the story. I don't know how much of it was real."

"Were you there?"

"No. No, I'd already left town. I think Charlie was missing me. He put me in a lot of his stories back then."

"Was Myles with him?"

"I'll be honest with you," Denny said. He rested his elbows on his knees and leaned forward. "I'm not sure Charlie was there. I think of that story as an allegory of some kind. For what, I do not know. But it was something that part of him felt the need to say."

The next guest to arrive was, to my surprise, Detective Broz. She looked as awkward as I felt and then some. Her shoulders were hunched, and she placed herself in the corner of the room farthest from the chairs, next to the coffee urn.

"Please, have a seat," Denny said.

She made an expression that I'm sure she thought was a smile. "I'm good. Thanks."

Jeremy came in, wearing what he'd been wearing on the roof of the Winnebago the night before. A faint but undeniable hint of cannabis wafted behind him as he passed my chair.

"Where's your friend?" he asked me.

"Somewhere else to be," I said. Jeremy didn't seem convinced, but he said nothing as he took his seat. When no one spoke in the minute or so after, he pointed at me.

"Tell your friend I think he might have had some experiences. He's got some of the signs. Tell him I'll be happy to hypnotize him."

"I will," I said. Jeremy nodded, satisfied. Denny was looking down to hide a smirk. It wasn't working.

Barbara came in on Myles Murati's arm.

Denny stood. "Myles."

"Denny." Myles offered a handshake, and Denny obliged. "Better circumstances," he added with a shake of his head.

"Indeed."

They sat. Barbara went to the open front of the chair circle. It was a tiny circle, a handful of chairs, and they had not been filled.

In China, for all I knew, they were weeping in the streets.

"I think this is us," Barbara said. "There's no… there's not a program. If anyone wants to say anything, please do. Or talk to each other. Have the food."

She seemed lost once she'd finished speaking, her role concluded. Denny stood and waved her to a seat beside his own.

"I'll say a few words," Denny said once Barbara was settled.

In a small mercy, at that moment someone else appeared in the doorway. He was dark-haired, not much bigger than Jess, and dressed in a plain business suit. Maybe forty, maybe fifty. As I glanced around the room, I could see recognition on Barbara's face, something between confusion and indifference on the rest, and Myles looking away.

"Barbara," he said. "I'm so sorry."

She reached out her hands, and he took them.

"Thank you," she said.

The man suddenly drew back, so far and so quickly that Barbara's hands fell from his and hit her lap with a slap.

"I'll come by the house to see you." His low, smooth voice had a slight tremor now. "Next week?"

"Yes, that's fine," Barbara said. "Is everything—"

"Next week, then," the man said and went out the door at speed. He nearly ran into Jess as Jess was coming in. Short walk, but it seemed to have done whatever Jess needed it to do.

Jess froze for a second as the dark-haired man passed, then turned and went after him. I saw Broz take a step toward the door. I understood. It was obviously worth talking to that man, but she also didn't want to miss whatever was going to happen in the room. I could see her decide to stay and let Jess track the running man down.

"What was that about? I asked.

"I don't know," Barbara said. "That was Charlie's agent, Gerald Chin."

"Now you know why Charlie only sells in China," Myles said. Eddie's mouth tensed at the corners, and he stared at the floor.

"That's really not fair," Barbara said. "Gerald isn't even from there."

Eddie's head dropped lower. I understood. I would also have liked to sink through the floor.

"He sells in China because they are receptive to the message," Jeremy said. "They have not been completely overrun by puppets."

"I didn't know Charlie's agent was local," I said to Barbara. "Or did he fly in from Vancouver?"

"Oh no, he's from Edmonton," Barbara said. "He's the one who got Charlie his first big deal. Charlie is— he was very loyal to people."

"And that's why he never had a Netflix series," Myles said.

"But he has put up with all of you," Jeremy said. "You, Eddie. Did you ever return all the long boxes you borrowed? Did you ever intend to? Or did you bring them to your employer so he could sell those issues to someone else? Maybe you split the profits. I don't know what you've done, but a man your age can't be making a living and renting his own two-bedroom apartment at minimum wage."

Eddie raised his head and stared at Jeremy.

"My parents help me out," he said. "You know that. I've never stolen anything from Charlie."

Jeremy faced Barbara. "Are you the executor? You should check for empty boxes. I think you'll find more than a few."

I stared at Jeremy.

He cast a sleepy gaze at me. "What is it, son?"

"Why didn't you tell me this last night?"

"It wasn't relevant. You wanted to know who murdered Charlie. I told you."

"You can't tell me you weren't eager for the money," Eddie said, more sharply than I'd have expected from him. "Every game night it was something else.

Winnie needs a new transmission. Your domain name and website are up for renewal. I guess I didn't think much of it because Charlie always gave you the money, but maybe you got tired of asking."

"Young man, my friendship with Charlie was worth far more than any amount of money."

"It could be said," Denny said to Jeremy, "that you have not been good for Charlie's mental health. Myles and I always did our best to support—"

"You and Myles were a pair of bullies," Jeremy said. "You liked having a buddy who thought you were the cool kid."

"You didn't know us in high school," Denny said stiffly.

Jeremy smiled. "I didn't have to. I know you now."

A text alert came to me. From Jesse.

meet us at the car

"This isn't why we came here today," Barbara said. "I think—"

"And you. Always thinking you're above your brother. Hiding his papers from the lunatic asylum in your basement and pretending you never consigned him there for the crime of being confused." Jeremy shook his head. "Shameful."

"I never—" Barbara started.

"Do not set in on her," Denny said, cutting off whatever Barbara had never done. "She was good enough to bring us all here, and I think we should respect that, and respect what this gathering is meant to be about."

"I've said what I came to say." Jeremy said. He got to his feet slowly and ambled out of the room. No one spoke.

"He loaned me those comics," Eddie said finally. Myles rolled his eyes.

"I'm going to go," Broz said. "Barbara, my condolences again. By the way, I hate to ask this now, but were you able to find the contact information for your brother's housekeeper?"

"I'm so sorry," Barbara said. "I've been so busy it slipped my mind."

"Get it to me when you can," Broz said. She said "Condolences" again and left. I took out my phone, as unobtrusively as I could, and texted her.

wait for me

She sent a thumbs-up in reply.

The friends and relations of Charlie Gudzyak served themselves sandwiches and cake. Denny and Myles began to catch up. Had they not seen each other since Denny came to town?

"Are you going?" Eddie asked me. "Are we going to the house?"

"Barbara," I said, "Eddie thinks he can get the footage from the doorbell camera. You can stay here as long as you like, but would you be able to give me the key?"

She nodded and took a house key off a sonic screwdriver key ring.

"This was Charlie's" she said, in case I'd mistaken her for the *Doctor Who* fan.

"Thanks. Oh, Denny, while I've got you here—a quick question."

Denny was back in his chair. Sitting like a menswear mannequin, legs crossed with his right ankle at his left knee, staring into the middle distance. It took him a moment to realize I'd been speaking to him.

"Um, yes. How can I help?"

"When did you get into town?"

"Friday. Late afternoon. Do you need the time?"

"No, that's good. Thanks. Barbara, I'll see you later."

Broz was outside on her phone, checking in with someone. I waved at her to follow me, and she walked and talked a few steps behind me and Eddie.

"No, not yet. We might want to check into a few more things. I'll call you later."

She caught up to us, which wasn't tough since Eddie preferred a relaxed stroll.

"Where are we going?" Broz asked.

"My car. I thought you might want to talk to Charlie's agent."

I led them through an alley to the parking lot where Jess and the agent were sitting on the hood of my car and having what appeared to be an amiable conversation.

I walked up to the car and extended a hand.

"I hear you're Gerald Chin," I said. "I didn't have a chance to introduce myself before. I'm Ben Ames."

Gerald looked amused. "So your friend here tells me. You know, I've heard that name before. On my phone. Your secretary is persistent."

My secretary. I could see Jess pressing his lips together, fighting a laugh. Izzy would be hearing about this later.

"Sorry about that," I lied. "I wanted to make sure you didn't miss the wake."

"Yeah, well," Gerald said, turning his head in the direction of the gaming café, "guess I missed it."

"You didn't miss much," I said.

"Not a lot," Broz said. "I'm Detective Alice Broz, Edmonton Police."

"I'm Gerald Chin," the agent said. He pointed at me. "He knows that. I was Charlie Gudzyak's literary agent."

"I'm Eddie," Eddie said. Gerald gave him a nod.

"You ran out of there pretty fast," Broz said. "You do track in college?"

Gerald laughed. "Sure. I was the fastest guy in Honours English."

"You looked like something surprised you," I said.

"Yeah." He turned to Jess. "Are we waiting for anyone else? I wasn't expecting a crowd."

"I think this is everyone," Jess said. "Go ahead."

"It's silly. I didn't need to take off like that. But I saw Myles Murani sitting there, and it threw me."

"Why's that?" Broz asked.

"No offense if any of you are friends of his," Gerald said, "but I had kind of a rough experience with him when Charlie first signed up with me. I'm not sure where to start. I guess I'll say that *Breakpath* wasn't going to be Charlie's first book. It's a great book, but Charlie had a novella the publisher wanted to put out first. It was nearly done—all Charlie would have had to do was flesh it out a little. Half a year's work, maybe. But he'd sold that novella to Myles for serialization in his shitty little magazine, and the guy would not let us buy it back."

"Okay, that must have been disappointing," Broz said. "But wasn't that his right?"

Gerald barked out a laugh. "Yeah. Yeah, that contract was solid because he paid Charlie the one hundred and fifty bucks he'd offered for it."

Broz looked at me. "That seems low. Is that low?"

"Small magazines don't have a lot of money," Eddie answered for me. "Charlie was probably just stoked to get published. I didn't know him at the time, but that's usually how it is."

"Except Myles didn't usually pay Charlie at all. He said he was going to, but he stiffed Charlie over ridiculously small amounts of money. Fifty bucks. Seventy-five. The only reason he paid Charlie for the novella was that he wanted to make sure the contract held up."

"That is some low-down behaviour," Broz said. "Any idea why Myles was so stubborn? Didn't he stand to make a lot of money if he sold you that book?"

"Some. It was Charlie's first book, so no one knew how well it was going to do. Myles sells back issues and reprints, and he does a good business in that, so he's probably made that much or more over time. That's not why he was such a shit about the whole thing, though."

"Why was that?" I asked.

"He wanted to be Charlie's agent. He thought he was a big deal because he runs that convention. He was holding on to that story to try to force Charlie to go with him. I always assumed Charlie had stopped speaking to him after that. But apparently not."

"That explains why you don't care for Myles," I said, "but it doesn't explain why you broke the five-minute mile getting out of there."

"Oh, that." Gerald hummed softly. Not a tune, just a humming sound. "I don't like the guy. I know you know that, but I really don't like the guy. He creeps me out. When all this shit was going on? Someone took a baseball bat to my car. I never knew for sure that it was Myles, but I always felt like it was."

He paused. His eyes tracked an empty drink cup as the wind took it across the lot into a patch of weeds by the payment machine.

"So," he said, "I decided to stay out of his way. I worked hard not to see him. This town's not that big. I hadn't run across him in years before I saw him in there."

"You took off because you were scared of Myles?" Eddie asked. He sounded like he'd caught Gerald running away from a tiny spider. Some people would, but those people would be ridiculous.

"I overreacted," Gerald said. "I feel stupid, okay? I'll apologize to Barbara again later."

"If you have evidence of unpaid debts," Broz said, "you can tell the executor, and they can pursue that. I realize these are small amounts, so it may not be worth it."

"It would be on principle if I did," Gerald said. "But I don't need to poke that guy. It's okay."

"Right." She turned to Eddie. "When we talked last night, you didn't mention that you had a substantial amount of Charlie Gudzyak's property."

"I don't. He lent me some comics to read. Jeremy's kind of nasty about anything to do with comics or whatever. He thought it was a waste of time."

"He must be interested in the money he'll be inheriting from the sale of the collection," Broz suggested.

Eddie shrugged. "We'll see how much it is, right? Anyway, Charlie said I could keep whatever I wanted and sell the rest, so maybe Jeremy shouldn't be such a dick to me. I could decide I want to keep the whole thing."

That had crossed my mind, but it surprised me to hear Eddie say it, his voice still quiet but with an edge I hadn't heard before.

This was where Jess would usually jump in with some comment about taking the high road. Instead, he regarded Eddie with flat silence, like he didn't have the energy to deal with this and wouldn't have wasted it if he did.

"We'll talk more later," Broz told him. To Gerald she said, "It must have been a shock, losing Charlie this way."

Gerald said it was, it was a huge shock, and Broz offered to walk him to his car. She wanted a talk with him, obviously, without Eddie around. Possibly without me or Jess around either.

"Did we want to talk to him more?" Jess asked as they walked away. "I asked him some of the things, like what he thought happened, when he last saw Charlie, whether he'd noticed anything unusual lately."

"That should do," I said. "I don't think this guy's in the loop. Did he say anything interesting?"

"No. He wasn't enthusiastic about the memoir, but he wasn't upset about it either. He said it was a blip. They'd publish it, it would sink like the *Titanic*, only faster, and Charlie would go back to profitable science fiction. He hasn't been at the house in years, and he and Charlie did most of their communication by phone. And he either didn't have an opinion about what happened or didn't want to give it to me."

"I never even met him before," Eddie said. He turned to Jess. "I didn't get a chance to say anything before, but Hailey asked if I'd recognized you. I totally didn't."

"That is often the idea," Jess said with a smile.

"I bet. Well, I won't harp on it, but it's cool to meet you. I saw somewhere that you were dating some PI from Calgary, so I guess this is that guy."

"That's me," I confirmed. "Now that we've got that straightened out, let's get to the house and check the camera."

Chapter Eleven

WE DIDN'T talk much on the way to the house. It was a short drive, by Edmonton standards. Ten minutes through downtown and south into the river valley. Eddie and Jess were on their phones for most of it.

The house was quiet when we arrived. Red-tailed bumblebees were jostling each other in Barbara's flower beds, and the AC buzzed from the south side. No one appeared to ask who we were or what we were doing as we let ourselves in.

"It sends a signal upstairs," Eddie explained, pointing at the camera as we went by. "It's wireless, so you can't find it by tracking the wires. Charlie wanted it upstairs because he was mostly worried about people coming onto the yard at night."

The upstairs had more breathing room than the main floor. An open landing space at the top held a throw rug, an end table with a landline phone, and had three doors leading off.

"Charlie, Barbara, bathroom," Eddie said, pointing at the doors. "I've never been in Barbara's room. It's funny now that I think of it, because I've been in this house so often. There's a whole room I've never gone in. Anyway. Right through here."

Charlie's room was neater and less cluttered than I'd expected, and decorated exactly how I'd have expected if I'd given it any thought. The bedspread featured one of the Starship Enterprises. The bedside lamp was a C-3P0 with a bulb for a head, and above the bed, a kid's model of the solar system hung from the ceiling.

"I wonder what Barbara is going to do with all of this," Eddie said, running a reverent hand over the bedspread. "Do you think she'll think of it as part of the collection?"

"That or a big donation to charity," I said. I did not mention that Barbara might not be thrilled to hear Eddie asking for things right on the heels of finding out that he might have been stealing from Charlie all along.

"This is it," Eddie said. He'd grabbed a small white-framed LED screen that faced Charlie's bed. It had that month's calendar covering most of the screen and the time of day in the corner. "It's like your basic time and day alarm clock, but watch."

He did something with buttons on the side and back, and the screen changed to show a wide angle of the front yard. Full colour and fairly smooth, though there could have been some lag.

"Interesting device," I said. "Usually those doorbells send to a unit with an SD card in it."

Eddie nodded. "I know. I told him I could hide that easily, but he preferred to have a screen he could use instead of transferring the card to and from his laptop, so I found this for him. There's this spy store in Toronto that has the coolest stuff."

"I'm familiar," I said. I was. I didn't buy much from them, but my clients frequently came to me with gear they'd bought and stories about using it. *I put this tracker on my husband's car and it went to the condo building where his old girlfriend lives—can I hire you to get photos of them? I bought this infidelity test kit and used it on my girlfriend's clothes, and now I need to know whose semen this is.*

"Is the footage from Monday still there?"

"Should be. It's a seven-day cycle."

Jess had wandered off while Eddie was tinkering with the screen. I couldn't tell if he was over whatever he'd been upset about, or whether he'd decided to shelve it for now.

"Yep, here we go. It's motion activated, so we've got... there's Barbara going out to water the flowers... and back inside. There's you and Jack... man, that is so weird. Sorry. I don't mean to, like, make it weird."

"Next one should be us leaving," I said.

"There you are... and here's Denny."

It was like Denny and Barbara had said. Arrival and departure as expected. I leaned forward. Whatever came up next would be someone we didn't know about—someone who wasn't on the list of people who'd come to the house that day. It wasn't a sure thing that this person would have been the killer, since anyone from the Jehovah's Witnesses to the Girl Guides might have stopped by, but I would sure as hell have questions if it was someone Charlie knew.

The next thing that appeared on the screen was...

The EMTs. They were rushing inside to get Charlie. Jess and I arrived after them, and the next shot was of them leaving. And then the three of us, me and Jess and Barbara, leaving the house for the night.

"It skipped something," I said. "There should be something between Denny leaving and the EMTs getting there."

Eddie pressed a few buttons, frowning, then set the screen back on the bedside table. "That's it."

"What do you mean? Did someone delete something?"

"No. I don't think so." He picked it up again. "The next day is there—see, there's the police. You don't think… did Denny Hill do it? For real?"

"I don't know," I admitted. "He wasn't here on Thursday, so he couldn't have taken the manuscript in the first place. And I don't think he knew that Charlie was rewriting it. So probably not. But I don't know for sure."

"Denny Hill," Eddie said, shaking his head. Whether he couldn't believe that Denny might have committed murder, or that he might have committed murder and not written a song about it, he didn't say.

"Did everyone leave after the game on Friday?" I asked.

Eddie thought about it. "You think someone hid out here the whole time? I doubt it. But anyway, we all left at the same time. I walked out to the street with them, and Myles gave me a lift home."

"Can you check who was in and out on the weekend?"

We ran through it quickly. There hadn't been much activity, and nothing unexpected. Someone had dropped off a flyer on neon-pink paper. A couple of food deliveries. Mostly Barb coming and going, likely to the folk festival.

The back door had been locked on Monday. It might have been open at some point on the weekend, but that was a lot to swallow—an unlocked door that was normally locked, plus someone using it to sneak in, unseen, and hiding somewhere, like the basement, until Monday afternoon.

The basement.

There'd been a window, ground level. Pretty small to me, so I hadn't inspected the thing. But maybe it was worth a second look.

"I'm going to check on something," I said.

Eddie nodded. He was peering into the closet, which was open and had stacks of old board games on the floor. Eddie would probably have called them vintage. I'd have to make sure Eddie didn't try to sneak any of them out under his shirt.

I passed Jess as I went through the upstairs landing. He was on his phone and beckoned me with a wave.

"In a sec," I told him and headed downstairs.

The basement was about as inviting as it had been the day before. If anything, it smelled mustier, like someone had left apples down there to rot. The cardboard boxes along one side had been disturbed: a few shoved to the side and one left open, as if someone had been rifling through it. Barbara, for example, digging for the old files on Charlie. I went to the box. There were a few more files that looked medical, along with worried notes on school letterhead about Charlie's mental state. There were also more ordinary keepsakes. Report cards and yearbooks and swimming badges.

I crossed to the window. It had a thick wood frame that was water damaged and splintering. It had swollen so badly that it had to be tough to fully close and latch, which might have been why it was open.

It could have been open all week. Or all month. The whole summer long.

All those paths in the woods leading to the back of the house, it would have been easy for someone who knew the area to approach without being noticed. Then they'd have to lift the basement window, which was probably easy enough, and slip inside.

An old garden bench was shoved up against the basement wall below the window. The bench made it easier to slide into the basement from outside and made it possible to get back out the window from the basement. The window's size was the only thing that made me question whether it was possible. I could picture Jess making it through, barely. Jess or someone about his size. Like Myles.

He fit the bill in a lot of ways. He'd known about the memoir and the rewrite. He had a temper. He knew the house. Kids being kids, I wondered if he might even know about the window. A way for Charlie to get back into the house after curfew or to sneak out while grounded.

But who killed someone over a hundred dollars? You could say it wasn't the money, that it was anger over Charlie going with someone else for an agent. Or a desire to protect his reputation as a fair dealer... if he even had that reputation in the first place.

I didn't like any of it. I believed he could have done it. Physically, logistically. Even his personality, that eerie moment when we'd first met him and he'd gone cold while talking about Charlie's paranoia, or the way he'd scared Gerald Chin badly enough that the guy had avoided him for years.

I'd told Jess before that motive wasn't necessary for an arrest or even a conviction, but I liked to see one that made sense. All I had was a few things I didn't believe anyone, even a guy with a temper, would kill over.

Was it the camping trip, the one that he might not have been on and that might not even have happened?

As I stared at the window going through these thoughts and back again, I heard the front door open.

Barbara, most likely, home from the wake. Maybe she'd think of something if I laid it out for her that I thought it was Myles but I didn't know why.

I went upstairs to find the main floor empty and kept going to the second floor. When I got to the landing, I nearly ran into Barbara. She'd stopped at the top of the stairs. Over her shoulder, I could see Jess regarding her with what I thought of as his expectant face—the one he got when he'd asked a question and damned well expected an answer. Eddie was watching from the sidelines.

"What's going on here?" I said.

"I just got off the phone with the maid," Jesse said.

"You found the number?" I asked Barbara.

"She had it the whole time," Jess said. "Of course she did. She hired the maid. She paid her."

"She has a new phone," Barbara said. "I don't remember the number."

Jess rolled his eyes. "The only reason I didn't ask you about this earlier was that you seemed determined to lie, so I didn't think I'd get anywhere. But here's what I found stuck to the mirror in the bathroom."

He held up a Post-it note with the name Nadia and a phone number written on it. Local area code. Scotch tape at the top, like it had fallen and someone had put it back up.

"The handwriting matches the papers on your desk. But wouldn't you have all the numbers you need in your phone?"

"Yep. It was for Charlie," I said. "So he could call the maid if he needed to. What did she say, Jess?"

"She said Barbara called her Thursday night and canceled the Friday booking."

Barbara took a deep breath.

Eddie was staring at Jesse. "What does that mean? Why would she do that?"

"Why'd you do that, Barbara?" I asked.

She stepped into the middle of the landing and turned to face me.

"How is that any of your business? I have every right to cancel a visit from the housekeeper."

Over her shoulder, I saw Jess going into Barbara's room.

"The police were through there," I told him.

Barbara wheeled and followed Jess into her room. I moved forward enough to see into the room, but not so far forward that I'd miss Eddie if he tried to steal the *Star Wars* lamp and make a break for it.

"Stay out of my things," Barbara ordered in what I assumed was her "I'd like to see the manager" voice. "I do not give you permission to go through my things."

He was studying the room, not opening anything, just giving a good look to one thing after another.

"They were," he said. "The police were through here yesterday. They didn't find anything."

"There's nothing to find," Barbara said. "Now I ask you to leave my room."

Jess and I saw it at the same time. It was only a question of who got there first, and he was closer and quicker.

"Do not open that!" Barbara said. Her voice was high and panicky as Jess bent down to unlatch the blue spinner suitcase she'd left the house with on Monday night.

"Holy crow," Eddie said. He'd moved forward, too, and was staring at the open suitcase along with the rest of us. Falling out from behind a set of PJs and a sleep mask was a plain grey laptop, power cord and all. Someone had torn off the back, and pieces were hanging out the sides. Jess used the pajama fabric to keep from leaving prints as he carefully went through the computer's guts.

"I think the hard drive is gone," he said.

Barbara was standing still, arms crossed and eyes moist with tears.

"It is," she said. "Someone took it."

"Is that Charlie's computer?" Eddie said, stepping closer.

"It's his," Barbara said.

"The first one?" I asked. "Or the new one?"

"The first one. I took it on Thursday. I went to the festival Friday night, and someone got into it while I was gone."

"Is that why you canceled the maid?" Jess asked. "So she wouldn't find the computer while she was cleaning?"

"It seemed easier," Barbara said. "I know. It was stupid. I wanted time to read the book, and I didn't want to have to avoid her or keep hiding it."

"And you put the computer in your luggage so the cops wouldn't find it when they searched your room."

She turned to face me. "I needed to know what was in that book. I thought if it wasn't that bad, I'd give it back."

"You didn't," Jesse said.

"Did it mention how you wrote books?" I said. "Did he talk about all the things you borrowed from him?"

"It wasn't about that," she said. "It was lunacy. It would have embarrassed him. He wouldn't have known it was embarrassing, but he would have looked like...."

"Like he was mentally ill?" Jess said, gently.

Barbara narrowed her eyes. "He didn't need people to know he was that way."

"Did you kill him?" Eddie said.

"No," she said, with her usual amount of concern for what Eddie thought about anything.

"Did Myles?" I said.

She turned to me again. "How would I know?"

"Charlie's agent says Myles is violent."

Barbara laughed humourlessly. "They're all messed up. This one works for that same crook that Charlie worked for. People got beat up all the time when Charlie first started there. That Jeremy idiot thinks half the people he meets are secret aliens. He punched a man in the face last year for following him. On a public street! Do you know what that sicko said? He said the guy had been following him around in different bodies. Did Gerald tell you that Myles broke his car windows? He has no proof."

"Do you think Myles did that?" Jess asked.

Barbara shrugged. "Maybe. He did things like that in high school. He beat a kid up with his algebra textbook because the kid called him something. A troll doll? Myles's hair was all over the place back then, and he was always shorter than everyone else. He knocked some teeth out of that kid. He chased someone with his car once too. Who knows what that poor boy said. He had a weapon collection he was very proud of, used to bring nunchucks to school, but many of the boys were like that. They grew out of it."

"Boys will be boys?" I asked.

She scowled at me. "What do you want me to say? His friends were weird. Charlie had *fucked-up* friends."

I didn't think I'd heard Barbara swear before, and in fact she had said the words as if she were repulsed to find them in her mouth. Jess glanced up from the suitcase, which he had been digging through as we talked.

"Why am I only hearing this now?" I said. "You had the book. You knew there were violent people in his life, and—"

"I hired you to find out who killed him, not to turn over every rock."

"Are you kidding me? That's how a murder investigation works. You turn over rocks until you find something."

"You were supposed to be good!" she said. "I thought you'd be more... surgical than the police. I thought you'd get it done quickly and I could move on!"

"Where's the flash drive?" Jess said suddenly. "There should be a flash drive in here with a backup of the book. It's not in your suitcase."

"It disappeared Friday night," Barbara said. "It would be the same person who broke into the laptop, I imagine."

"I imagine that too," I said. "Eddie? You were at the game. Did anyone leave the table?"

"We were all there for the whole game," Eddie said.

"Are you sure?" I asked. "There's no bathroom downstairs."

"Oh yeah—that's different. Everyone uses the bathroom," Eddie said. "It's a long session. The game, I mean. Everyone came up here."

"It wouldn't take long to pull open a laptop," I said. "Not if you didn't care about it ever being put back together. But he'd have had to find it first."

"How would they know she took it?" Jess asked.

"A hunch?" I said. "Barbara had access. She wasn't happy about the book. You wouldn't even have to be sure—you'd only have to be suspicious. Maybe you wouldn't toss the place unless you were certain, but you might poke around a little. And it doesn't sound like it was that hard to find."

"It was in my dresser," Barb said. "I knew Charlie would never search for it in my room. He was so sure it was the aliens. I didn't move it to my spinner until Monday night, when I was packing to leave. And then I left it in the spinner because of the police. Like you said. Because they were going through my room."

"How long was Myles upstairs?" I asked Eddie. "Do you remember? Do you remember anyone being up here for, I don't know, ten minutes or more?"

"Probably all of us?" Eddie said. "That's not much time. You have to get upstairs, use the washroom, go back down."

That made sense. At Eddie's pace, the back and forth might have eaten up some time. Not for Myles or Jeremy, though.

"The basement window is open," I told Barbara. "I don't know whether that's news to you."

"Oh, that window," she said, wrinkling her nose. "I kept telling Charlie to have it fixed. It doesn't latch properly anymore."

"I couldn't fit through it," I said, "and Eddie couldn't, but I bet Myles could."

"The window!" Eddie said. "That's why no one showed up on the front-door camera!"

"He's about my size," Jess said. "I could try it."

The offer was not made with enthusiasm, and I didn't blame him. He'd likely come out of the experience needing a new T-shirt and a tetanus shot.

"The problem," I said, "is that I don't understand—"

A shrill noise broke in from below. Barbara was the first to realize what it was.

"It's just the smoke alarm," she said.

"Could something be on fire?" Eddie asked politely.

"Oh, I doubt it. That thing goes off if someone is cooking or—"

I didn't wait for the rest. No one was cooking or whatever else Barbara was going to say. I tore down the stairs and smelled smoke once I was about halfway. It was coming from the basement, seeping under the door to the basement stairs.

"Jess! There's a fire!"

Eddie had followed me down, and I expected him to go to the front door like a sensible human, but I had misjudged him. He went, instead, into the kitchen. To the back door? I went after him and saw him making a hard left turn to the pantry. The floor was getting warm and the smoke was thickening, wisps of it coming into the hall.

"Eddie! The house is on fire!"

"Yeah, I know! Gimme a sec!"

I thought about leaving. Eddie was a grown-up. No one would have blamed me.

Damn it. I would have blamed me.

I went through the pantry and dining room to find him in the gaming room, looking through a long box.

"Leave it and get moving!" I yelled.

"In a sec!" Eddie yelled back.

It was getting uncomfortably warm, and I didn't know how long we had before we started losing floor.

"Now!"

He ignored me.

He was a big guy but poorly balanced, so I figured I had a chance to shift him. I grabbed the back of his shirt in both hands and pulled. He reeled back and threw a leg sideways to steady himself, which half turned him toward the door. I used the momentum and kept him turning, then gave him a shove forward.

I kept him going, shoving and pulling. My shoulders were going to punish me for it later, but at least they wouldn't be on fire. The smoke was thick in the hall outside the kitchen, and I couldn't tell whether the front door had been opened. Jess had to be out by now. He wasn't an idiot like this guy.

Eddie had gotten a lungful of smoke and wasn't giving me trouble anymore. He was leaning against the kitchen wall and coughing so hard it doubled him over. Once I got the back door open, I lined Eddie up. I did not, strictly speaking, have to plant my foot on his ass and kick him into the yard, but I felt like I'd earned it.

Eddie sprawled into the shrubs at the back of the yard. It wasn't the safest place, with the house starting to spit sparks and all that wood dry from so many hot days, but he was mobile and could get himself free.

I ran around to the front of the house and found Jess on his hands and knees on the lawn. The front door was open. Barbara was standing in the middle of the yard, crying like a child. I went to Jess, knelt beside him, and put a hand on his back.

"Are you okay?"

He coughed and nodded. I rubbed his back and brushed ash from his hair as I called 911.

"SHE WENT back," I said, "for jewelry."

"Once again," Jess said, "yes. Her mother's wedding ring."

We were in the hotel restaurant, showered and changed and barely coughing anymore. The fire department had arrived in good time and had done better than Barbara deserved. The house would need to come down, but a lot was unburned in the soggy rubble, so she might get some keepsakes back eventually. Maybe even that stupid ring.

I was trying not to think about how close it had been because of her going back into her bedroom for the ring. Jesse following her in and wrestling to get her out, the way I'd done with Eddie, but with less leverage and with lungs that were still a little touchy about the pneumonia he'd had a year before.

"Did she fire me at any point?" I asked. "I felt like we were heading there when you opened the suitcase."

"You're not fired," Jess said. He had a beer and a water in front of him and drank some of each before continuing. "I can't guarantee she'll pay up, though, so you might want to cut your losses and quit."

"It's a fucking thought."

We let that fucking thought hang between us, enjoying a few moments of thinking I'd actually do it. Our charcuterie board arrived, and Jess batted my hand away from the brie.

"It's Myles, right?" I said.

"Seems like it," Jess said. "Everything fits."

"Over a hundred dollars? Or a grudge he's had for, what, twenty years?"

"Did you tell me that motive wasn't—"

"I take it back. Okay? I retract that statement. I need a reason why."

We ate and drank some more. It was cool and dark in the restaurant, and I felt like staying for a century.

"Do you think he started the fire?" Jess said. "He can't have been downstairs the whole time we were there. You were in the basement. You'd have seen him."

"I was only down there for a few minutes. I don't know. I have a hard time believing that two different people killed Charlie and started that fire. Then again, until two hours ago, I thought the same person had stolen both laptops, so I'm an idiot. You can't go by me."

My phone rang. Broz. I knew I'd forgotten something.

"Ben Ames," I said.

"Ben Ames, did it not occur to you to tell me that the Gudzyak home was burned down?"

"It was still standing when I left," I said. "More or less."

"Is this your idea of keeping me in the loop?"

"Sorry. Smoke inhalation is bad for the brain."

She sighed so loudly that Jess turned his head at the sound. "I heard you were in the house. Are you both all right?"

"Been better. Been worse. Do you have any word on how it started?"

"Arson. I'm sure that's not news. Mix of accelerants. Acetone, lighter fluid. Looks like it started along the east wall."

"Rotten fruit," I said.

"Pardon me?"

"I was in the basement right before the fire started. I thought I smelled rotting apples."

"Yeah, that could have been the acetone. You're lucky whoever started it waited for you to go back upstairs. What were you doing down there anyway?"

"There's an open window. I've got the front-door camera footage, and it doesn't show anyone going in after Denny left. I think Myles let himself in through the basement window on Monday afternoon."

Silence. Was she driving? I thought I could hear cars going by.

"You think it was Myles Murani."

"I've got means and opportunity. Still working on a motive that makes sense. I feel like you might find a laptop and two flash drives if you searched his home and office."

"Noted. You wouldn't have any idea why someone would start a fire in that basement?"

The east wall. That was where the cardboard boxes had been. The files on Charlie.

"Maybe," I said. "There were old records about Charlie. Some medical files from when he was in a psychiatric hospital in the early nineties. Jeremy mentioned the files at the wake today, and all my suspects heard him."

"Why would they want to destroy those?"

"I don't know," I said. "But I think it has something to do with something that happened in 1992 at a place called Chip Lake."

"Something? That's pretty specific."

"Charlie told his parents that he saw someone get attacked by a bear. They didn't believe him. I guess he used to see things. Jeremy thinks Charlie really saw a UFO. I've searched for bear attacks and UFO sightings in that area in the early 1990s, and I'm not finding anything. I don't know what Charlie saw. Maybe nothing. But I have one of his medical files from back then, and it's full of drawings of a bear attack at what seems to be Chip Lake. Kind of. They're not great drawings, and we were matching it against maps online."

"You think something criminal happened out there?" Broz asked. "Something that someone might want to cover up?"

"Maybe? Right now all I've got is Myles ticking all the boxes without a motive beyond being mad about something that happened over a decade ago and owing Charlie a hundred bucks he was never going to pay."

"I can look into it. I've got to go."

"I'll text if anything comes up."

We hung up. Jess was frowning at me over the wild-boar sausage.

"What?" I asked.

"You didn't tell her about Barbara stealing the first manuscript."

"She's still my client," I said. "And the investigation is about murder."

He seemed like he had thoughts about that, but he didn't share them. He went back to picking through the food. Like any charcuterie board, it had high and low points, but it was pretty good overall—though we both gave the smoked gouda a pass.

"Does your chest hurt?" I asked once we'd put most of the food away.

"It's okay," he said. "I'll live."

"If you need to lie down—"

"I don't."

I put my hand on his. "I'm sorry. I keep getting you into this kind of thing."

He smiled. "You keep trying to shove me out of this kind of thing."

"Well," I said. "That is for reasons."

"It really is okay. Overall I would say my life has been healthier since I came to live with you."

"I wish I could say that was a strong endorsement."

He laced his hand with mine. "About earlier—in the car. I'm sorry about taking off like that."

"I'm sorry for whatever I said," I told him. "I realize that's a bad apology."

He took a breath so long and deep that I decided his lungs might be okay after all. "You didn't know. And I know you don't get it."

"Tell me anyway."

He thought about it. He might have been thinking about what to say, how to phrase it. But I suspected that, instead, he was considering whether to tell me at all.

"You'll like this news," he said. "I can't write."

At first I thought he meant he couldn't physically write, with pen and paper, and that was ridiculous because he'd been taking notes for two days. Then I got it. Music. He was talking about music.

"What, you have… is there a musician's writers' block?"

He scowled and twisted one of the napkins our server had piled up beside the food. "You know what I do in that place I rented? I stare at the piano. When I get tired of that, I stare at the guitars. Please don't say it."

"Say what?"

"That I should quit."

It was hard not to say it, and I realized it had become a reflex for me. When Jess complained about his work, the label, being harassed, the handful of genuine stalker types who showed up when he toured and the one I'd chased away from our front yard in May, I always said the same thing. Quit. If he didn't like the job, and he shouldn't, why have one at all? He was rich. The solution was obvious.

"You're not on a timeline," I said carefully. "You might need a break before you can write again."

He raised his brows. "So quit for now?"

"You can do whatever you want, Jess."

"Except write. I realize you think that's no great loss."

I finished my beer. I might need a couple more before this conversation was over. "I have never said that. I'm not Jack Lowe's biggest fan, but I think you've written excellent songs. Some of them you gave to other people. You've also written stuff I didn't care for, but so what? You have people all over the world who love everything you do, and despite what you seem to think, there are a lot of people who respect your work, so why do you need that from me? You'd be the first to say I'm not an expert. I'm not."

He was looking at his own beer like it was a knife he'd brought to a gunfight. He knew this place had some decent whiskey. I'd seen him check.

"Is it stupid to want your boyfriend to respect you?" he asked.

I cocked my head. "What makes you think I don't respect you? I respect you the most of probably anybody, and I thought you knew that."

"But you think my music is a waste. And I don't. You tell people I went into it to outearn my father, and I'm not denying I enjoyed that, but it's not why I went into music. I care about it."

"Good. You're the one who needs to. I think you could have done anything and done it well, except professional basketball. What you chose to do with your life is your business, and you're the only one who needs to get it."

He said nothing. He was, in fact, staring in the direction of the bar.

I took his other hand. "Jess."

He turned to me.

"I always thought it would be reassuring to you that I don't care about the rock star thing. You don't have to worry about whether I love you for you."

"But it's not as distinct as that. You're saying you love me and you respect me, but you don't really care for the thing I do best, and actually you'd prefer I stopped doing it."

I hadn't thought of it that way. I waved the server over and ordered us drinks, another beer for me and something harder for Jess.

"Enabler," he said once the server had gone.

"Have you thought about stand-up?" I asked. "You're a funny guy. I don't know what to tell you. Most people don't care that much what their partner does for a living, as long as they're happy. I don't think you care that I'm a detective, do you? Aside from thinking it's fun to get involved?"

He considered that. "I care that you're trying to help people. I care that you're interested in justice, like, actual justice. And I enjoy watching you do it well." He looked me in the eye. "It's attractive."

"Okay, don't do that or we will not get through this conversation," I said. "It is attractive how good you are at your job. You command the stage. You make difficult things seem like you barely had to think about them. But I see those things in you all the time."

He pressed my hands, then let go. "This probably isn't a you thing. This is probably a me thing. I'll work on it."

"I'll work on it too," I said. "In case it is me."

He kissed me in a way that was appropriate to a public space, but only barely.

"I'm sorry you're having trouble writing," I told him. "Sincerely. I don't like it when things make you miserable."

"I wrote for him," Jess said. The whiskey came, and he drank with moderation. I finished his beer.

"You mean Jack?" I asked. There had better not be some other him.

"Yeah. I wrote Jack Lowe songs, and I wrote songs for other people. I don't know how to write as me."

"You were writing songs before you started using that name," I said.

"Yeah, but I was building him out even then. I don't know how to do music without the whole—" He waved his hands like he was strewing confetti. "—thing."

"That's what Reiss meant when he said you'd figure it out?" I said.

He nodded.

"I second that. You'll figure it out. Take a break if you need to—not because I want you to stop. Because you spent years becoming Jack Lowe and you're not going to unbecome him overnight."

He blinked at me. "That was helpful. You're right."

"Please stop looking so surprised."

He gave me a kiss on the forehead. "Be right more often."

"Stand-up, I tell you," I said. "Do you want more helpful advice?"

"Yes."

"First, spend more time with other musicians. I don't understand art or artists because I'm not one. You need to fly some of your friends out here. Do that. Invite them to that studio you rented to do whatever the hell it is you weirdos do."

He pushed the whiskey away and stole my second beer. "I've been embarrassed," he said.

"That's dumb. You can't be the first musician to have composer's block. Invite people you trust."

"Okay. I could do that."

I nodded. "Second, and please don't get your back up—"

He smiled with wary eyes. "That never goes anywhere good."

"No, just listen. You're depressed. You said so yourself. You may think you're depressed because you can't write, but maybe it's the other way around, or maybe it's some of both. This is another thing I don't personally get, but from what I've read, clinical depression is not the creative wellspring some people think it is. Talk to your therapist and see about adjusting your meds, and maybe you'll find that things get easier."

"Okay."

We had a good twenty minutes of peace after that, to finish our drinks and take a walk around downtown, watching people playing Ping-Pong and giant chess in the civic mall. Giving money to buskers. It wasn't getting us anywhere with the case, but it was nice, and anyhow, I didn't know what my next steps should be. Get into Myles's home and office to search for a laptop and hard drive that could be anywhere? Search his car for a receipt for a case of nail polish remover? I wasn't optimistic about either.

When my phone rang, I showed Jess that it was Broz, and he nodded and wandered off while I took the call. Not to give me privacy but because a man was reading a book with a giant snake hanging around his shoulders, and Jesse had apparently decided to go talk to him. No matter one's opinion of Jess, it was difficult to deny that I was dating a crazy person.

"Ben Ames."

"I called a friend in the RCMP and asked them to do a search for Chip Lake, 1992. He found something, but I don't know if it's any help to you."

"What was it?"

"A body. Unsolved homicide, kind of."

I moved away from a woman with twins in a stroller and found a bench where no one would overhear what might not be a family-friendly conversation.

"How do you have a kind of unsolved homicide?"

"He was in a motorcycle club. He was found in the woods near a campsite. He'd been beaten and stabbed. The knife was found near the body. Spring-loaded switchblade, which some of the local bikers had been carrying around that time. The assumption is he got into some kind of dust-up with his own club or another club. There was an investigation, and like I said, it's officially unsolved, but it looks like club business."

"Do you have anything else?" I asked. "When the body was found? An estimate for how long it had been out there?"

"Yeah, hang on." I heard a tapping sound of nails on her screen as she swiped to something else, then came back. "Found in mid-November. Probably there a couple of weeks. Hard to be specific—you've got weather below zero, predation...."

"Late October," I said.

"Sure. Late October sounds right. What are you thinking? That Charlie saw what happened? And, what, told everyone it was a bear attack? I guess that's possible, but I'm not buying that some motorcycle gang found out about this book decades later and took Charlie out. This is sounding pretty tenuous."

A girl with a pair of dark braids went by on a rental scooter, so close that I had to pull my feet up onto the bench to avoid getting run over. She waved at me as she sped away, a gesture that I chose to take as an apology.

"Was there anything distinguishing about the guy?"

"He had a club tattoo. He was in the Griz MC."

"He had a tattoo of a bear? And you're not seeing a connection?"

"It would have been covered by his clothes. He was fully dressed. Jeans, boots, one of those plaid work jackets."

Plaid work jacket. Like a plaid shirt.

"Oh, and he had a walking cast. Probably made him an easy job for whoever took him out."

And a misshapen leg.

"Charlie Gudzyak was there," I said. "I don't know what happened, but he was there. And I think Myles Murani was there too. That's why he burned the files in the basement."

"Slow down. We don't know why the fire was set or who set it. You're making leaps all over the place."

"Maybe. I need to think. Thanks for this."

"Don't make me regret it."

I hung up and waved Jesse over. He was all smiles.

"That was a nice snake. Boa constrictor. I met one at a video shoot once."

"I'm glad you're able to enjoy them in public and not in my home."

"Don't you think Frank would like to have a friend?"

"I got him a friend," I said. "You're just not home right now."

Jess laughed and sat next to me on the bench. "What did Broz have to say?"

I told him. His eyes got wider with every sentence.

"That's it," he said. "Charlie saw someone get killed."

"And no matter what the cops think, I think Myles is the one who did it. He has a temper. Maybe this guy did or said something he didn't like."

"Called him a troll doll," Jess said.

"That's motive. Not the troll doll thing. The murder. If Myles killed someone and Charlie knew."

"But Charlie thought it was an alien abduction."

He picked up a ball that had rolled up to us and tossed it back to a pair of boys. Neither had nunchucks or switchblades so far as I could see.

"Maybe Myles figured it would be close enough for someone to put it together. Someone who remembered the case. That guy's family could still be around."

"Or a nosy detective."

I put an arm around Jesse's shoulders.

"The question is, what do we do now?"

"Get him to confess?" Jess said. "We're not going to find evidence at this point—not for that murder. Charlie's dead. We have the drawings, and maybe you could convince someone that Charlie saw the murder, but that doesn't link in Myles. Unless we can get him to say he did this, and killed Charlie, I don't know if Broz is going to feel like arresting him."

Unless, unless…. I stood up.

"Where did we leave the drawings?"

"I brought them to the room. I didn't want to leave them in the car."

"Come on. I need to see them again."

CHAPTER TWELVE

"ONE OR three. Never two." I had the pages spread out on the bed and was pointing at the tents. "Charlie draws one tent or three tents at his campsite, but never two tents. When he remembers being there with some-one else, it's two friends. Not one."

"Could one tent belong to the victim?" Jess asked.

"Then it would never be one tent."

"Right. Okay. And the most likely person to have been out there with Myles and Charlie is Denny. Except it couldn't have been Denny. Because he'd already left town."

"That's what he says."

We looked at each other. I picked up my phone and placed a call.

"Ben Ames Investigations Research Department."

"I have a question for you."

"And we have answers at a reasonable rate," Izzy said. "What's your question?"

"At dinner, you said Denny talked to you about what it was like being a teenager in the Stone Age."

"Oh yeah. Pterodactyl burgers, going to the cave with a date to watch the paintings flicker."

"In actual fact, though," I said, "did he ever tell you when he left Edmonton? Was it right after high school?"

"What?" she said. "Where'd you hear that? He was here for a couple years after he graduated. He started university, dropped out, went up north to plant trees, came home, started a band, fought with them, they broke up—that's pretty relatable. Finally his parents told him to go away and not come back until he'd stuck with something for at least a year."

"Would he have been here in 1992?" I asked. "He would have been about twenty years old."

"I think so? He told me about him and his parents watching Clinton get inaugurated. Was that… I know it was the early nineties."

I checked on my phone. "Ninety-three. January. Thanks."

"No problem. Was that all you needed?"

"That's it. From here out, don't talk to anyone on this case. Even Denny."

"Even Denny? What the hell?"

"Just don't. Okay? I promise you will get the whole story, but not right now."

"Jesus. Fine."

"Thank you." I set my phone down. "He was still here in ninety-three. That thing about leaving town right after high school is part of the Denny Hill legend."

"And an alibi," Jess said. "How much do you think he knows?"

"He has to at least suspect that Myles killed Charlie. I don't know if he was involved in Charlie's death. There's only one way to find out."

Jess lay back on the bed, stretching his legs out over the drawings. "It might be easier to get him to confess. To the thing in 1993, anyway. Even if he only saw Myles do it, he didn't report it."

"And he helped gaslight Charlie about him and Myles not being there."

Jess closed his eyes. "He may not want to talk to us. He shouldn't. I wouldn't if I were him."

"We'll see."

I called Denny and got voice mail. I left a message saying that I wanted to ask him some questions and could we meet. Nothing scary about that.

"If he doesn't return your call, we could have Barbara call him," Jess said.

"We can give him some time. You look like you could use a nap."

"No, I'm okay." He opened his eyes. "Stupid depression."

"I remember," I said. "You used to sleep for days in Toronto."

"And you thought it was drugs. Goes to show, a guy can be a drug fiend and have a mental health problem at the same time."

"And a person can be psychotic and still be right sometimes," I said. "He did see someone get killed."

"Or abducted from Earth, I guess," Jess agreed.

"Jeremy wants to hypnotize you, by the way. He mentioned it at the wake."

Jess laughed. "He wants to uncover my lost memories of alien abduction? I'd settle for lost memories of my first European tour. Actually I take that back. I probably don't want to know."

"I know I don't."

He rolled onto his side to face me. "Can you believe Barb took Charlie's book? I mean, I believe it, but... man. That is a deeply shitty thing to do. Even if you do think you're saving someone from embarrassing themselves."

"I find it hard to believe," I said, "that it was his embarrassment she was worried about. But I called this right from the start. It was the Brasher fucking Doubloon. The client knew who took it."

"Oh my God, you're right. I guess you should always go with your first instinct."

My phone rang. Jess stared at it. I took a deep breath, in and out.

"Ben Ames."

"You called me."

It was Denny, but not as I'd heard him before. His words were mushy, and his voice was soft.

"I did. Are you all right? You sound a little—"

"What did you want?"

Drunk. He sounded drunk the way people did when they weren't playing it up for their friends at the bar.

"I have a few questions. It'd probably be easier if I came to see you. Are you at your hotel?"

The thought flashed through my mind that I hadn't asked Barbara where she'd go after her house burned down or whether she needed anything. But Jesse had gotten a lungful of smoke and nearly been trapped in the fire because she'd thought she needed her special ring, so maybe I hadn't owed her anything. Maybe it was enough that I hadn't called her a selfish bitch or taken her purse away and thrown it into the fire.

"I don't want to see anyone," Denny said. "Sorry."

"It won't take long," I said. "I'll come to you. Are you at a bar?"

I listened as I waited for him to speak. I could hear music in the background, too quiet for me to make out the song. No other voices. No clinking of glassware. There was, maybe, the sound of a roadway.

He said, "I have nothing for you."

Something about the way he said it told me there wasn't any point to pretense. "Denny, I don't think that's true."

He hung up. My hand, still holding the phone, dropped to my lap.

"What happened?" Jess said.

"He's drunk. Somewhere. He may be driving."

"Oh, that's great. Do we know what he's driving? Can we have Broz send someone after him?"

"Weirdly, I don't think she thinks she works for us."

"That is weird." Jess started to gather the drawings and put them back into the folder. "Why do you think he called you back if he doesn't want to talk to you?"

"He might have thought I had some kind of news."

"Maybe he wants to tell us what he knows. Even if he thinks he doesn't."

"I'm not going to get that over the phone. We have to find him first."

I called Barbara, who was at her friend's house and not thrilled to hear from me. She still didn't fire me, and I wasn't going to quit. She also didn't know where Denny was, or so she said. She said she'd call me if she heard from him.

Broz hadn't seen him and, as predicted, did not think it was her job to find him. She also said she'd call me if she happened to find out where he was.

Jess took the time to do some chores, checking his socials and answering what he needed to.

"Someone got a picture of me in the parking lot, talking to Gerald," he said. "I didn't even see that happen.

Oh cool, they're speculating about whether I'm cheating. Because I'm talking to some guy in a parking lot."

"The running narrative of your life on social media…," I said.

"…is often more interesting than my actual life," Jess finished. "If I—"

"What?" I said.

"Hold on."

He was doing something on his phone, or seemingly four or five things at once. Jess was the only person I knew who kept updating his phone, not for a better camera or some new feature, but because he couldn't find one that could keep up.

"Ha! I'm not the only musician getting photographed around here!"

I crossed to the other bed and turned his phone to me.

Someone had posted a photo of Denny from early in the afternoon. He was wearing shades and a panama hat, neither of which he'd worn into the event room at the wake. He must have left them at the café's outside door. He was getting into a red Mustang convertible, with the downtown skyline for a backdrop and the hot dry wind catching his linen suit jacket. By a mile, it was the most glamorous photo I had ever seen taken in a surface parking lot.

"That's near the gaming café. He must have rented a car. I think? Can you rent a car like that? They always give me a surprise sedan."

Jess smiled. "Some rental places have a luxury fleet. What do you mean by surprise sedan?"

"You've never rented a car, have you? Of course not. Why would you?"

"Most of my traveling has been done on tour," Jess said.

"They tell you that you're booked for a sedan, and you don't know what you're driving until you get there and they give you the keys. They probably don't know either. You get the car that's ready when you show up. I didn't even know you could ask for something specific."

"Maybe you get a surprise sports car. Is it a Mustang? Is it a 'Vette? Could be a Miata." He laughed. "Yeah, no. Anyone who bothers to rent a luxury car is going to want exactly the car they asked for."

"It's going to make him easy to spot," I said. "Where is he now?"

"Not sure. Gimme a sec."

I had things to do—clothes to sort out, receipts to file in the hopes that Barbara would pay up—so I looked after that while Jesse did the work.

"There! He was at a gas station twenty minutes ago."

Buying sunflower seeds and a bottle of vitamin water. Same hat and shades.

"Where is that?"

Jess pulled up a map. "Yellowhead, west of the city. Outside of Entwhistle." He pulled in the directions tab. "Twenty minutes from Chip Lake."

"He went to the lake."

Jess nodded. "He's probably there right now."

"Maybe there's evidence out there? After all this time? What, did he carve his initials in a fucking tree?"

"Maybe he felt like he needed to be there," Jesse said.

"Well, we need to be there." I grabbed my phone and keys. "How far out are we?"

"Hour and twenty minutes."

We didn't waste any time getting to the car. Jesse texted Broz while I got us onto the highway and on our way out of town.

"You gonna speed?" he asked as soon as we were clear of the city.

I glanced at him. "Should I have let you drive?"

"We could pull over and switch."

I preferred to go with the flow of traffic on the highway, and no one was speeding a lot on that road. It wouldn't save that much time to push our speed ten or twenty kilometers over the limit. But I didn't know what Denny was doing out at that lake—probably still drunk, maybe alone, maybe with Myles, and minutes could be the difference between finding him there or missing our chance.

We moved smoothly between semis and SUVs and the occasional plucky little hatchback. The road was wide, and most of the intersections were flyovers instead of junctions, so it was easy to keep up a good clip.

"No mountains yet," Jess observed.

"I told you. It's three hours to Jasper from Edmonton. I think you can see them once you get a little way past Chip Lake."

We passed turn-offs for a half-dozen lakes and a deep gorge to the Pembina River that made Jess crane his head for a better look. I could see why a shallow lake, probably weedy on top of that, wouldn't attract a lot of people when they had better options all around. Why the guys had gone there in the first place, and in October, was a mystery. It might have been as simple as having pot. Cannabis had still been illegal back then, and they might have wanted to smoke it in a place where they were unlikely to be disturbed.

Jess had brought the drawings and used them to pick an access road that would get us close to Charlie's vantage point, near the river and facing an oddly shaped island.

We saw the lake before the turn-off. It was wide and empty—no boats, not even kayaks or canoes. A train flew by along the lakeshore. One more reason it might not have been popular. No one liked a train whistle in the middle of the night.

The train was nothing but shipping containers, stacked double height and going on forever. It would cross the mountains into BC, and out to the ocean from there. Moving things across the provinces.

Like Charlie's old boss.

"The victim was stabbed with a switchblade," I told Jess.

"Is that important?"

"They've been illegal since the fifties. It's the kind of thing Nick Antonis might have been moving around between his stores. Maybe Charlie picked some up for his friends."

We went past the turn-off the first time. It wasn't marked. Jess was following the map and figured it out before we'd gone far.

"Hard to find," he said. I nodded.

I took it slow on the access road. It was gravel and bone dry, which made it a little slippery, but I also wanted to minimize the noise I was making. We crept around a spiderweb of narrow roads, seeing no one. Not a tent or a boat or a lonesome angler.

Jess saw the car first. He tapped me on the shoulder and pointed. He could have spoken, since there was no chance he'd be louder than my car, but I appreciated the effort.

The red Mustang was parked in a small dirt lot not far from the shore.

We moved slowly down to the edge of the lake. It was weedy, as I'd expected, with the musty smell and oil-slick look of blue-green algae near the shore. I'd pointed the algae out to Jess before, since it could be deadly to dogs and my dog enjoyed throwing himself into anything bigger than a mud puddle.

I set my phone to record, with a continuous upload to a shared folder I kept for occasions like these. The Wi-Fi signal wasn't bad out here, so close to the highway. I slipped the phone into my back pocket.

Once we got past the thick brush leading to the shore, I turned north and found Denny Hill a few hundred feet away. He was sitting on a lichen-covered rock on a small silty beach, gazing out at the water. His linen suit was going to be a write-off after this, but he didn't seem like he cared.

My low expectation of him had been that he'd have a guitar when we found him, writing something mournful about the tragedy of not reporting a murder and gaslighting your mentally ill friend. Or maybe breaking out some Gordon Lightfoot, with the passing trains as his choir. He was doing neither.

I didn't see empty bottles or cans around the rock either. He was sitting there, alone, sobering up and watching the weeds sway underwater. I could see a little tension in his back when he noticed our footsteps, but he didn't look our way. When we stepped onto the beach, he said, "There's a good spot for burbot back there. My father and I would go ice fishing here sometimes."

"I wouldn't have thought this was a good fishing lake," I said. He raised and dropped one shoulder.

"Only sometimes. How did you know I was here?"

We moved closer. Jess crouched beside him.

"People put it on the socials when they see you," he said. "You know how it is."

Denny nodded. Jesse stared at the lake.

"Have you been out here since that night?" Jess asked.

Denny shook his head. "No. I couldn't—I didn't want to."

"Charlie stopped going outside after that," I said. "He never went anywhere."

"I know."

"It must have been cold," Jess said. "When you were here." He'd dropped one hand to the beach and was raking lightly through the pebbles. Strumming a guitar instead of drumming.

"It was a cold fall. But we wanted to get out of the city for a night. Myles got into the water anyway. He wanted to see how far out he could walk. He said he was Jesus of the North."

"You didn't expect to see anyone else," I suggested.

He nodded. "We didn't know. We thought no one would be here. But because it was so quiet, the biker gangs would come out here sometimes. Meet up. Do business. There was one guy with his radio. One of those things they used to call ghetto blasters. It's a bad name, I know. I forget what the better name is. He was running it off a twelve-volt, playing some country station."

"Just the one guy?" Jess asked.

"Yes. He might have been meeting someone later. Or picking something up."

"They could have had a dead drop out here," I said.

A crow swooped by, close enough to ruffle my hair, and landed above us in a towering spruce. Denny watched him go, the first he'd moved since we'd arrived.

"I thought it was a raven," he said, as if he had to explain his interest. The shame of turning to look at something as common as a crow.

"He wouldn't have liked you being here," Jesse said. "The biker."

Denny's mouth twisted. "I don't know. He might not have cared. He didn't come to the campsite. Myles went to him."

I felt my joints locking into place and my breathing slowing. He was there, back in October of '92, and the slightest thing might scare him away. Jess sensed it too and didn't push. We waited.

"He hated country music," Denny said. "That started everything. He went to the shore to tell the guy to turn his radio off."

I could picture the standoff. In fact, I didn't have to. Charlie had drawn it. A man in a plaid work jacket. A radio. A bear.

"He wouldn't turn off the music," Jesse said, so softly that it was more of a breath.

"He told us to fuck off. Fuck off out of here. I've thought about this—do you think he was trying to do us a favour? He might have been telling us to leave before his friends arrived."

"Could be," I said. "No way to know."

"Myles never stands down. Never does. He's a little guy. Like you, Jack. So much front from a little guy. They fought like bears. They were clumsy like bears. That's where I got the idea for what to tell Charlie. Afterward. We told him over and over about the bear."

"He had a walking cast," I said. "The biker. Is that how Myles won the fight?"

"He had a cast," Denny said. "That was part of it. But it was three on one. It might have been the same even without the cast."

Three on one. Denny and Charlie had gotten involved. Trying to break it up, maybe, or throwing themselves in because it was cold and remote and everyone was a little feral that night.

"And Myles had a knife?" Jess said.

Denny's mouth twisted again, and I realized it was a try at a bitter smile. "Myles was jealous. Charlie had helped his boss unload some knives that morning, and his boss gave him one. Charlie didn't even want it, except to make Myles eat his liver."

Jesse stared at Denny. I could hear him struggling to keep his voice low and calm as he said,

"Charlie had the knife?"

Denny said nothing. He'd been saying nothing about this for decades, so why start saying anything now?

"It was Charlie," I said.

"It was Myles," Denny said with a flare of anger that brought him, for a moment, fully alive. "Myles couldn't stand the radio station. Myles wanted a fight."

They'd been protecting Charlie all this time. And themselves. The law wouldn't see these three much differently from one another, not after they'd left the body behind.

"Did Charlie ever tell anyone the truth?" Jess asked.

Denny picked up a rock and threw it into the lake. A loon cried.

"I don't know," Denny said. "But who would have believed him?"

"The two of you weren't even there," I said. "If he said otherwise, he was imagining things again. You and Myles stuck to that line the whole time. And you told anyone who'd listen that you'd left town right after high school. If anyone had gotten ideas about you being at the lake that night, all they had to do was check Wikipedia and they'd be convinced otherwise. Hell, Jess and I were convinced until we realized you'd been lying."

Denny looked at me. "Am I going to jail?"

"Not for me to say," I told him.

"I didn't kill Charlie," Denny said. "I never even read his book. I never wanted to."

"Why did you hire me to find it? It would have been better for you if it had stayed lost."

"For Charlie," Denny said. "Firstly for Charlie, like I always told you. It wasn't fair to take his book from him. I didn't know it was Boosh who took the first draft. I thought it might have been Myles, or Charlie's buddy from the store. I never trusted anyone who worked there."

"And secondly?"

"It was stupid to mess around with it. You think it would have been better for it to have stayed lost? Imagine if no one had taken it. Or if you'd found it. Charlie would be alive. Boosh would have her brother and her house. It would be published, and no one would care. Not even in China. All this and for what, to silence a man no one would ever listen to? Hasn't anyone heard of the Streisand Effect?"

I had. Jess had schooled me on it one night when I'd asked him why he, a man with access to lawyers, was shrugging off a particularly nasty piece of libel. The idea was that it was dangerous to try to suppress things on the internet, because the attempt itself could become a flashing neon sign over the thing you were trying to bury.

Or it could become a police investigation into a murder you'd committed in the hopes of covering up a manslaughter, or something like it, that had been forgotten almost as soon as it had happened. One that would likely never, book or no book, have been laid at anyone's door.

"Did Barbara know?" Jess asked. "Did she know what happened out here?"

Denny shook his head. "No, that was—she was part of why we lied. It was better for her and Charlie—and yes, for Myles and me, of course. It was better for us to keep this a secret, but it was also better for Charlie to spend some time in a hospital than to spend years in prison. He really was ill. He should have been treated before. And Barbara? What good would it have done her to see him be locked away? All of that misery, three lives ruined and hers as good as ruined, over a dead man from a biker gang? Why should we all suffer over a criminal like that?"

I had answers, plenty of them, but I didn't think Denny really wanted to hear them.

"You wanted Ben to stop whatever was happening with the book," Jess said. "And with Charlie. Before it all went to hell."

"Her brother," Denny said sadly. "And her home. She loved that house. I wanted not to fail her, but I think… I did."

Denny stood. He had a wobble to him, and Jess got up quickly to steady him.

"We'll give you a ride back to town," Jess said.

When we got back to the lot by the shore, I thought at first I was seeing things, like Charlie saw bears. A spectre of a little man with a temper, sitting in a folding lawn chair next to a stand of caragana. The sun glinting off the candy-apple car behind him.

But it was real. Myles Murani, in front of Denny's car, a beer tucked into the cup holder of the blue vinyl chair.

Denny wobbled again, and I caught him this time.

"Good God, Myles," he said. "What are you doing here?"

"Eavesdropping a little," Myles said easily. "You didn't leave too much out, did you, Denny?"

"What would be the point?" Denny said. "They know."

"You accuse me of stirring the pot," Myles said. "Meanwhile you hired a motherfucking private investigator. Do you even know what a secret is, Denny? Do you understand the word?"

"How did you know Barbara had the laptop?" Jess asked suddenly. Myles cocked his head.

"I didn't. But think about it. The laptop went missing on Thursday. Who was even in the house on Thursdays, besides Barbara? Denny wasn't in town yet. So Friday night, middle of the game, I went upstairs for a bathroom break and searched Barb's room. Found the laptop, took the hard drive and the flash drive, problem solved, right? Except I got back to the gaming table and Mr. Obsessive was saying he was already rewriting the book. Because there was no getting it back from the aliens."

"Or from Barbara," Denny said. "I think on some level he knew it was her. He told himself it was aliens because that was easier than thinking his sister took his book."

"Yeah, who gives a shit." Myles said. "Charlie and Barbara and their fucking psychodrama. Hey, you want to take seats or something? This is awkward, you all standing around looking at me. Pull up a rock… or a log."

None of us sat, but Denny did scan for something suitable, like Myles was the boss of him.

"You let yourself in through the basement," I said to Myles, "which you probably all did as kids. That's the kind of thing kids would do. You're still small enough to get through the window. And you knew about the doorbell camera—you'd need to avoid that. You killed him, took the new laptop and flash drive and the safe. Where's the safe, Myles?"

"In the river," Myles said. "It went down like a brick of steel. Glug, glug."

I hoped the laptop and flash drive were still on land somewhere. Myles's car or home or office. Not that I'd need it with everything I was recording, but more evidence never hurt. The safe might be findable, too, since Myles would likely have ditched it at the river end of a trail that led from Charlie's backyard.

"And you set that fire in the basement because you thought Charlie's psychiatric files were there," Jesse said. "But you could have stolen them anytime. Why didn't you?"

"Didn't need to," Myles said. "As far as I knew, everything was cool. Denny and I understood that it was smart to keep our mouths shut. We had Charlie convinced he'd seen a bear. The cops thought the guy dying out here was part of some dust-up between motorcycle gangs. Everything was fine until Charlie decided to write that fucking book. I still don't know what the hell possessed him."

"Jeremy Gustafsen," I told him. "He thought the bear story seemed like a screen memory, so he hypnotized Charlie and helped him to remember an alien abduction instead. You know it was possible to talk Charlie into that kind of thing."

Myles made a funny noise. He was, I realized, laughing. This had to be his real laugh, not the one he put on to sound like a regular guy.

"Jeremy is a goddamned idiot. I love it. He's an inch from the hole, and he misses the putt."

"See?" Denny demanded. "Do you get it, now? Jesus, Myles, Charlie would have said that the bear story was a screen memory for an abduction. That's two whole stories away from what really happened. And he sounds like a lunatic. None of this had to happen."

"I know what he said," Myles said. He wasn't laughing anymore. "I know how he sounded. I read the book. I took the flash drive from the first draft, remember? It was too close. He named the lake. He said which campground we were in. He gave the month and the year. All you'd have to do is whatever these two goobers did and you'd find the truth. He even brings up the topic of a screen memory! So you read that and think, gee, maybe that alien abduction thing didn't happen, because that's stupid, but what if it's a screen memory for something else? And not that stupid bear story either because that's also stupid. You think someone in China wasn't going to figure that out and make a fucking true-crime podcast about it? It takes one, Denny. Do you have any idea how many motherfuckers there are in China? How many fans he had? You need one intersection between crazy fan and true-crime podcaster and you and I are cooked. Unacceptable."

"So you did it your way," Denny said. "And that went so much better. You killed him! Did he know it was you? He did, didn't he? He trusted you. That's how he died, knowing you were the one killing him."

Myles grinned. "Relax. I'm sure he told himself it was aliens."

Denny's eyes narrowed, and he shook my hand off his arm. His hands were starting to curl into fists.

"I guess you were entertaining enough in high school, but you know something, Myles? You've always been a piece of shit."

"Get ahold of yourself, Den," Myles said. Casually he reached behind the chair and pulled out a rifle. He stood and pointed it at the three of us. "I need Ben and Jack here to understand a few things."

"What the hell, Myles?" Denny said. "Is that your dad's old gun? Put that away."

"No, I'm going to keep pointing this so you all listen. Denny, do you want to tell these two that I can shoot? I'm not a marksman, but from this distance I'm not going to miss."

Denny gave us an expression that was almost sheepish.

"He used to go hunting with his dad."

"So we're all clear on this," I told Myles, "the police know we're here."

"So you say," Myles said. "Denny, come on over here."

Denny hesitated, then went to stand next to Myles.

"This is what happens when you don't keep your mouth shut," Myles told Denny. "Things get serious."

"Stop talking like this is my fault," Denny said.

"Stop talking," Myles returned. "Christ, you have never stopped talking since we met. You gonna write a fucking song about this too?"

He probably would at that.

"Myles," I started. He shook his head and raised the gun a little.

"Just listen. We did what we did for Charlie, and for Barbara. Charlie killed that guy, and we all know he was out of his head when he did that. He probably thought he was stabbing General Zod or something. All Myles and I did was protect a mentally ill person who killed someone accidentally. Do you really think it would have been better to let Charlie go to prison?"

"He could have plead not criminally responsible," I said. "That exists for a reason."

"It would have been a nightmare for everyone," Myles said. "Not good for his mental health. And Denny's right. He and I are both productive members of society. I admit he's a little more productive than I am. It would not have done anyone any good to make us guests of Her—shit, His—His Majesty. Hers at the time. Whatever. We were more useful to the world on the outside. Charlie too. We're not burdens. And we weren't a danger to anyone."

"I don't know about that," I said. "I don't know what else you've done."

Myles shrugged with one shoulder.

"Do you figure we can all walk away?" Myles said. "That could be good. I'll take my chances on the cops figuring out what happened with Charlie. Which I didn't enjoy having to do, by the way. My consolation is he got to have a pretty good life outside of prison instead of spending that time locked up."

"He was scared to leave the house," Jess pointed out.

Myles made that laughing sound again. "Sure, and a prison cell is the size of that house, so it's all the same. Right? You get to keep all your Wonder Woman figurines in prison. Come on. We did a public service taking out a criminal, and we all went on to be good citizens."

Jess and I said nothing.

Myles took a forest's worth of spruce-scented air in through his nose. "Yeah, you're right. Even if you did tell me you were on board with keeping this quiet, I can't trust you. I have to kill both of you because Denny's a fucking tool."

"Stop blaming this on me!" Denny yelled. Myles didn't even flinch. When he spoke again, Denny's voice was under control. "It's okay if they talk. They can't prove it. We can say they're making it all up."

"You're giving me a headache," Myles said. "Denny, I came out here hoping you'd kept your mouth shut. The gun was just in case. But you killed these people when you yapped. It was fun to dick them around and see if they were craven enough to pretend they'd cover our shit up, but I can't stand around here playing games all day. This isn't a game. This is prison."

"Maybe we deserve that," Denny said. "Maybe we're lucky we got these years before it caught up with us."

"Oh, fuck off. Stop being a romantic troubadour for ten seconds and really try to imagine what this is going to be like. Day after day. Forever. Do you think you get a morning breakfast tray with cucumber slices for your eye bags in prison? You think you get to headline the folk festival? You think you get to have a guitar? And that's the rest of your life at this point, Denny. It's a lot of never agains."

Denny looked sick, a pale green reflection of the lake. He dropped back until he was leaning against the side of the car.

Myles shook his head at me. "Maybe this is a weird thing to say to someone in your profession, but you should have learned to mind your own business. The way I had things set up, it wasn't the worst for anyone. Even Charlie. He died quick and at home. Between you and blabbermouth here, you've made me burn a house down, and you've gotten two more people killed. Namely you and your boyfriend. You've made the whole situation a lot uglier than it had to be."

"You can shoot us," I said. I felt Jesse tense beside me and wished I could touch him, but it wouldn't have been smart to move. "I can't stop that. But it's not going to solve anything for you."

"Au contraire, mon frère," Myles said. "It'll plug up the hole in the dam."

"I've recorded everything Denny said," I told him. "And everything you've said. You can check my phone if you don't believe me."

Myles cackled. "Are you telling me I have to pry the back off another piece of consumer electronics?"

"I'm telling you you've been hanging around Charlie too long," I said. "Because you've forgotten that most people have no problem using the cloud. I've been uploading the whole time. There are audio files in a shared folder that a number of people can access, and they know to go there if I disappear."

That was it. He was done and he knew it. He'd confessed to everything, and if he had missed anything, Denny had covered it. Everything the police needed was sitting, safe as unburnt houses, on a server far, far away.

It was a good argument for Myles to back down and give up… and I should have known better than to say it. Hadn't Denny told us those were two things Myles would never do?

His eyes darkened, and I heard Jess take in a sharp breath. This was the temper, the reason Charlie's agent had avoided him for years. Myles didn't care what happened to him, or how much worse anything became, so long as he punished the people who'd made him lose.

There was nowhere to run. A lake to dive into, not even a foot deep off the shore. Trees on either side, too far to get to before the first shot. Someone was getting shot here, if Myles could aim at all. The light was clear and even. We were close enough that he could have thrown a rock and hit us.

But if I moved and drew fire, maybe it would give Jess a chance to run? Would he have the sense to do it, or would he come back for me like an idiot?

I should have convinced Broz to meet us here. I should have convinced her we were right instead of waiting to get the confession. I shouldn't have let Jesse get involved, again, after telling myself I'd never let that happen. I should have minded my own business, like Myles had said.

He aimed. My throat ached, and my legs were on fire. It was the only chance either of us had. I had to run.

I was turning, and Myles was turning the gun toward me, the way I'd known he would. An amateur drawn to motion. He'd take me down. I could almost feel it.

It never came.

The gun went off and I felt nothing, and then I was ice clear through. He'd gone for Jess instead. I turned around, nearly falling, and saw Jess standing, staring at Myles. No blood.

Myles was on the ground. The gun was lying a few feet away from him, and Denny was behind him with a guitar case in his hand.

Jess and I went for the gun together, the way we'd gone for Barbara's spinner case, and he outraced me this time too. He handed the gun to me, and we backed away. Denny was looking from me to Myles and back. Myles was gripping his leg and cursing. He'd shot himself in the calf. Denny must have hit his gun arm with the guitar case, forcing it down as Myles pulled the trigger.

Jess came to stand close to me and took out his phone to call the RCMP.

"Like old times," he said. Because we'd held a gun on someone before, waiting for the cops to show up. And that was funny to him.

"Am I going to jail?" Denny asked again.

"I told you," I said. "It's not up to me."

Jess was shivering, despite the warm day. I moved closer so he could lean against me.

"You okay?" I asked him.

"Relatively," he said. I knew what he meant. I put an arm around his shoulders.

"I've been thinking lately," I said, "That your job might not be so bad after all."

"I CAN'T BELIEVE it. I cannot believe it."

That was Izzy, lying next to me on the grass. She and Jess and I were at the festival grounds, or the park that the grounds had gone back to being. Izzy had brought beach mats and sunscreen and mosquito repellant. Jess and I had brought booze and food.

"What exactly can't you believe?" I asked.

"Oh my God, all of it. You got into another murder case with famous people? You're starring on social media again? Denny Hill helped kill a guy in the nineties? Denny freakin' Hill? For real, he was so nice to me."

"He's not the worst person who ever lived," I said. "If he were, we'd be dead."

She shuddered. "That's scary shit."

I glanced at Jess, who was sitting up, watching traffic flowing over the bridge to downtown.

"It is," I said pointedly. "It's very serious."

"I know," Jess said serenely. "That's why I'd rather you weren't alone."

"I hope my not-real-dads aren't going to get into a fight in front of me," Izzy said.

Jess smiled. "We can save it for the car."

"How is that Barbara chick doing?" Izzy asked. "This is, like, nine kinds of fucked for her."

It was. She'd lost her brother, her house, and a childhood friend, depending on what she thought of Denny once the dust had settled. I knew from my call to her after Denny and Myles had been arrested that it was going to be some time before she considered speaking to Denny again. Myles might have burned down with her house for all she cared, and she'd told me, in so many words, that she would have preferred it. She was also a top-billed social media star for all the reasons she'd always hoped not to be.

"She'll live," I said. If she didn't appreciate that as much as she should have, she could try getting a gun in the face sometime.

"Reiss says he and Brennan are going to your studio," she said to Jess. She sounded wistful.

"It's not mine. I'm renting it. We're going to… I don't even know. I've got a block I have to get through."

"Sounds nice," Izzy said softly.

Jess glanced at me. I busied myself putting on more sunscreen. This was Jesse's business.

"Isobel?" he asked.

"Yes?"

"Did you want to come?"

Izzy grinned. "I wouldn't want to intrude."

"You can stay in the guest room," I told her. "But this is not an adoption. We're sending your ass back to Edmonton once this music… whatever, session is done."

"You'd better. I don't want to be stuck in Calgary."

Jess lay back on the grass and laughed. I leaned over to kiss the top of his head, which turned into some rolling around that Izzy politely pretended not to see.

"What are you going to do now?" Izzy asked me. I lay back and closed my eyes. Soaked up sun under a cloudless sky. There was no blues band playing, but it would do.

"I am," I said, "on vacation."

Coming Soon

The Woman Who Went on Midnights

Ben Ames Case Files: Book Four

Radio is becoming the deadliest gig in town when the bodies pile up at CGNU Saskatoon. P.I. Ben Ames isn't looking for an out-of-province adventure, but his musician boyfriend has connections that put them both on the trail of a killer at the Gnu.

Scan the QR Code Below to Preorder!

Keep Reading for an Excerpt from
The Dominion
Book #1 in the Seven Leagues Guides Series,
By Gayleen Froese.

FOREWORD

I HOPE YOU'RE not waiting for *Seven Leagues Over the Dominion* to come out. If you are, you'll be waiting a long time, and you can blame my editor. Or maybe you can blame me, for bringing an uninvited guest to lunch.

I was meeting my editor for a nice business lunch three months after my trip to the Dominion. We were both enthusiastic about a Seven Leagues book covering the most magical place on Earth. At a certain point, if you're writing adventure travel guides, there's no excuse not to go there. The local crime lord will rip your heart from your chest, werewolves can legally eat you, and they had to rebuild City Hall because a dragon burned it down. It's incredibly dangerous, more so than any war-torn republic or 8,000-metre mountaintop. No tourist should ever go there. That's why it was unmissable for me.

She was looking forward to hearing about my trip and to helping me decide what parts I should write about. The Seven Leagues books are pretty strictly structured, with sections about travel to and from the destination, travel within the destination, where to stay, what to eat, how to avoid trouble with the law… all the information you'll need to go places you shouldn't. I know the formula because I created the formula. I'd even written some of the book before our meeting, knowing what would need to be there.

Still, there's room to focus on what's special about a destination, such as the Dominion's lively college scene, or its hallucinogenic wastelands. That's the sort of thing we discuss when we get together.

That day I thought it would be a good idea to bring my photographer along. Karsten Roth was new to the Seven Leagues series, and he was a hell of a catch since his photos had been on the covers of everything from *National Geographic* to *The Cryptid*. I guarantee you've seen his work. You probably don't recognize his name, and you certainly wouldn't recognize his face because he likes it that way. My editor was a fan, and even she couldn't have picked him out of a police line.

She was thrilled to meet him. I told her that would wear off fast, and Karsten hit my arm with his camera bag.

He was polite and dour and funny. He brought her flowers and said he was in awe that she could put up with me. She was charmed.

She insisted we both tell her everything, every detail about our trip, and we stayed so long that we ate dinner at that table too. Over dessert, she declared that *Seven Leagues Over the Dominion* could wait.

I was shocked to say the least. She'd spent hours enraptured by our story. Why wouldn't she want the book?

It turned out she wanted a different book. She wanted a travel memoir, not an adventure guide, about me and Karsten and what happened to us in the Dominion. She wanted both of us to tell the story, not just me. I didn't write that kind of book, and Karsten didn't write at all, not professionally, but that didn't matter. She'd hire a memory extractor, one of the best. All memoirs were created that way these days, she said.

Karsten was horrified at first. Everyone gets their minds read all the time—by customs agents and cops and bored telepaths standing next to us on the sub-way—but memory extraction is more intensive than any of that, and Karsten is a private guy. He refused, first in his proper Oxford English and then in his more colourful German. Miri, my editor, patted his arm and said it was fine. He didn't have to do it. She'd rather have his perspective and his version of events, but the book could be done without it. Being the evil genius she is, Miri had no doubt guessed what his reaction would be. There was no way he was going to let me tell the story of our trip without his input. He said I was a scoundrel and a fantasist and some word that was long, German, and probably slang, since I didn't recognize it. My version of anything required a second opinion.

Also, though he didn't say it to Miri, there were things that had happened between us that even his so-phisticated European sensibility might not want spelled out for everyone to read. If he wasn't part of the book's creation, he'd have no say in what did or didn't wind up on the page. The truth is, I wouldn't have embarrassed him. But he didn't need to know that right then.

As for me, I had mixed feelings. I'd gone to the Dominion planning to write a certain kind of book. I wasn't sure I wanted to change things up.

But the evil genius reminded me that I'd grown up on memoirs of travel and adventure. She said I'd had the real thing in the Dominion—mysterious deaths, a cun-ning villain, a monster the size of a city block... even my own near demise. It would be a shame to squeeze a story that big around the edges of a travel guide. Be-sides, we could still do the travel guide, and then I'd have the chance to get two slots on the bestseller lists.

In case that wasn't enough, she waited until Karsten had wandered off to the washroom, then leaned forward and said, "You can find out what he really thought of you right from when you met."

I told her Karsten didn't exactly leave people in the dark regarding his opinion of them. But you'll notice I did the book anyway.

-Innis Stuart, writing from Dawson City, Yukon Territory, Canada

Introduction: A History of Memory

AROUND THE mid-1960s, when most North Americans had become comfortable with magic, some people got the idea that it was ridiculous to have limitations. Old-fashioned, even. If you'd ever been carrying groceries and wished you had a third arm, you didn't have to just wish for it anymore. You could hire someone to make it happen. Why drag a scuba tank around to explore the ocean? Why study for exams when you could pay to never forget anything you'd seen, heard, or done? It was an exciting time in which it seemed as if we'd all be able to be anything we wanted, provided we had the money. Why not?

Today, we know why not. There were the spells that went wrong and the shady operators who would give you a third arm and then leave town before you discovered you'd be growing an arm a week from then on. More importantly, though, there were things we found we could not change.

Take memory for example. We should have known we wouldn't be happy remembering everything. We should have known because there were people in the world before magic who could. They hadn't purchased a spell or potion. They'd simply been born with hoarding brains. You could ask these people what they had eaten for breakfast on a specific day thirty years earlier and they would tell you without hesitation. It's tough to verify an ordinary breakfast that's thirty years gone, so the subjects—as these people were known—would be asked about the weather on a certain day or the newspaper headlines. They were never wrong.

They were also unhappy. They felt rootless and detached. Without momentum. They were haunted by a million small things.

Eventually, the people in the '60s and '70s who bought perfect memories came to feel the same way. It seems there are things we are not built, in psychology or temperament, to be.

These days if you want to remember everything about a part of your life, you pay for a memory extraction instead. The best extractors in the business will find everything you remember and everything you'd forgotten about for a week or a month or, if you can afford it, a year. No one I know of offers more than a year. It's too much effort, too much magic, and too much information.

The police were the first to use this service. It was unheard of at first, so it was legal everywhere. Then it was challenged in court after court and became illegal in most places. Then it was necessary in solving a few downright devilish cases, and people started thinking it wasn't such a bad idea. Now you'll find it used in most places that allow any magic at all.

If something is used for one thing, people will find a way to use it for a hundred. If you're well-off and living in a place where magic is used casually, you may even have bought an extraction yourself. Maybe you wanted to present your child with the story of her birth or preserve your wedding day. Everyone has photos and video of these events, but a good memory extractor creates something more personal. It's your perspective—your memory, your thoughts, in your voice—translated to text. The first extractions read like witness statements, and it was said they'd never replace writing for thoughtful evocation and grace of prose. But the process has developed over the past few decades, and now memory extracts are indistinguishable from the sort of literary works and memoirs that were written two hundred years ago.

Except, of course, that they are accurate. They are coloured by what the subject saw and noticed and by the subject's way of thinking about these things. They reflect misunderstanding and obliviousness. But they reflect these things honestly and without prejudice.

I would be lying if I said I didn't feel a romantic pull toward the image of a lone man at his journal or keyboard, trying to capture his memories of travel and adventure before they flew away. Those are the books I read as a boy living on Canada's boundless prairie. I would read on the porch at my grandmother's farm, then set the book down, look at the horizon, and itch to go there. I had the idea I would write about what I found.

And I do. I write my Seven Leagues books alone at a keyboard, wrestling with memory and sometimes getting it wrong. Sometimes getting it wrong on purpose because, let's face it, adventure travel should be an adventure, in life and on the page.

This book, though, has all the adventure it needs without any help from my imagination. It's about the Dominion and Karsten and me and what happened to us and why and how we're still alive. I didn't want it to be a mistake or a lie.

What you are about to read, ladies and gentlemen of the jury, is the whole truth and nothing but the truth. So help me.

SCAN THE QR CODE BELOW TO ORDER!

GAYLEEN FROESE is an LGBTQ writer of detective fiction living in Edmonton, Canada. Her novels include the Ben Ames detective series, the superhero novel Lightning Strike Blues and urban fantasy The Dominion from DSP Publications, and Touch and Grayling Cross from NeWest Press.

Gayleen has appeared on Canadian Learning Television's A Total Write-Off, won the second season of the Three Day Novel Contest on Book Television and, as a singer-songwriter, showcased at festivals across Canada. She has worked as a radio writer and talk show host, an advertising creative director, and a communications officer.

A past resident of Saskatoon, Toronto, and northern Saskatchewan, Gayleen now lives in Edmonton with novelist Laird Ryan States in a home that includes dogs, geckos, snakes, monitor lizards and Marlowe the tegu. When not writing, she can be found kayaking, photographing unsuspecting wildlife, and playing cooperative board games, viciously competitive card games, and tabletop RPGs.

Gayleen can be found on Facebook @ GayleenFroeseWriting

and on Instagram at @gayleenfroese

Follow me on BookBub

GAYLEEN FROESE

THE GIRL WHOSE LUCK RAN OUT

Can a disillusioned former cop track
down a missing girl before it's too late?

Can a disillusioned former cop track down a missing girl before it's too late?

Seven years ago, criminologist Ben Ames thought he'd change a big city police force from the inside. He failed. Now he's a private detective trailing insurance frauds and cheating spouses through the foothills of the Rocky Mountains. Like police work, the job would be easier if he didn't have a conscience.

When university student Kimberly Moy goes missing, her sister begs Ben to take the case. But before Ben can follow up on any leads—What does the Fibonacci series have to do with Kim's disappearance? What do her disaffected friends know? And where is her car?—chance and bad timing drop his unexpected ex, Jesse, into the mix.

Ben doesn't have time to train Jesse into the junior PI he seems determined to become. Amateur sleuths are always trouble. Unfortunately, this is turning out to be the kind of case that requires backup, and his intuition is telling him Kim's story may not have a happy ending...

SCAN THE QR CODE BELOW TO ORDER!

GAYLEEN FROESE

THE MAN WHO LOST HIS PEN

Everybody freeze.

Calgary PI Ben Ames expects a relaxing evening off as he supports his boyfriend, Jesse, one of the star performers at a charity concert. But it turns out relaxing isn't on the program.

When last-minute guest Matt Garrett shows up, it creates a frenzy backstage. An A-list movie star with an ego to match, Garrett has bad blood with many of the performers—Jesse included. So when Garrett turns up dead, Ben begins to dig for the truth, both to protect Jesse and to satisfy his own instinctive curiosity.

So much for his night off.

When the police arrive, emotions backstage heat up, but no one can step out to cool off, because the Western Canadian winter is so cold that hypothermia waits outside. With such a high-profile crime, the lead detective seems poised to make a quick arrest... and Jesse's a prime suspect. Ben has his work cut out for him to solve the murder under the police and paparazzi's noses before Jesse's reputation becomes collateral damage.

SCAN THE QR CODE BELOW TO ORDER!

LIGHTNING STRIKE BLUES
GAYLEEN FROESE

WARNING: CAPE DOES
NOT ENABLE USER TO FLY

On Friday, Gabriel Reece gets struck by lightning while riding his motorcycle.

It's not the worst thing that happens to him that week.

Gabe walks away from a smoldering pile of metal without a scratch—or any clothes, which seem to have been vaporized. And that's weird, but he's more worried about the sudden disappearance of his brother, Colin, who ditched town the second Gabe accidentally outed himself as gay.

Gabe tries to sift through fragmented memories of his crummy childhood for clues to his sudden invincibility, but he barely has time to think before people around town start turning up dead, and Colin is the cops' number-one suspect.

Gabe is sure Colin is innocent, but even he has to admit the evidence is compelling. Especially once the home he shares with Gabe burns to the ground.

When Eli Samm, a mysterious and attractive stranger, shows up looking for Colin too, Gabe thinks he might finally have an ally. Except it turns out Eli thinks Colin is a supervillain, and his mission is to put him down....

SCAN THE QR CODE BELOW TO ORDER!

For more
great fiction
from

DSP PUBLICATIONS

visit us online.
WWW.DSPPUBLICATIONS.COM